# ST. MARTIN'S

## MINOTAUR

### MYSTERIES

W9-BEM-563

### GET A CLUE!

Be the first to hear the latest mystery book news…

With the St. Martin's Minotaur monthly newsletter, you'll learn about the hottest new Minotaur books, receive advance excerpts from newly published works, read exclusive original material from featured mystery writers, and be able to enter to win free books!

Sign up on the Minotaur Web site at:
www.minotaurbooks.com

# Praise for Joan Hess
# and her Claire Malloy Mysteries

"A wildly entertaining series."

—*Mystery Scene*

"Claire Malloy is one of the most engaging narrators in mystery."

—*The Drood Review*

"If you've never spent time with Claire and her crew, I feel sorry for you. Stop reading this nonsense and hop to it. You'll see wit and humanity all wrapped up in a nifty murder mystery."

—Harlan Coben, author of *Just One Look*

"Joan Hess is seriously funny. Moreover, she is seriously kind **as** well as clever when depicting the follies, foibles, and fantasies of our lives. Viva Joan!"

—Carolyn Hart, author of *Death of the Party*

## OUT ON A LIMB

"Witty plot twists and hilarious exchanges...You can't go wrong with a Joan Hess novel."

—*Mystery Lovers Bookshop News*

"Joan Hess writes this series with a wickedly funny sense of humor. Anyone looking to be amused by a wildly entertaining series will have a good time."

—*Mystery Scene*

"With her wry asides, Claire makes a most **engaging** narrator. The author deftly juggles the various plot strands...The surprising denouement comes off with éclat."

—*Publishers Weekly*

# The Claire Malloy Mysteries
# by Joan Hess

# A HOLLY, JOLLY MURDER

## A CLAIRE MALLOY MYSTERY

## Joan Hess

St. Martin's Paperbacks

A HOLLY, JOLLY MURDER

Copyright © 1997 by Joan Hess.
Excerpt from *Damsels in Distress* © 2006 by Joan Hess.

ISBN: 0-312-34916-5
EAN: 9780312-34916-5

Printed in the United States of America

Dutton edition published 1997
Onyx edition / November 1998
St. Martin's Paperbacks edition / November 2006

St. Martin's Paperbacks are published by St. Martin's Press, 175 Fifth Avenue, New York, NY 10010.

10 9 8 7 6 5 4 3 2 1

# CHAPTER 1

"My mother was a very strange woman," the customer said, "and so was my father."

In that we'd done no more than make bland observations regarding the weather, I was not prepared for her abrupt pronouncement. I edged behind the counter, wishing there was at least one other customer in my dusty bookstore. As usual, there was not. Farber College had ended its fall semester, and the earnest young students had fled home for the holidays. I was reduced to selling books to stray Christmas shoppers like the one standing in front of me on this gray afternoon. "Stray" was an appropriate word; she appeared to be in her sixties or early seventies, with wispy gray hair in a haphazard bun, an ankle-length print dress, sandals, heavy wool socks, and a scarlet cloak. All she lacked to fit the stereotypic portrayal of a gypsy was a gold tooth and a wart on her chin.

"Oh, really?" I said.

"It was due, I should think, to her unconventional childhood. Mumsy was never quite at ease among the cannibals." She wandered behind the paperback fiction rack. "She remained a vegetarian until she fell to her death some years ago."

I resisted the urge to pinch myself as I watched the

top of her head bobbling above the rack. "She fell to her death?" I said, futilely trying to come up with a scenario that entailed cannibals and trapezes.

"As did my father, as you must have guessed. Where do you keep the New Age books, dearie? All I'm finding are covers with buxom women in leather underwear and boots."

"You're in the fantasy section," I said, "but it's the closest I carry to New Age material. You might try one of the bookstores out at the mall."

This had to be the first time since I'd bought the bookstore in the old train station that I had discouraged a customer, and I could almost hear my liver-spotted accountant hissing in disapproval. There were months when business was adequate to pay the bills and make nominal contributions to the credit-card companies, but there were also months when I endangered my relationship with the various publishers, as well as with the local utility companies, the above-mentioned accountant, and my daughter, who has a black belt in consumerism.

The woman reappeared and gave me a reproving look. "I do not patronize the merchants at the mall. The place is permeated by a negative energy field that makes me queasy. I have often suspected that the music blaring from unseen speakers masks subliminal messages. My name is Malthea Hendlerson, by the way. What's yours?"

"Claire Malloy," I said. "Would you like me to find out if I can order books for you?"

"I have a list," she said as she began to dig through an immense satchel made of bright fabric patches. "This store, by contrast, has a very well balanced energy field. It must be situated on a ley line."

"Only if the railroad tracks qualify."

Malthea finally produced a scrap of paper covered with tiny writing. "See what you can do. I sense you have a very determined nature and will not allow yourself to be daunted by a challenge."

I put on my reading glasses and peered at the paper. "*Celtic Mysticism in the Second Century? Applied Magick? The Encyclopedia of Pagan Rituals and Initiations? Symbols of Irish Mythology? A General Introduction to the Fellowship of Isis? Pagan Spirituality in the New Age?*" Seriously daunted, I looked up at her. "I'm not sure I can locate these. They're not mainstream titles."

"Making the books difficult to acquire is an insidious form of censorship perpetrated by the religious right. After all, I am hardly a satanist."

I made sure the scissors and letter opener were not within her reach. Her expression was benign, almost twinkly, but during the course of my civic-minded attempts to aid the police in the apprehension of miscreants, I'd learned the wisdom of prudence. "Shall I call you if I have any success?" I asked.

"That would be very nice," she said. Her hand once again plunged into the satchel. I held my breath until it reemerged with a rectangle of stiff, if somewhat soiled, paper. "Ah, yes, I knew I had it here somewhere."

She put it on the counter, nodded, and sailed out of the store before I could respond. I picked up the dog-eared card and read: "Malthea Hendlerson, Arch Druid of the Sacred Grove of Keltria." Beneath this announcement were a mundane street address and a local telephone number—although, of course, the address might prove to be a vacant lot and the telephone attached to an oak tree.

I dutifully scanned the microfiche for the pertinent titles, found all but one, and called in the order to a distributor in Nashville. The woman at the other end may have sniggered, but she promised the books would go out that afternoon. I was wondering how the employees of the mall bookstores would have reacted to the Arch Druid of the Sacred Grove of Keltria when I was pleasantly diverted by a customer in search of a coffee-table book. He was more interested in size and weight than content. In that I had no reservations about selling books by the pound, I sent him away with the most expensive of the lot.

After that, diversions were few and far between, and by late afternoon I was reduced to watching the traffic crawl down Thurber Street. The merchants' association had done what it could to battle the magnetism of the mall, but we all knew it was a matter of time before the pasteurized chains put us out of business; wreaths on streetlights were no match for Muzak and parking. A few people were drifting into the bar across the street in anticipation of happy hour, which was much happier when the beer garden behind it was open and conversations could be conducted under a thick canopy of wisteria vines (and a thick haze of exhaust fumes).

I was somewhat pleased when my daughter, Caron, and her steadfast companion, Inez Thornton, came careening into the bookstore like a pair of dust devils. Caron has my red hair and fair, lightly freckled complexion, but at the moment her face was flushed with excitement. Inez was more muted; the two made a wonderful example of bipolar attraction. Inez is a placid lake, deep and sometimes unfathomable. Caron is, in all senses of the phrase, a babbling brook.

"We got the most fantastic job," she began, her hands swishing in the air. "You won't believe it! We not only get minimum wage—we get commissions, too! It works out to more than ten dollars an hour."

"That's a lot of money," I said mildly.

Inez nodded. "If we work ten hours a day until Christmas, we'll make as much as six hundred dollars—less taxes and withholding."

Caron began to pirouette. "What's more, we don't have to wear dweebish paper hats and ask people if they want fries. We tried all the boutiques and department stores, but they weren't hiring. Inez wanted to try the shoe stores, but I wasn't about to spend eight hours a day bent over smelly feet and end up with hoof-and-mouth disease. The lady at the gift-wrapping booth said we'd have to come back when the manager was there and wrap packages so we could be rated on speed and aesthetic effect—as if some snotty little kid's going to sit there Christmas morning and admire the bow instead of ripping into it. Give me a break!"

Although I wasn't at all sure I wanted to know, I forced myself to say, "What's this fantastic job?"

Caron twirled to a stop and gave me the vastly superior smile she'd perfected on her sixteenth birthday in hopes, perhaps, of being conscripted into the British monarchy. "We're working for a photographer at the mall. The girls who were working for her quit, and she was so desperate that she came up to us at the frozen yogurt stand and offered us the jobs. Starting tomorrow, we work from ten till eight. We each get a twenty-five-cent commission for every portrait."

"In a department store?" I asked.

"Oh, no," inserted Inez, who occasionally found the

nerve to undertake a minor role in Caron's melodramatic presentations. "We're assistants in Santa's Workshop. It's this gazebo kind of thing in the middle of the mall, with a bunch of fake snow, plastic elves, and Christmas lights. We collect money from the parents and steer the children up the steps to sit on Santa's lap."

"At which time," Caron said, regaining the limelight with negligent ease, "the photographer takes the shot, we stuff a candy cane in the kid's mouth and hustle him back to the rope, and then go for the next one. Santa gets regular potty breaks, but we can still run twenty to twenty-five kids through the chute every hour. Maybe more, if she'd let us use cattle prods. I don't think she will, though. She's anal."

"I should put in an application, too," I said. "Of course I'd have to go on unemployment on December twenty-sixth unless I was offered a permanent position at the North Pole."

"Doing what?" Inez asked, staring at me.

Caron grabbed her arm. "Come on, let's go to my house and look at fashion magazines. I am Sick And Tired of Rhonda Maguire feeling obliged to tell us the brand name of everything she wears from her sunglasses to her shoelaces. When school starts back up, she's going to look like a bag woman compared to us."

"Wait a minute," I said with a frown. "You are not going to spend every penny you earn on clothes. For one thing, you still owe me a hundred dollars for the traffic ticket and defensive driving course."

"I already explained it wasn't my fault," Caron retorted. "The whole thing was stupid."

"But also expensive," I said. "What's more, the other day I gave you ten dollars to put gas in the car. I did not intend for you to put in a gallon and pocket the change."

Her lower lip crept out as she considered her response. She eventually opted for pathos, one of her favorites. "Then you should have said so. I assumed you didn't want me to be the only student in the entirety of Farberville High School who had to stand in the hall and beg for lunch money—or root through garbage cans for crusts of bread and moldy carrot sticks."

"Or have pizza at the mall," I said, unimpressed by the performance. "The first one hundred and nine dollars of your wages have my name written all over them."

"That's a violation of the Child Labor Act."

"So report me." I made Caron hand over the car key, shooed them out the door, and went to find a guide to boarding schools in Iceland.

At six o'clock, I locked the Book Depot and drove home to the duplex across the street from Farber College. As always, I glanced at the venerable landmark that had housed the English department and provided my deceased husband with the privacy he required when tutoring distaff students in fields not related to twentieth-century American literature (with the possible exception of *The Tropic of Cancer*). On a winter night not unlike the present one, Carlton had had an unfortunate episode with a chicken truck on a mountain road, leaving me a widow without a viable source of income.

I still didn't have one, but life (mine, not Carlton's) had been . . . well, lively since then. Being suspected of murdering a local romance writer had led not only to the dawning of my talents as an amateur sleuth but also to an ongoing relationship with Lieutenant Peter Rosen of the Farberville CID. Ongoing and off-going, to be precise, since Peter has been known to object to my well-intentioned assistance in situations in which I've felt obligated to involve myself. I've never walked the mean streets in hopes of capturing a drug dealer or thwarting a mugger, nor have I advertised my services in the yellow pages. Things just kept happening.

As I let myself into the top-floor apartment, I could hear a heated fashion debate emanating from Caron's room. I plugged in the lights that decorated the runty Christmas tree in the living room and glumly regarded the few packages around its base. Caron had been much easier to gratify as a child; cheap plastic toys and new crayons had thrilled her, as had a tricycle gleaned from a garage sale.

These days, however, she had the eye of a real estate appraiser, and I was worried that my scant offerings—paperback classics, a sweater, a pair of earrings, and a CD that Inez had recommended—would fail to elicit delirious gratitude. A key to a red convertible, yes. Her very own copy of *Pride and Prejudice*, no.

There was nothing I could do about it short of holding up a convenience store, so I poured myself a drink, found the mystery novel I was currently reading, and retreated to the bathroom for a bubble bath.

I was immersed in hot water and genteel mayhem when Caron knocked on the door. "Peter called about five minutes before you got here," she said, making it clear that this constituted a grave intrusion on her right to privacy. "He was at the airport, and said to tell you he has to fly to Rhode Island to deal with his mother. He doesn't know when he'll get back to town."

"What's wrong with his mother?" I asked.

"He didn't say."

I listened to her stomp down the hallway and close her door with just enough forcefulness to convey her displeasure at being coerced into service as a social secretary. I wasted a few minutes speculating about Peter's family crisis, then took a sip of scotch and settled back to outwit Scotland Yard. It was not as difficult as one might surmise, at least for those of us endowed with perspicacity and a keen nose for red herrings.

Peter called the next afternoon. Since I was alone in the bookstore, we exchanged steamy sentiments involving potential physical entanglements before I asked him about his mother.

"She's getting married," he said morosely.

"What's wrong with that?"

"So now you're advocating marriage? That doesn't seem to be your attitude whenever I suggest that you and I give it a whirl. Something about compromising your independence and sacrificing closet space, I recall. Oh, and let's not forget shelves in the bathroom cabinet and razor stubble in the sink."

"That's different," I said.

"Why?"

Lacking Caron's talent for extemporization, I fumbled for an answer. "It just is, so let's not talk about it anymore. Doesn't your mother deserve companionship at her age? If she were blissfully married, she wouldn't be threatening to sell the mansion in Newport and move to a retirement community to be near her only child."

"It's more complicated than that. The guy's given

her so many flowers that the house looks like a funeral parlor. She's gained ten pounds from all the fancy chocolates and champagne. She gets all moony-eyed when she talks about him, as if she were a ditzy adolescent with a crush on a rock star. In fact, Myron's the only thing she's been talking about since she picked me up at the airport last night. She didn't even ask about my flight."

"Then they ought to be very happy together," I said, feeling more forceful now that the topic was back on the right track (or ley line)."

Peter sighed. "My mother and I had lunch with him today. I could tell the moment I saw him that there's something phony about him. He was more deferential than the maître d', and oilier than the raspberry vinaigrette on the salad. He was nervous, too. Only people with guilty consciences are nervous around cops."

"That's not true. Whenever I pass a police car on the street, I get a lump in my stomach because I'm sure I'm inadvertently doing something illegal. Furthermore, you were probably glowering at him so furiously that he was afraid you were going to stab him with a butter knife."

"I wasn't glowering," he said huffily. "Don't I have an obligation to scrutinize the man who wants to marry my mother? His name's Myron, for pity's sake. What kind of name is Myron? Have you ever met anyone named Myron? He's probably a Mafia accountant."

"Why don't you ask him for a DNA sample so you can determine if he's related to Jack the Ripper?"

After a moment of silence, Peter said, "I certainly will run a background check before this nonsense gets serious. My mother's too besotted to ask him anything more illuminating than his preference for lemon or milk when she pours his tea."

"Give it your best shot, Sherlock. I'm sure you can dig up some dirt and destroy your mother's last chance for happiness. Think how grateful she'll be, knowing she was saved by her son, who chooses to live two thousand miles away and has to be reminded to send flowers on her birthday."

Instead of engaging in a civil discussion about the transparency of his motives, he hung up. I replaced the receiver and examined my own motives, which were by no means transparent. Peter is very attractive in a rugged, vulpine way. His bite is significantly worse than his bark; countless convicted felons would agree. When angered, he can be ruthless. When the anger's directed at me, he can be irrational as well, but at other times, his eyes turn to pools of golden brown molasses and his amorous expertise leaves me breathless. He's divorced, rich, physically fit, accustomed to picking up his dry cleaning, and devoted to old B-grade movies.

If he'd only stop battling the marital status quo, he'd be close to perfect.

I glanced up from my book when Caron exploded into the living room that evening. I opened my mouth to ask her about her first day in Santa's Workshop, but I didn't get a chance.

"That woman is a tyrant!" she said as she flung herself into a chair. "She is incapable of listening to reason, and she is a slave to her stupid manual. She probably keeps it under her pillow at night."

"What's the problem?"

"Costumes. I could Just Die right here and now. I

have never been more mortified in my entire life, including the time I was dragged to the animal shelter simply because of the gorilla suit. Adults have no flexibility. Not a shred."

Steeling myself to maintain a sympathetic look on my face, I said, "What kind of costume?"

"Reindeer, if you must know. Furry brown tunics, tights, boots, and a collar with a bunch of jingle bells—which means we sound as idiotic as we look."

"I'm sure you look adorable."

She crossed her arms and glared at me. "And these hoods with droopy felt antlers. Rhonda Maguire and Louis Wilderberry were at the mall with some of the other kids. Rhonda yelled something about Blunder and Stupid, and everybody started laughing so loudly that I'm surprised mall security didn't come racing down the hall. Even the tyrant thought it was funny."

"Oh, dear," I murmured, determined not to smile.

"Is that all you can say?"

I rubbed my chin to control my trembling lips. "I can understand why you were embarrassed, dear. It must have been ghastly. However, you're making a lot of money, and by the time school starts in January, everybody will have forgotten all about it."

Caron groaned. "I won't. I'll remain traumatized for life and spend years in psychoanalysis coming to grips with my scarred psyche. Christmas will become an annual ordeal that evokes an overwhelming sense of humiliation. Hearing 'Jingle Bells' will reduce me to tears. I might as well join a convent and save you the cost of college."

I could think of nothing to say as she dragged herself to her feet and stumbled down the hall to her room. Maternal platitudes would not have been appreciated when all she wanted was for me to offer to put out a contract on the evil Rhonda Maguire.

Both of us knew I was too broke.

Peter did not call back that evening. I wasn't exactly brooding, but I was feeling rather grumpy the following afternoon as I unpacked a shipment and found the books I'd ordered for Malthea Hendlerson. Out of curiosity, I flipped through several of them and learned that the original Druids weren't nearly as romantic as I'd assumed and had never pranced around Stonehenge for the benefit of camera-wielding tourists. They'd been members of the ancient Celtic priesthood, serving as scholars, judges, and philosophers. They'd utilized divination via animal and human sacrifices, but their traditions were oral and almost nothing was known about them. By the end of the fifth century A.D., they were history (so to speak).

The contemporary ones, properly known as neo-Druids, sounded like stepchildren of the 1960s' social insurrection. Like their predecessors, they had rites and rituals aimed at a pantheon of Celtic deities, but they'd replaced the grisly sacrifices with fir branches, cake, and drops of wine. One reference book declared contemporary Druidism to be an alternative religion; another declared it to be a path to spiritual enlightenment. I was unable to make much sense of the blithe references to metaphysical principles and festivals with peculiar names like Samhain, Imbolc, Beltaine, and Lughnasad. I was familiar with the less mysterious concepts of the summer and winter solstices and the spring and autumn equinoxes, although I had no idea what was de rigueur on such occasions. A photograph

of naked bodies cavorting around a bonfire gave me
a clue.

I found Malthea's card and called her. When she answered, I told her that her order had arrived.

"How splendid," she said. "Do you need instructions?"

"I don't think so," I said, staring at the photograph
in the encyclopedia. If I were struck with an urge to
dance around a bonfire in my birthday suit, I could
figure out how to go about it on my own.

"Most people do."

"I'm not into paganism," I said tactfully.

Malthea chuckled. "Instructions how to find my
house, Claire. My car is in the shop, awaiting a part,
and it's a bit too far for me to walk to the bookstore.
You may keep the books if you wish, and I'll come by
when I can. However, I was hoping to get some decorating hints for the holiday season. I do so love to deck
the halls with boughs of holly."

"You celebrate Christmas?" I asked, somewhat bewildered. "I wouldn't have thought Druids ... did
that."

"Why, of course we celebrate the birth of Jesus. We
also welcome Dionysus, Attis, Mithras, and Baal with
song and dance. We have an absolutely lovely ritual,
then share a splendid feast, with my special 'Tipsy
Tarts' for dessert. Why don't you join us this year?"

I took a deep breath. "Thank you for inviting me,
but I'll have to check my schedule. I have a daughter,
you see, and she and I always—"

"Rainbow and Cosmos will be delighted to make a
new friend. Morning Rose and Sullivan believe in home
schooling, and I often worry that the little ones miss out
on opportunities to socialize with their peers."

I had a feeling Caron would not appreciate being cast in that particular role. "Well, we'll see," I said. "If you'll tell me how to find your house, I'll drop off the books on my way home this evening."

She obliged, and an hour later I pulled up in front of a one-story beige brick duplex in a neighborhood that had once been staunchly middle class. Now the majority of the residences were rental properties that housed college students and marginal derelicts. Station wagons had been replaced with motorcycles, and porch swings with chairs salvaged from the local dump. Landscaping was mostly aluminum.

Malthea's duplex was tidier than the ones on either side, although the sidewalk was cracked and paint bubbled off the trim. She'd told me her apartment was on the right, but as I raised my hand to knock, the other door opened and she said, "Over here, Claire."

I obediently went into a living room crammed with chairs, a love seat, a bulging sofa, and a dozen teetery tables holding potted plants of every sort, from dangling vines to exotic cacti. The walls were covered with amateurish watercolor paintings and overly ambitious macramé hangings.

Malthea beamed at me as if I'd made it across a minefield. "This isn't where I live," she confided in a low voice, her eyebrows wiggling jauntily.

"It isn't?" I said.

"I have a cat."

"Do you really?" I murmured, wondering what on earth we were doing in someone else's home. I was not inexperienced in breaking and entering (I have an eclectic rap sheet), but I preferred to do so with adequate provocation.

"And a very fine cat she is," Malthea said. "Why don't you sit in this chair by the radiator and get comfortable? It's so drafty here that we might as well be outside."

It was indeed drafty where we stood, but I could feel a veneer of perspiration forming on my forehead. "Who lives here, Malthea?" I asked in a shaky voice.

"Her name is Merlinda. It's a play on Merlin of the Arthurian folklore."

"Merlinda who?" I persisted. "What are we doing in her home?" I did not add: and what have you done with her? I was glancing over her shoulder, however, and remaining close to the front door.

"I don't understand, Claire," Malthea said, her smile fading as she approached me. Creases appeared between her eyebrows and cut semicircles from the corners of her mouth. "I think you'd better sit down and have a cup of something. I'd hate to think of you driving in this condition. If you're coming down with a cold, I can fix you a very nice fresh gingerroot infusion with a touch of honey. Nothing's nicer than clearing one's sinuses."

I kept the bag in front of me as I edged backward. "I promised my daughter that I'd—have dinner ready when she gets home from work, so I'd better be on my way. I'll leave the books on this table and you can mail a check when you get the chance."

"At least a cup of tea," she said sternly.

"No, thank you," I said, groping behind my back for the doorknob. "It's so kind of you to offer, but I must be going. As I said, I'll just leave the books—"

The doorbell rang. Malthea froze, but I'm embarrassed to say I gasped as if a slobbering monster in a

horror movie had just leapt out from behind a headstone. I glanced wildly at Malthea, then spun around
and yanked open the door.

The situation did not improve.

# CHAPTER 2

Standing on Malthea's or Merlinda's or whoever's porch was a teenage boy who exemplified every mother's nightmare. He was not exceptionally tall or heavy, but he had stringy black hair that hung to his shoulders like some species of slimy seaweed. His eyes were dark, close-set, and wary. His worn leather jacket was unzipped, exposing a black T-shirt with a depiction of distorted white faces and the words: SATAN RULES. To make matters worse (if such a thing were possible), he was holding a hammer.

"Who're you?" he asked in a deep voice that made it clear puberty was a thing of the past.

My mouth was so dry that the best I could do was croak, "Nobody, really. I came by to drop off some books."

"Why, Roy," Malthea chirped from behind me. "Do come in. Claire and I were about to have a cup of tea."

He didn't move. "Mr. Chunder sent me over to fix the back steps. I would've made it earlier, but I had to run some errands for Morning Rose. You know how she can be."

I wished I could slide into the bag between *Applied Magick* and *The Encyclopedia of Pagan Rituals and Initiations*. Malthea was right behind me, and the boy she'd called Roy appeared to have taken up permanent residence in the doorway. Neither of them had said anything remotely menacing, much less implied I was in danger of physical assault (one of my least favorite things). I did not, however, have a fuzzy feeling about the situation.

I turned around as I heard footsteps. Entering the room was a gaunt woman with a narrow nose and thin, colorless lips. Her gray hair was pinned up in a braided bun, but unlike Malthea's, not a wisp dared to stray. She inspected me through wire-rimmed bifocals for a long moment, then said, "What's going on in here?"

"Claire came by with some books I ordered," Malthea answered, "and Roy's here to repair the back porch steps. I was just suggesting we all have a cup of tea."

"With the front door wide open? This room is by no means easy to keep warm, and my heating bills are exorbitant. Can you imagine paying over seventy dollars a month to heat a one-bedroom apartment?"

I stepped aside to allow Roy to come into the living room. "I'll be on my way, if you don't mind," I said to Malthea. "There's a receipt in the bag."

"Do allow me to introduce you to two more members of our grove," she said. "This is Fern Lewis, my neighbor, and this is Roy Tate, who's currently living in Nicholas Chunder's carriage house. Claire owns a bookstore just down the hill from the campus. When I was there, I could feel it breathing."

"Nice to meet you," I mumbled mendaciously, inching toward the door in hopes of escaping before the unseen Merlinda burst out of a closet with a bloody ax.

Roy acknowledged the introduction with a nod, then

brushed past me, saying, "Is there a light on the back porch?"

"Come along," said Fern as she started out of the room. "It would have been much more convenient if you'd come here earlier, but I suppose I should be grateful that you came at all. I called Nicholas well over a week ago. It's a miracle the step hasn't given way and sent me crashing into the side of the greenhouse. I shudder to think of the cuts and abrasions . . ."

Her voice diminished as they went into the back of the house. Malthea shook her head. "Fern is still having difficulty coping with her husband's death. He was a very competent handyman who could fix anything. Now that her circumstances have changed, she's frustrated at the need to rely on others."

"I'm sorry to hear that," I said as I put down the sack and tried once again to retreat. "Please let me know if I can order books for you in the future."

"Of course, after hearing her story, I began to speculate about his death. It's not to say that men of a certain age don't have severe gastric attacks, but Fern grows some plants known to cause a variety of disagreeable symptoms. She's particularly proud of her lilies of the valley and euphorbia. She said she gave him nothing but meadowsweet broth. I can't help wondering, though."

"You believe Fern murdered her husband?"

"Suicide was more likely," she said darkly.

"I truly must leave now," I said with all the resolve I could muster.

Malthea sat down on the sofa and opened her satchel. "Let me pay you for the books. It was so thoughtful of you to drive all the way over here to bring them to me.

Are you sure you won't have one cup of tea before you go back out in the cold?"

The redolence of cash was too much to resist. "I can stay for a minute," I said, "but then I'm leaving. The total came to one hundred twenty-seven dollars and forty-three cents." I sat down on the other end of the sofa and smiled brightly at her.

"Let me put on the kettle first," she said, then left the room before I could protest—not that I thought it would do any good. I resigned myself to a cup of tea and a brief conversation about whatever wacky idea popped into Malthea's mind.

From the back of the house, I could hear hammering as Roy did the repair work under Fern's supervision, and from the kitchen, water running as Malthea filled the tea kettle. I'd come to the conclusion that I was in Fern's half of the duplex, so I wasn't surprised not to hear any whimpers or pathetic scratching from a closet that might be serving as Merlinda's temporary dungeon. All I had to do is gulp down the tea, get the money, and head home for a drink and a dose of the nightly news.

I was beginning to relax when the doorbell rang and I nearly slid off the sofa. As I caught myself, Malthea called, "Would you get that, please?"

Rather than pretend I'd been struck by an acute hearing affliction, I went to the door and opened it. The man on the porch stared at me for a moment, then said, "I don't believe we've met."

"Neither do I," I said.

"I'm Nicholas Chunder, the owner of this property. I came by to have a word with Fern Lewis."

I didn't have a response to that, so I waved him inside and closed the door. Nicholas Chunder was of the same generation as his tenants, but he was clearly in a much higher income bracket. He had a neatly groomed mustache of the sort favored by nineteenth-century politicians and military men. I hadn't noticed a limp, so I presumed the gold-knobbed walking stick he carried was an affectation, as were the ankle-length black overcoat and fur hat.

"Nicholas," said Malthea as she came into the room, "you're just in time for tea."

He gave her a small bow. "Not tonight, Malthea. I stopped by on the way to a genealogy meeting to make sure Roy repaired the steps. Has he been here?"

"He's here right now. Did you introduce yourself to my friend Claire?"

"Claire Malloy," I murmured, extending my hand.

He squeezed it briefly. "Delighted, I'm sure. If you will excuse me, the meeting begins at seven and I'm presenting a paper on utilizing the Internet to access documents around the world. It's quite amazing."

"Tell Claire all about it while I fetch the tray," Malthea said as she made another unanticipated exit.

In that my technological prowess went no further than calculators and microwave ovens, my smile may have been unconvincing. "Please do, Mr. Chunder."

"Are you interested in genealogy?"

I sank back down on the sofa. "I've been told it's a very popular hobby."

"You're Irish, I suppose?"

"Someone in my late husband's family must have been."

He winced at my offhanded reply. "I have traced my ancestry back to early-eighteenth-century Wales. One of my distant cousins was influential in the formation of *Uileach Druidh Braitreachas*." When I merely looked at him, he added, "It was the first meso-Druid group to be organized after so many centuries of disrespect and ignorance resulting from the libelous writings of the Romans."

"Claire's not a neophyte," said Malthea from the doorway. "She's a bookseller."

Chunder frowned at me as if I'd misrepresented myself. "Then you must forgive me for boring you," he said coolly. "I should not have assumed you desired to join the grove. Few people do because of the erroneous idea that Druidry is associated with black magic and animal sacrifices. That, too, goes back to the writings of Julius Caesar and others of the era."

Malthea shoved a cup in my hand. "You really should join us for the winter-solstice celebration so you can see for yourself that we harbor no evil within the Sacred Grove of Keltria."

"Or so you say," Chunder muttered as he ignored the proffered teacup and went to the front door. "Tell Roy that as soon as he's finished, he's to go home and wait for me. We have something to discuss. It may have a profound effect on the grove, Malthea. Do not be surprised if there's an upheaval in store for all of us."

"Whatever does that mean, Nicholas?" she asked as if she were a nanny humoring a recalcitrant child.

"The grove has been tainted by depravity." He thumped his walking stick on the floor, then bowed and left.

Malthea waited until the door closed before permitting herself a fluttery little sigh. "It sounds as if there is unpleasantness in the ether. Roy's a good boy at heart, but like so many of his peers, he has taken an unhealthy interest in certain aspects of the occult. I can tell Nicholas is upset with him, most likely with justification."

Curiosity got the better of me, as it's been known to do. "You mentioned that Roy lives in his carriage house?"

"Nicholas owns a large estate at the edge of Farberville. On the property is an old carriage house with an upstairs apartment. Roy's father and stepmother are cultural anthropologists at Farber College, and they took a six-month sabbatical to Borneo or one of those peculiar places. They didn't want Roy to miss school, so they arranged for him to stay with a family. When that didn't work out, Nicholas offered the carriage house as lodging." She peered into her cup as if deciphering the tea leaves. "If Roy's done something to upset Nicholas, perhaps I in my capacity as Arch Druid should intervene. We must maintain harmony and positive energy fields in order . . ."

The sound of the back door opening ended her musing. I hurried to my feet and said, "Just drop off the money at the bookstore after your car is fixed."

This time I succeeded, and I was at home pouring myself a drink when Caron came into the kitchen. "I thought you were supposed to work until eight," I said.

"I was." She opened the refrigerator and glumly studied its contents. "There's absolutely nothing to eat. Can we order a pizza?"

"Then why are you home so early?"

"I wasn't fired, if that's what you're thinking," she said as she took out a pitcher of orange juice. "This smells funny. How long has it been in here?"

"Not that long—and what happened at the mall?"

She replaced the pitcher and sat down at the table.

"Santa got sacked. Since nobody's going to pay fifteen bucks for a photo of a kid sitting on a chair, Mrs. Claus sent Inez and me home. If she can't find a replacement, I'm out of a job."

I took a gulp of scotch. "Let's start at the beginning. Santa got sacked? What did he do—bash Mrs. Claus with a candy cane?"

"I wish he had, but it was a lot worse than that. He's this old geezer they probably found living under a bridge. If I were a kid, I wouldn't get within fifty feet of him, but he was doing okay with the 'ho-ho-ho' bit and Mrs. Claus was keeping a real sharp eye on him. She couldn't follow him into the men's rest room, though. Inez and I both noticed he was weaving when he came back from a break, but we didn't dare say anything. I'd just wrestled these three-year-old twins into his lap when he started bawling about his misspent boyhood or something ridiculous like that. Before anybody could figure out what was going on, half the kids in line were bawling, too. Both twins wet their pants, and so did Santa. Mrs. Claus hustled him off to the employee lounge, and when she came back, she told us she'd fired him."

"Poor old Santa," I said.

"At least he can go back to his bridge. What am I supposed to do about all the clothes on layaway?" She realized what she'd said and hastily stood up. "I'll think of something. Maybe I can still get a job wrapping presents or pushing fries."

"Hold on," I said, aiming a finger at her. "Didn't I tell you that you weren't going to spend—"

"Mrs. Claus is going to the unemployment office first thing tomorrow morning to interview some guys. She's going to call us if she finds a replacement."

I let my finger drop. "Let me ask you about a boy I met this afternoon. Do you know someone named Roy Tate?"

"Where did you meet *him*?" she said in a horrified voice.

"I delivered some books to a customer's house. He came by to do some repair work."

Caron stared at me as if I'd described a casual social encounter with Hitler. "Roy Tate is a freak."

"A freak? He may not have been attractive, but he looked ordinary in the physical sense."

"Oh, Mother," she said, "you are so far out of it. A freak is someone who's all creepy and weird. Roy Tate has to be the freakiest guy who's ever gone to Farberville High. He drives an old hearse and hangs out in the basement by the boiler room. He never speaks to anyone, including the teachers. They kept giving him detention, but finally resigned themselves to his occasional grunts. Emily had to sit behind him in European history at the beginning of the semester, and she just about threw up every time she looked at his hair. She was terrified she'd get cooties."

"He didn't seem that bad," I said, "and he explained why he was late."

"Selling drugs at the playground, I'll bet," Caron said with a sniff. At some point preceding adolescence, she may have had a speck of compassion, but hormones had flushed it out of her system. "I cannot believe you're defending Mr. Mortician. Inez is going to absolutely howl when I tell her."

Her mood much improved, she went down the hall to call Inez. I accepted the futility of convincing her that nonconformity was not the worst of personal attributes; maturation rather than maternal enlightenment would be required. I did feel a bit sorry for Roy Tate, but there was nothing I could do short of inviting him for dinner. I wasn't anywhere near that sorry for him.

I was heading for bed when Peter finally called. Our greetings were chilly, but I decided to be magnanimous and forgive him for his previous childish behavior.

"How's your mother?" I asked.

"Still jabbering away about Myron. She's eager to elope, but I convinced her to think about it for a few days. She may very well forget her promise to me, though; she barely notices that I'm here. Maybe I ought to change my name to Myron."

"Oh, Peter," I said with a flicker of irritation, "you're behaving like a jealous toddler. Your mother is capable of making up her own mind. If she wants to get married, she should hop on the next flight to Las Vegas and haul Myron down the aisle of a wedding chapel. Maybe they can find an Elvis impersonator to do the honors."

"I don't trust him. He's probably after her money."

I did not point out that he'd ignored my astute psychological diagnosis. "There's nothing wrong with her wanting some excitement in her life. You yourself were complaining that all she ever does is have her hair done, shop, play bridge, and have dinner at the country club. If Myron has swept her off her feet, more power to the both of them."

"You're hardly in a position to encourage someone to climb out of a rut," he said.

"Would you care to expound on that remark?"

"You get up in the morning and go to the bookstore. If we don't go out, you spend your evenings at home

with a book. I'll admit you've stuck your elegant nose
into some risky situations, but for the most part,
you're in a rut somewhat deeper than, say, the Grand
Canyon."

I was not pleased to be characterized as a total
bore, even though there was an iota of truth in what
he'd said. I could have pointed out the situations had
been more than risky, but this might have led to another of his tedious lectures about meddling in police
investigations.

I waited until I could trust myself not to bark at him,
then said, "So I prefer as much order as possible in my
life. What's wrong with that?"

"It's hypocritical of you to say my mother ought to
elope when you won't even go to a movie until you've
read a dozen reviews. The only times you've done
anything remotely spontaneous were when you were
hot on the trail of a murderer."

"That's not true," I said in such a cold tone that I
hoped icicles were poking out of his receiver. "I happen
to be a very spontaneous person when it suits me."

He snickered, fully aware it would infuriate me. "Do
you have a block of time on your calendar marked off
as 'be spontaneous from one till three'?"

"If you're quite finished, I suggest you sponta-
neously stick a fork in a light socket."

This time I was the one who terminated the conversation by banging down the receiver. I gave him a
moment to call back and apologize, then stalked down
the hall to my bedroom. When I glanced in the mirror
above the dresser, I was surprised at how composed I
appeared to be. Unlike Caron, I prefer to internalize
my anger—an unhealthy habit most likely picked up
from Carlton, who'd preferred sarcasm to histrionics.

I was still studying my reflection when Caron came into the room and collapsed across my bed.

"What were you shrieking about a few minutes ago?" she asked as she inspected her fingernail polish for infinitesimal flaws.

"Peter annoyed me," I admitted as I sat down beside her and massaged her back. "Was I really shrieking?"

"No, you were slightly strident, which is about all you ever are. When I tell my friends how you smacked somebody with a chair or barely escaped being blown up, they don't believe me. They think you're too stodgy for anything like that."

Great, I thought as I gave her neck a final (nonlethal) squeeze. According to popular consensus, I was in a rut, boring, stodgy, and incapable of raising my voice. Forty seemed too young for me to retreat to a rocking chair, but it sounded as though Peter, Caron, and her friends might beg to differ. They'd no doubt agree that knitting would be a suitable pastime—as long as the needles were too dull for me to hurt myself if I knitted when I should have purled.

I poked Caron's rump. "Call me in the morning if Mrs. Claus wants you back, dear. I'll close the store and take you and Inez to lunch in the food court at the mall."

"You won't close the store. Every time some emergency comes up and you have to go galloping off, you moan and groan about the sales you might be missing. I'll call you if Santa gets kidnapped or Mrs. Claus is found dead on the toilet, okay?"

I tried not to sigh. "Well, I do need every sale I can get. The post-Christmas season is bleak until the spring semester starts in the middle of January. Maybe I should close during that period. You and I can jump in the car and simply go wherever catches our fancy. The beach might be fun, don't you think? Or how about New Orleans? You've never been there."

"Oh, Mother," she said as she rolled over and gave me a piercing look, "you know perfectly well that we won't go anywhere. Spare me the long-winded excuses about Christmas bills and the checking-account balance. Inez and I are already resigned to cleaning out her closet. If I find that blue sweater I loaned her last year, I may pass out from the excitement."

I sent her away, then climbed into bed and tried to read. The words failed to capture me. I finally closed the book and spent several hours in critical self-examination before falling into restive sleep.

The following morning I felt somewhat proud of myself as I opened the Book Depot fifteen minutes later than usual, proving to one and all that I was not a slave to routine. Instead of automatically starting a pot of coffee, I sat down with the morning paper and turned to the entertainment page. There was a long column of movie offerings. I could go to any one of them I chose, I thought defiantly, even if I'd never heard of it. Or better yet, I could go to a country music bar, guzzle beer, and dance with bowlegged good ol' boys. I could respond to a personal ad and meet a stranger in a secluded spot. I could pull an Ambrose Bierce or a Judge Crater.

I was still entertaining myself with possibilities when the bell above the door tinkled. Entering the store was a petite woman with waist-length black hair and an exceedingly determined expression on what otherwise would have been a pretty face. Even in her wool coat and field boots she couldn't have weighed a hundred pounds; she would have made a perfect undercover agent in a junior high drug investigation. Trailing behind her were two small children of indeterminate gender, since they were swaddled in coats, mufflers, and knitted caps.

All three of them examined me from just inside the doorway. The woman finally said, "Are you Claire Malloy?"

"Yes," I said cautiously.

"Malthea Hendlerson told me you'd ordered some books for her. I'd like you to try to find one for me."

I felt a twinge of apprehension as the children disappeared behind the racks. Grubby little fingerprints do not enhance the value of books. "I'll do my best," I said. "Do you have the title and author?"

She glanced in the direction of her offspring, shook her head, and then came to the counter. "I'm looking for *Psycho-Sexual Transitions in Wiccan Initiation Rituals*. I'm not sure of the author, but I doubt the title's all that common."

An aroma of muskiness accompanied her. It brought back memories of my college days, when those of us who were adamantly antiwar staged demonstrations with temporary allies who wore flowers and beads in their hair and nothing at all on their feet. The woman across from me was much too young to have participated, and in fact was more likely to have found a bottle of patchouli oil in her mother's belongings.

"I'll try the microfiche," I said, glancing over her shoulder to check on her children, who were as silent as commandos on a covert mission. I slid the plastic sheet into place and scanned titles as quickly as I could. "No, I don't see it. Do you know the publisher?"

She shrugged. "A small press, I should think."

I took out *Books in Print* and started flipping pages,

mindful of minute rustling from the far side of the store. "Yes, here it is. I can order it from the publisher, but it may take several weeks to arrive."

"Mother!" howled a high-pitched voice. "Cosmos tried to bite me."

"No, I didn't, you pig-faced lump of dung!" said another. "But maybe I ought to."

The first speaker was not intimidated. "I'll yank off your penis, chop it into pieces, and throw them in the composter!"

The woman gave me a proud smile. "Children can be so forthright, can't they? They're blessed with a naive ignorance of societal conventionality."

I assumed this meant she approved of their nasty mouths and graphic threats. This further confirmed my hypothesis that she was the member of the grove who home-schooled her children. Since it was not a home I cared to visit, I said, "If you'll leave your telephone number, I'll call you when the book comes in and you can pick it up. As I said, it may be several weeks."

As the level of insults escalated from behind the rack, she unhurriedly wrote a name and telephone number on a piece of paper and handed it to me. "Do you have children?"

I winced as the rack shuddered. "A sixteen-year-old daughter." Who, in contrast to the present barbarians, was a veritable paragon of restraint and decorum.

"Such a perfect age," the woman murmured, looking into my eyes as though planting an idea in my mind.

It was not going to germinate, I thought as I watched her collect her children and leave. The musky smell lingered, but now it seemed to imply malevolence rather than flower power. *Psycho-Sexual Transitions in*

*Wiccan Initiation Rituals* was not likely to be a New Age version of the Girl Scout handbook. I picked up the piece of paper and read her name: Morning Rose Sawyer. One of the children had referred to his or her sibling as "Cosmos"; I couldn't remember the other's name.

Not that I cared, I concluded as I wrote up an order to Peanut Brittle Press and stuck it in an envelope. For that matter, I didn't care if the book ever came. My profit on a nine-dollar trade paperback would cover the cost of postage, but it would not impress my accountant.

I was straightening the cookbooks when Caron came into the store. "The tyrant called," she announced. "She found another Santa and wants us to report as soon as possible. Inez's mother has a meeting, so she can't take us to the mall. Can I have the car?"

"There's not much gas," I said as I gave her the key. "You may have to spend a couple of your own dollars if you want to make it home tonight."

She politely overlooked my ludicrous suggestion. "What's that awful smell?"

"It's from a customer who left a few minutes ago."

"Well, I didn't think you were wearing some peculiar perfume. All you ever smell like is talcum powder."

After she was gone, I tried to reimmerse myself in fantasies, but it was futile. What was wrong with smelling like talcum powder? It was preferable to smelling like ripened roadkill or rotten eggs. Peter had never objected, much less commented on it. He'd never given me a bottle of perfume, for that matter.

But he had, I remembered with a guilty start. I'd thanked him profusely, then tucked the bottle away in a dresser drawer. Maybe the time had come to shatter the aura of predictability that surrounded me like a scratchy wool blanket. In that I couldn't afford to enroll in a flight school or book a trek to Nepal, I took Malthea's card out of a drawer and dialed her number.

# CHAPTER 3

W hat had seemed like a moderately eccentric thing to do the previous day seemed downright insane as I walked across the wet pasture. Frost crackled beneath my feet as though I was crushing glass. The diffused light from the eastern sky was adequate for me to avoid stepping in or on anything, although I was more concerned about snakes and mice than I was about livestock droppings. Minutes earlier I'd driven through a subdivision of treeless lots and prefabricated houses, but I was not at all convinced I wouldn't encounter a dinosaur, or at least a woolly mammoth, before the sun rose.

If the sun rose on places this desolate.

As per Malthea's instructions, I'd parked my car on a dirt lane in the company of a rusty van, an antiquated white subcompact, and a bicycle propped against a fence post. I would have dressed more warmly if I'd realized how far I had to walk. Okay, to be candid, I most likely would have stayed in my cozy bed until I heard Caron leave the bathroom after a ritual that was longer and more complex than anything Druids could ever dream up. I am not what is commonly called a morning person; the idea of hopping out of bed before dawn, jogging several miles, and arriving back home just as the newspaper is plopped into the front yard is inconceivable. I do not enjoy unnecessary physical exertion any more than I do bran muffins, and I prefer to stay in touch with my outer child, who does not care to sweat.

My shoes were making squishy noises by the time I reached the edge of the woods. My disposition had fared no better, and I sharply reminded myself that I was here by choice. Not a good choice, mind you, but without coercion of any kind. Malthea had been pleased, if not rhapsodic, when I'd called and accepted her invitation to attend the winter-solstice ritual. What I hadn't anticipated was that said ritual would begin at sunrise; the winter solstice, being a technical kind of thing when the sun reaches its most southerly point in the sky, can happen at any time during the day, including midafternoon. Malthea had informed me that they were using calculations from an eighth-century Celtic calendar. I hadn't thought they were relying on *TV Guide*.

An unfamiliar woman stepped out from behind a tree. Her anemic brown hair had been chopped off by what was clearly an untrained hand; uneven bangs obscured her eyebrows (presuming she had them). Her skin was sallow and scarred from acne, her cheeks concave, her countenance more sour than her thirty-odd years of life merited.

"Malthea asked me to meet you," she said. "I'm Gilda D'Orcher."

"Thank you. I wasn't quite sure how to find the grove."

"Those who genuinely come to seek enlightenment shall not stray. The Mother Goddess watches over us. Blessed be."

· She turned and walked quickly into the woods. I followed as best I could, catching an occasional branch in the face and tripping over vines and rocks. There were no birds to be heard; birdbrained though they might be, they had enough sense to sleep in.

I was breathing heavily as we detoured around a fallen tree trunk and came into a small clearing defined primarily by oaks and scruffy firs. In the center was a stone altar made of two vertical pieces and a horizontal slab; it had been decorated with branches of holly and clumps of mistletoe. As far as I could see, there were no faded bloodstains or remnants of animal entrails on its surface.

Despite the imminence of dawn on what I gathered was a major holiday, the Druids were not in a festive mood. Malthea and Fern were on the far edge of the clearing, deep in a conversation that obviously disturbed both of them. Roy Tate sat on a log, his shoulders slumped and his hands twitching as his eyes flickered around the clearing. His hair was either wet or a good deal greasier than it had been when I first met him. Beyond him was the woman who'd ordered the book about Wiccan initiations; after a moment I remembered her name was Morning Rose Sawyer. The man beside her was small and wiry, his thin, receding hair a contrast to her profusive black mane. He stared at me as though I'd stepped in something in the pasture and brought an obtrusive fetor into the grove.

All of them, to my disappointment, were wearing conventional coats and gloves, including Malthea, who'd eschewed her scarlet cape for dowdy tweed. It was much too early to be confronted with naked flesh, but I'd been hoping for ornate robes and headdresses to spice up my subsequent accounts of my adventure (preferably interrupted by frequent gasps of admiration for my derring-do).

Gilda gestured at a stump. "Sit there."

"What's going to happen?" I asked her.

"How should I know? You'll have to ask the Arch Druid. She's made it clear *she's* in charge."

I went around the perimeter of the clearing and approached Malthea and Fern. In that I was not well versed in orthodox Druidic greetings, I opted for a commonplace, "Good morning."

Malthea gave me a forced smile. "I'm surprised to see you."

"Why should you be?" snapped Fern, her sharp chin quivering with annoyance. "You invited her, even though we have a covenant to ban skeptics. That was probably what pushed Nicholas over the brink. He's been fussing and fuming for the better part of a month, but he was not intractable. You must bear the responsibility for this, Malthea." Her eyes filled with tears, fogging up the lenses of her bifocals. "To think after all these years . . ."

"Now, now," Malthea said, patting Fern's shoulder. "We must not give up hope that Nicholas can be persuaded to change his mind. I may have erred, but Gilda and Morning Rose share the responsibility. Roy is not completely innocent, either. He refused to tell me why Nicholas was so angry earlier in the week. That well may have had something to do with the current calamity."

It seemed I had stumbled into something more multifarious than a sacred grove. "What's wrong?" I asked, as much to remind them of my presence as to meddle in the muddle.

Fern took a tissue out of her coat pocket and wiped

her eyes. "Forgive us, Claire. You're here in anticipation of our celebration to embrace the primacy of the Earth Mother and honor the Celtic deities. The 'calamity,' as Malthea calls it, has nothing to do with you."

I glanced at Malthea. "If it would be politic of me to leave, please say so. I won't be offended."

"There's no point in that now," she said with a shrug. Raising her voice, she said, "Roy, did you see Nicholas this morning? The sun will be up soon, and I don't want to begin without him."

Roy rose to his feet and came across the clearing to join us, walking with the same indolent slouch that was epidemic in the halls of Farberville High School. "I came directly here. There was a light on in the kitchen, so maybe he's having a last cup of coffee or something."

"Or he's not coming," added Morning Rose. "After what happened last night, he may have decided to boycott the ritual."

The Arch Druid hesitated, then threw back her shoulders and said with great regality, "Nicholas would never do that, no matter how upset he was. The cyclical celebrations are very meaningful to him. This is not to say he might not take petty pleasure in arriving at the last minute in order to alarm us."

Gilda glided up. "Perhaps someone ought to go ask him if he's coming. My shift at the hospital starts at eight, and it'll take me half an hour to get there on my bicycle." She looked at Morning Rose. "Did you put some kind of curse on him?"

"Of course not," Morning Rose said, ignoring Malthea's sudden intake of breath. "Sullivan has forbidden curses because of the children. Besides that, I don't know any specifically suited for this situation. Do you?"

Sometime between leaving my car and arriving at the Sacred Grove of Keltria, I'd lost my mind, I thought as I edged out of the circle of decidedly peculiar people. What's more, they were in the midst of a conflict among themselves that had unpleasant undertones. I'd hoped to come away with a diverting narrative, but at that moment all I wanted to do was leave without incurring any curses.

"Do you want me to go to the house?" asked the man who was apt to be Morning Rose's husband, or at least the father of her children.

Malthea nodded. "Yes, Sullivan, I think that's what needs to be done. If Nicholas does not intend to participate, then there's nothing to do but get on with it."

After he left, Malthea and Fern drifted away to continue their conversation. Roy resumed his seat and Gilda faded into the woods, leaving me with Morning Rose.

"Where are your children?" I asked her.

"At home. They got into a tussle last night and knocked over a bookcase. Sullivan was furious enough to ground them for two weeks. He doesn't believe that they should be allowed to express their aggressive impulses. I'm afraid they're becoming stifled. Cosmos, in particular, needs to act out his inherent urge to compete with his father for tribal dominance, which is all he's doing when he attacks Rainbow. She, on the other hand, must deal with her sexual attraction to her father and her resentment toward me." She touched a bruised semicircle below her eye. "She was so upset last night that she hit me. She cried afterward, but I assured her that she was only acknowledging her basic instincts."

I tried to hide my revulsion at her psychobabble. "It's a shame they'll miss the ritual."

"Perhaps not," she said. "Last year Cosmos ate so many tarts that he threw up in the van."

Malthea clapped her hands to get our attention. "The sun is going to rise with or without Nicholas's presence. I do not intend to allow him to put a cloud on this glorious day when we seek Herne, who at Samhain promised to protect us through the dark months of winter." She pulled off her coat. To my delight, she was wearing a silky white robe with embroidered symbols.

"What about us?" asked Gilda as she came back into the clearing, her smug expression leading me to wonder if she'd been casting the odd curse or two. "As I said, I'm going to celebrate in the manner I prefer."

Malthea frowned at her. "It was decided last night that Wiccan elements will be excluded from today's ritual. I believe we should continue to abide by that."

"Nicholas is the only one who objects," retorted Gilda, her hands on her hips, "and he's not here. I should be allowed to affirm my traditional beliefs. Go ahead and expel me from the grove. I don't care. I won't be here for Beltaine anyway."

"You'll catch your death of cold," said Fern, sounding more like a grouchy great-aunt than a joyful solstice celebrant.

"The first thing I did this morning was to cast a spell to protect myself from the cold," Gilda said, "and it's none of your business, anyway. I warned all of you when I joined the grove that I would continue to practice my religion."

I glanced at Morning Rose. "What's the issue?"

"Gilda wants to perform the ritual skyclad. So do I, but Sullivan would have a fit. He's incredibly surly when I insist on engaging in certain observances in the backyard. He thinks they're a bad influence on the children. He's being ridiculous, of course. Children come into the world without the artificial restrictions of clothing."

Sullivan staggered into the clearing. "There's been a terrible accident," he said in a raspy voice. "It's Nicholas. He's—" We all gaped at him as he leaned against the altar to steady himself. After a deep shudder that threatened to put him on the ground, he added, "He's badly hurt or even dead."

"Nonsense," said Malthea.

"When he didn't answer the doorbell, I went around to the back of the house to see if he might be in the kitchen listening to the radio. The door was locked, but I could see his body on the floor. There was blood."

Malthea gestured at Gilda. "It may well be a practical joke, but we must act. You hurry ahead on your bicycle and see if there's anything you can do. The rest of us will follow as quickly as we can."

No one commented on the sudden eruption of sunlight through the foliage as we ran toward the vehicles parked on the road. I could see Gilda pedaling across another pasture as I dove into my car and scrambled to find my key in the bottom of my purse. After a significant amount of maneuvering, we formed a procession and drove back to the highway, and then turned almost immediately on a driveway lined with poplars.

Nicholas Chunder's house wasn't a castle, but it was nevertheless impressive in its size and ivied stone facade. A separate building, also of stone and perpendicular to the house, was more likely to have sheltered cars than carriages, but it added a stately pseudo-Regency touch. I parked in front of a row of marble statues of bearded men and comely women, and beyond them, a nonfunctioning circular fountain. Sullivan, Roy, and Morning Rose were already running around the corner of the house as I caught up with Fern and Malthea.

"What are *you* doing here?" said Fern.

Rather than answer, I dodged around them and hurried toward the back of the house, where I saw Gilda peering through a window. Sullivan was seated on a wrought-iron chair, bent forward while Morning Rose held his head between his knees. Roy stood apart, with hands in his pockets.

Gilda straightened up. "He's lying on the floor, and like Sullivan said, there's blood on his face. What should we do?"

"Is the door locked?" I said.

"Yes," Sullivan whimpered. "I tried it earlier. The front door's locked, too."

Morning Rose released the back of his neck, picked up a flowerpot, and smashed the window in an unsettlingly proficient manner. "Roy, crawl through here and unlock the door." As he carefully climbed over the sill, she handed a small metal box to Gilda. "This is the first-aid kit we keep in the van. It's probably a little late for a Band-Aid and Mercurochrome. You'd better leave the smelling salts on the table for Sullivan."

Malthea and Fern arrived as Roy unlocked the back door, and with the exception of Sullivan, we all jostled our way into the kitchen. Gilda dropped to her knees and put her fingers on Nicholas Chunder's neck. I took a quick glance at his bloodied forehead, vacant eyes, and limp, outflung limbs. Suspecting it was a great deal more than a little late for a Band-Aid, I continued through the kitchen and into a hallway, where I found a telephone on an antique escritoire.

I dialed 911, explained as best I could what had happened and where the house was, and then returned to the kitchen in time to hear Gilda say, "I can't find a pulse."

"Don't touch him," I said. "I've called for an ambulance, and there's nothing we can do until the paramedics arrive. We need to wait outside."

"Oh, dear," groaned Malthea, the words bubbling from deep inside her. "This is dreadful. Nicholas was a stickler for propriety. It seems . . . blasphemous to leave him in this undignified position. Let me find a blanket to cover him."

"No!" I said with such forcefulness that they all stopped staring at the body and looked at me. "The police will want the scene to remain exactly as we found it. They'll be upset as it is that the window's broken and everyone has trampled all over the floor. Now we need to move outside."

After I'd repeated this several times, Gilda rose and we retreated to the flagstone patio. Morning Rose hauled Sullivan to his feet and steered him across the lawn to a bench beneath a bower covered with dried vines. Fern sank down in one of the chairs and plucked at the buttons of her coat. Gilda announced she would await the ambulance in the driveway. The sun was above the treetops and shining brightly, but no one seemed in the mood to herald the dawn of the winter solstice by embracing the primacy of the Earth Mother. I most assuredly was not.

Malthea drew me aside. "Do you think it was necessary to summon the police? Nicholas had a heart condition that forced him to retire last year. Isn't it likely that he had an attack and hit his head on the edge of the counter as he fell?"

"All I know is that the police have to be notified in this sort of situation," I said. "If he had a heart attack, the autopsy will reveal it. Do you know who his next of kin might be?"

"You'll have to ask Fern. She's been renting from him ever since her husband passed away some ten years ago. I myself moved into the duplex only two years ago. I used to live in a little house of my own, but the maintenance became too much of a burden. It was a difficult decision, but I finally sacrificed my view of the cemetery and accepted Nicholas's offer." Her gaze shifted to the kitchen door. "He was not the most assiduous landlord, but I tried to be tolerant because of his willingness to allow the grove on his property. I do miss my midnight strolls among the headstones and marble cherubim, however, and the ease in which I could join funeral parties during interments."

I tried not to think how I would have reacted if a figure wrapped in a scarlet cape had appeared out of the fog as Carlton's casket was being lowered. "Did Nicholas live alone?"

"I believe so," she said.

Roy, who'd disappeared during the transition to the patio, came around the far corner of the house. "I found a broken window in his study. There are footprints in the flower bed, but they're so jumbled I can't tell how many burglars there might have been."

"Burglars?" said Malthea.

"Looks like it," he said. "I told him he should have an alarm system put in or get a couple of dogs to patrol the grounds. I mean, a rich old guy living by himself in the middle of nowhere—that's asking for trouble."

No one refuted his final statement, or did much of anything until Gilda came back to the patio in the company of two paramedics with a gurney and an equal number of uniformed police officers.

One of the officers followed the paramedics into the kitchen, but the other, a shiny-faced boy who looked as if he were Caron's age, stopped and stared at me. His plastic name tag identified him as Corporal B. Billsby.

"I know you, don't I?" he said.

As much as I wanted to resort to nothing more than name, rank, and serial number, I managed a nod. "I believe we encountered each other last summer on Willow Street," I said coolly. "We were never formally introduced."

He took off his hat and scratched his head for a moment. "Oh, yeah, you're Lieutenant Rosen's girlfriend—the one who keeps butting into his investigations and trying to get herself killed. One of the dispatchers is keeping a scrapbook."

"Goodness," murmured Malthea, sounding awed and to some degree, appalled.

The other officer came to the doorway. "The homicide team's on the way. Keep an eye on things while I go meet the sergeant and let him know what's going on."

Corporal Billsby sized me up with such arrogance that I wanted to shove him into the nearest flower bed.

"Are you some kind of magnet for murder, lady? I've been on the force for six years, and I've only seen two cases. Funny that you were in the immediate vicinity both times, isn't it?"

"I wasn't in the vicinity this time," I said.

Malthea nudged me aside and opened her coat to expose her white robe with its colorful yoke. "Claire merely asked to participate in our winter-solstice ritual across the pasture in the Sacred Grove of Keltria." She raised her arms as if indicating a touchdown had been scored. " 'The geese fly high this solstice morn, the woods are bare, the snow is deep. We wait for Herne to sound his horn to wake his children up from sleep.' Isn't that lovely?"

"Yeah," he said as he pulled a notebook out of his pocket. "Is this one of those oddball cults where you all get naked and have orgies?"

Malthea swept across the patio in a bustle of white ripples and stuck her finger perilously close to his nose. "Your ignorance is shocking, young man. Druids worship nature, and we gather on holidays to invoke the inspirational presence of the Spirit. We chant, we dance, we meditate, and we offer benedictions to all the deities. We do *not* get naked, as you so crudely put it."

"And Wiccans rarely have orgies," said Gilda.

Corporal Billsby stared at her. "I thought she said you were Druids—whatever the hell that means."

"Well, I'm not, and if I could find a coven, I wouldn't be here. I prefer the structure and exclusivity of the Wiccan religion." She glanced at me. "We never allow gawkers to intrude on our ceremonies, and in particular, our initiation rites."

"Which are orgies?" said Billsby, visibly confused.

Gilda smiled. "That's an oversimplification of a religio-magical tradition that goes back more than five thousand years to the clay goddesses and cave paintings of the Neolithic era. Within the divine is a duality that is both male and female, and when the Great Mother Goddess and her consort, the Horned God, are reconciled ultimately in a divinity which is one, we achieve transcendency. It's as much spiritual as it is sexual. Want to give it a try some time, big boy? You can wear a mask and a cute little fur codpiece."

I wondered if Corporal Billsby might shoot me in the back if I attempted to dash around the house. It seemed likely, I concluded. His expression was that of someone awakening from a coma surrounded not by loved ones, but by large, green, tentacled creatures. Regrettably, I could tell he'd placed me in the latter group.

"Listen up," he said, backing toward the kitchen door. "No one moves till the sergeant gets here. Don't talk to each other, either." His eyes swiveled nervously toward Gilda. "And don't go taking off any clothes. The sergeant won't like it, and he'll already be pissed on account of getting a call at this hour."

I felt a wave of relief as I realized Peter would not be arriving momentarily to take charge of the crime scene. My presence at past crime scenes had never made his eyes light up and his lips curl into a smile of delight. One would think he'd appreciate the observations of an intelligent, perceptive witness, but that hadn't happened to date. On more than one occasion, he'd visibly bristle like a hedgehog. This time, I thought, I'd be spared the lecture and admonishments to mind my own business.

And there was no reason for me to involve myself in this investigation. I barely knew any of the Druids, and had met the victim only briefly. The winter solstice had arrived without dramatic fanfare, and all I wanted to do was to depart in the same fashion. However, Corporal Billsby had recognized me, so there was little hope my name would slip through a crack in the reports. The media would lapse into an unattractive feeding frenzy when details were made known to them; words such as "witches" and "pagan rituals" would dominate the headlines. The dispatcher could anticipate several new pages in the infamous scrapbook.

As soon as Billsby was safely inside the house, I sat down next to Malthea and gave her an encouraging smile. "Don't worry too much about this. The medical examiner is the only person qualified to attest to the cause of death. He'll probably determine that Nicholas had a heart attack and there was nothing unnatural about his death."

"But there was," she said.

My eyes instinctively widened. "Why do you say that? Does it have to do with whatever happened last night that resulted in what you referred to as a 'calamity'?"

"No one ever forgets where the hatchet is buried."

"I suppose not," I said carefully. "What exactly took place last night?"

"We gathered in Nicholas's living room to decorate for the climactic finale of our celebration to be held this morning. Fern and I brought bushel baskets of holly, ivy, and whatever greenery we could procure at this time of year. Morning Rose and Sullivan brought tinsel and string. Roy had cut down mistletoe from the oak trees surrounding the grove. We draped all the furniture with sheets, then hung garlands everywhere. It looked so peaceful, like a secluded glen on a snowy morning. I could sense the approval of the deities and the blessing of Mother Earth."

"But Nicholas was not happy?"

"I think he'd been exasperated by certain members of the grove for quite some time. He fancied himself to be a purist in matters of Druidry, although he based his interpretation on the nineteenth-century revival. That was absurd, of course, since they were heavily influenced by Freemasonry—and attracted some unsavory occult practitioners as well. 'Balderdash!' I said to him time and again. 'Rosicrucians and cabalists were no more Druids than the poets who frequented Mumsy's salon in Budapest.' "

I heard voices from the front of the house and made an effort to steer her back to the subject at hand. "What did Nicholas do that upset you and the others?"

"I was not upset, dearie," she said chidingly. "I was concerned. Fern, on the other hand, did seem agitated as we drove out here this morning. I clutched my crystal all the way so that its healing power might soothe her. It's so important to conduct rituals with the proper attitude, you know."

The voices were growing louder. I gave up trying to get a coherent response from her and moved across the patio to a neutral, and I hoped inconspicuous, spot. The first person to come around the corner was a rabbity little man with a medical bag. He went into the kitchen as Sergeant Jorgeson and several other men arrived on the patio.

Jorgeson was Peter's minion, which no doubt explained his dyspeptic nature. He gave me a discouraged look, then gestured at the rest of the crime-scene team to follow him into the house. I tagged along, and despite a scowl from Corporal Billsby, squeezed my way into the room.

"From the looks of it, I'd say he died maybe six to eight hours ago from a bullet wound to the chest," said the man I assumed was the medical examiner. "The shot was fired from less than three feet away. Any sign of a weapon?"

"No, sir," said the other uniformed officer.

Jorgeson squatted down to study the bloodied face. "He was beaten before he was shot." He looked up at the officer. "Anybody else live here?"

"No, sir. Only one bedroom appears to be occupied; the others are kinda dusty. But you ought to take a look at the front room. I don't know what this dude was into, but it sure wasn't interior decorating. It's spooky, if you ask me."

Jorgeson stood up. "Rather than asking you, why don't I take a look? Would you like to join me, Mrs. Malloy? You'll undoubtedly do it anyway unless I have you handcuffed to a tree."

"I did not come in here in order to interfere, Jorgeson. I simply want to ask that the people outside be allowed to wait someplace warm. Two of the women are elderly and beginning to turn a bit blue. Hypothermia is not conducive to cooperating in an investigation."

He gave me a dry smile, then said, "Billsby, you and Cliffern get their names and addresses, then send them to the station to give statements. I want all of them to be available the rest of the day if I have questions. Mrs. Malloy, why don't we have a look at the living room?"

As we went down the hall, I said, "Roy said there's

a broken window in Nicholas's study. Have there been other burglaries in the area?"

Jorgeson stopped so abruptly that I almost bumped my nose on his shoulder. Without turning, he said, "Mrs. Malloy, the only reason I've allowed you this much leeway is because you seem to have some idea of who these people are. Once you have shared that with me, you will be free to go home and have a nice hot cup of coffee. I'll need to get your statement when we have time. God knows I'd pay big bucks to be able to see the lieutenant's expression when he hears you were here. His nose will light up like that reindeer's."

"He's terribly worried that his mother is going to elope with a gigolo named Myron. There's really no reason to add to his troubles."

"I'm not going to lie to him," Jorgeson said as he resumed walking.

I caught up with him in the doorway to the living room. I'd planned on an insightful comment about the subtle difference between sins of commission and those of omission, but I found myself speechless. The room had been decorated as Malthea had said, and it did bear some resemblance to a forest glen—if said glen had been seized by hyperactive elves obsessed with pine-scented disinfectant.

"What's the deal?" Jorgeson asked me.

I told him about the aborted celebration in the clearing, stressing that my presence was motivated solely by my adventurous spirit and openness to novel experiences.

He raised his eyebrows. "Does the lieutenant know you're a closet Druid?"

"I am no such thing," I said. "Perhaps you don't need my cooperation after all. Start with the Arch

Druid. The only thing you're liable to get out of her is a long-winded account of her mother's childhood among the cannibals. The boy in the black jacket, known around the high school as Mr. Mortician, has a reputation for refusing to speak to authority figures. Fern's snappish, but Morning Rose will be happy to share her skewed take on developmental psychology, and—"

"Okay," he said, holding up his hand, "I get the point. Let's find a less leafy room where you can tell me who these people are and why"—he glanced into the living room—"they do whatever it is they do."

"So that you can tell the lieutenant how deeply involved I am?"

"You are obligated to cooperate fully with us, Mrs. Malloy. Anything less could be construed as impeding an investigation."

"Our definitions of 'fully' may differ, Sergeant Jorgeson. I will certainly give a factual accounting of any interaction I may have had with those people. It won't take long."

Peter would have had me hauled to an interrogation room and left me to ponder my transgressions over cold, oily coffee and a floor show featuring fleas.

Jorgeson grimaced. "All right, I won't say anything to Lieutenant Rosen, but I can't falsify the reports or drop your statement in the trash. When he gets back, he'll have to be briefed."

But only if the investigation had not been concluded to the prosecutor's satisfaction, I told myself in a slightly optimistic voice. Otherwise, Peter would have plenty of ongoing cases that he'd temporarily abandoned. Someone in the police department might take a wicked pleasure in telling him all the details of the case. I might even do so myself—when time has blunted the impact.

I nodded at Jorgeson. "Shall we take a look at the broken window in the study?"

# CHAPTER 4

Jorgeson allowed me a quick look at Nicholas Chunder's study, but the room was unremarkable except for the broken shards of glass on the hardwood floor. It was all very masculine, as I'd expected. The desk was large, with a computer and printer protected by plastic covers, neat stacks of folders, and an expensive-looking gold pen and pencil on a block of marble. There were bookcases against three walls, an antique globe on a wooden stand, assorted leather chairs for visitors, and between the two windows behind the desk, a framed chart of a multilimbed family tree. Oak, no doubt, with lots of acorns.

"Six to eight hours ago," I said as we walked toward the kitchen. "That would put the time of death between midnight and two. I suppose after they'd decorated the living room, the others left and Nicholas turned off the lights and went to bed. When he heard the window break, he went downstairs to investigate. Bad decision."

"Could have happened that way," Jorgeson commented.

"Which means," I continued, "that the members of the grove had nothing to do with this."

"Didn't say they did."

I held in a growl of frustration. "They're not your basic Sunday-morning congregation, and their beliefs are out of sync with traditional theology, but that doesn't make them a gang of cold-blooded killers."

Jorgeson toured the front rooms and made sure all of his men were busily dusting for fingerprints, taking photographs of the scene, and measuring pretty much everything in sight. The paramedics had put Nicholas's body in a bag and transferred it to the gurney. The medical examiner mumbled a promise to do a preliminary autopsy as soon as possible, then followed the squeaking gurney out the door. We continued into a dining room with wainscoting, drab wallpaper, and a somewhat menacing chandelier above a table that could accommodate two dozen guests without any bumping of elbows.

We sat down next to each other rather than at opposite ends of the table, where megaphones might be required to communicate. Before Jorgeson could open his notebook, however, one of the officers came into the room. "I checked out the broken window," he said, shaking his head. "The dust on the sill hasn't been disturbed. Somebody broke the glass, but nobody came into the house that way."

"What about the locks on the doors and windows?" said Jorgeson.

"All the windows on the ground floor are locked, and the dead bolts on the doors are sturdy. We're still looking for signs of a forced entry. I'll be damned surprised if we find anything, though."

"The back door was locked when we arrived," I volunteered.

Jorgeson sat back and eyed the chandelier. "So the victim either admitted the perp, or the perp stayed around after everybody else on the decorating committee left."

For some odd reason, I was offended at his aspersion on the grove, since it was impossible not to share a sense of camaraderie with those with whom one rendezvoused before dawn. What's more, their potential as steady customers at the bookstore could not be easily dismissed.

"Isn't it more likely," I said, "that someone came to the door, posing as a stranded motorist, and asked to use the telephone? Besides that, he knew plenty of other people who might have been invited for a late-night drink. I'm sure he was a member of all sorts of organizations, like the genealogy society and the historical society and the"—it was getting tougher—"the Sons of the Celtic Revolution. He used the Internet, too. There have been numerous stories in the newspaper about people who strike up an acquaintance and then discover they're electronic pen pals with inmates in prisons and serial killers."

"Very eloquently put," said Jorgeson. "Tell you what, Mrs. Malloy—you go on home and write down anything you think might be helpful. Don't leave out any theories, including leprechauns, the CIA, and the Mafia. I'll send someone by later to pick up your notes."

"What about the others?"

"They'll be home within an hour. Until we get some feedback from forensics and the medical examiner, we can't do much more than try to get an idea of what happened last night. The weapon may turn up and be covered with lovely, legible prints. One of the neighbors out on the road may have seen a hitchhiker—or better yet, disgruntled Boston basketball players."

"Jorgeson," I said as I stood up and buttoned my coat, "you've been working too long with Lieutenant Rosen. Your feeble attempt at humor is indicative of the depth of your neuroses. Caron's announced she's entering a convent. Shall I inquire if it's coeducational?"

"Good-bye, Mrs. Malloy. Drive safely."

Vowing to order my own copy of *Applied Magick* so I could cast some ingenious curses, I went through the kitchen to the patio. The Druids were no longer present. I continued to my car and drove back to Farberville at an immodest speed, although I wasn't sure that ending up in a ditch would prove I'd climbed out of a rut.

I stopped by my apartment to change into dry shoes. Caron had left a note saying that—despite the indignity and source of further humiliation associated with the need to rely on public transportation—she'd taken the bus to the mall, and that she might linger after work to look at the Christmas decorations. Under no circumstances would she shop.

And I, of course, might get an apology from Jorgeson and a teary request to conduct the investigation into Nicholas Chunder's premature departure.

I drove to the store, started a pot of coffee, and sat down on a stool behind the counter to write down a few observations for Jorgeson. After nibbling the pencil and staring at a blank page, I concluded that I knew next to nothing about any of the Druids. I knew where Malthea, Fern, and Roy lived, but that information had already been recorded. All I really knew about Morning Rose and Sullivan was that they disagreed in matters of child rearing, curses, and skyclad performances in their backyard. Gilda rode a bicycle, worked at the hospital in some unspecified capacity, and trimmed her hair in the dark.

None of it seemed worth writing down, but I wrote a brief synopsis of what interactions I'd had on the slight chance that Jorgeson would keep his word, which meant Peter would not be immediately informed that I was involved in even the most minimal way. It would be best if the death turned out to be a suicide, but the team had not uncovered a weapon— and it was hard to envision Nicholas breaking the window, then beating his face on a kitchen counter before shooting himself with an invisible gun. He could have, I supposed, although my theory of a late-night visitor seemed more likely. Roy might have seen or heard something, including the shot; whether or not he'd share it with the police was debatable.

I paced up and down the aisles, pausing to rearrange paperbacks and tidy up the rows of thin yellow study guides that accounted for much of my income during final exams. When I realized I'd covered the territory more than once and was mindlessly tapping the edges of the same guides, I went into my cramped office and called Luanne Bradshaw, a divorcée of a comparable age who owns a secondhand clothing store and has been responsible for a couple of my forays into deduction.

"You'll never guess where I went this morning," I began coyly.

"Then there's no point in trying, is there?" she said, not nearly as enthralled as I'd hoped. "I'm having a few people on Christmas Eve for nog and nonsense. Caron's welcome to come, but she'll probably go into a coma at the suggestion. Can you and Peter make it?"

I told her where he was and why, then said, "He

sounded as though he'll stay there until either his mother stuffs a negligee in the pocket of her mink coat and vanishes, or Myron is exposed as a polygamist with weeping wives scattered across the country like fast-food franchises."

Luanne chuckled. "Maybe this'll cause him to rethink his position on matrimony and stop bugging you to tie the knot and don the gay apparel of leg-irons and joint tax returns."

"Maybe," I said, then changed the subject by telling her about Caron's job at Santa's Workshop. "Do you want to go to the mall with me this evening?" I added. "For fifteen bucks you can sit on Santa's knee and whisper your kinkiest fantasies in his ear."

"I might. What does he look like?"

"Well, Luanne, his nose is like a cherry and the beard on his chin is as white as the snow. When he laughs, his little round belly shakes like a bowlful of jelly. All in all, he's a right jolly old elf."

"Ho, ho," she said without inflection. "Pick me up at six and we'll check him out. Under all that fur and felt and excessive facial hair may well be a muscular bimboy who'll fill my stocking on Christmas Eve."

After I'd hung up, I realized I'd never told her about my early-morning activities. I was curious to find out what progress Jorgeson had made—if any—but I suspected he might not appreciate a telephone call any more than Peter would have. Malthea had not elaborated on her comment that Nicholas's death might not have resulted from natural causes, and had never really given me a clue as to the source of the friction the previous evening. Nicholas had objected to Gilda's desire to celebrate the winter solstice without "the artificial restrictions of clothing," to use Morning Rose's phrase. The conflict, however, seemed more a matter of squabbling over policy than a calamity of measurable magnitude. What's more, the remarks in the grove seemed to imply Nicholas had emerged the victor.

I pushed aside the sparse notes and propped my face on my hands, wondering how I'd react if Peter came home and never again mentioned matrimony. Relieved—or rejected? Could our relationship continue indefinitely until the time came when we were more interested in sharing our beds with heating pads than with each other?

The telephone jangled me out of my thoughts. As soon as I'd picked up the receiver, Malthea said, "Would it be possible for you to come to my house? I just don't know what I should do, and Fern's no help whatsoever."

"I might be able to come by tonight," I said.

"That may be too late."

"Why, Malthea? I have a business to operate, and I can't leave a note on the counter asking customers to write themselves a receipt and make change from the drawer. I'd come back to empty shelves and an emptier cash register."

She snorted. "If that's your attitude, then I shall walk to the store. My arthritis will slow me down, but I should arrive there in an hour or so—unless, of course, it begins to rain. In that case, it may take much longer. At my age, I must be cautious about falling and breaking a hip. When that happened to a neighbor of mine, her husband put her in a nursing home and took up with a woman who allowed their Siamese cat to choke to death on a chicken bone."

I looked out the window at the cloudless sky, sighed, and said, "I can't stay more than half an hour."

"That should be adequate. I'll fix some sandwiches and we'll have lunch while we talk."

At noon I hung the "closed" sign on the door and drove to Malthea's duplex. I again raised my hand to knock on the door on the right; this time it opened before I could make contact. Malthea pointed at Fern's door, put her finger on her lips, and pulled me inside.

"I don't want Fern to know you're here," she whispered as she propelled me through the living room and into a cramped kitchen. "Sometimes I get very annoyed with her, as I'm sure her husband did before his excruciatingly painful demise."

"Why did you call me?" I asked bluntly.

"Sit right here," she said, gesturing at a dinette set with two place mats, forks, and paper napkins. "You do like tuna fish salad, don't you? Merlinda's very fond of it. I considered making deviled eggs, but it didn't seem right after what transpired this morning. The police officer assured me that he died instantaneously."

I assumed she meant Nicholas had died instantaneously, as opposed to Corporal Billsby. "What else did he say?"

"Not very much." She took a plate of sandwiches from the refrigerator and turned on the burner beneath an aluminum teapot. The telephone began to ring in the living room, but she seemed oblivious of the sound. "The young woman at the police department asked me a number of questions, but I couldn't really tell her anything useful. We finished putting up decorations shortly before nine o'clock, relaxed for a few minutes, and then said good-night and left. Fern's car was a bit balky, so we were still sitting there when

Sullivan and Morning Rose drove away and Roy went up the stairs to his apartment."

"Don't you need to answer the phone?" I asked.

"The caller will try again."

The rings stopped as if on cue.

Somewhat nonplussed, I returned to the topic. "Was Gilda there?"

"She'd planned to come on her bicycle, but Morning Rose insisted she ride with them. Yes, we were all there—our happy little grove. The eve of a major holiday is always so invigorating to the spirits, isn't it? We sang ancient pagan songs like 'The Holly and the Ivy' while we sat around the fire and had tankards of mead. Nicholas made his own every fall in preparation for Samhain, using honey from a very special apiary in Salisbury. I do hope I'll be able to find a recipe."

I waited until she'd poured boiling water into teacups and brought them to the table. "I'm sure you had a lovely evening," I said, grinding out the words as politely as I could, "but you and Fern alluded to some hostility that also took place. She was in tears this morning, and none of you looked the least bit like a 'happy little grove.' If you don't want to tell me what happened, that's fine. Did you tell the officer who took your statement?"

"No, I don't seem to think I did. That doesn't mean someone else might not have mentioned it. I hope not, though. Nonbelievers often have difficulty understanding the dynamics of a group such as ours. I'm sorry to have to say this, but Wiccans can be a teensy bit stubborn."

I pulled back my cuff to uncover my wristwatch. "I am leaving in eighteen minutes. If you desire, we can pass the time debating the recalcitrance of Wiccans or looking through cookbooks for mead recipes. You can expound on why Fern's husband might have sprinkled belladonna instead of blueberries on his cereal. It's entirely up to you—but in eighteen minutes I'm going to go out to my car and drive back to the Book Depot."

"It doesn't really have anything to do with last night," she said. "I'm concerned about Roy. He can't stay out there by himself, not at his age. When his parents left, they asked Sullivan and Morning Rose to look after him. Nicholas then took charge of him. Now I don't know what to do. It's impossible to get in touch with his parents, who're conducting field research in a remote area. There's no room for Roy here or in Fern's apartment, and neither of us has any idea how to deal with someone that age. My niece is well over thirty now, but when she was a girl, she was a quiet little creature who was more worried about braces and social clubs than—"

"When are Roy's parents returning home?" I asked as the tuna fish I'd eaten came to life and started struggling to swim upstream.

"Sometime in the spring. I know his outward appearance is not appealing, but underneath his belligerent posture beats a good heart. You were here when he came to repair the back porch steps, weren't you? He was very polite at the time."

"My daughter told me that he drives a hearse."

Malthea took a sip of tea. "Well, there is that. I should think it's nothing more than a petty affectation, shouldn't you? He's merely trying to make a statement."

The statement Roy Tate was most likely trying to make had to do with the role of Satan in secular soci-

ety, I told myself as I finished my sandwich. "My suggestion is that you talk to Morning Rose and Sullivan
about taking him back in until his parents return.
That, or perhaps you and Fern can share one side of
the duplex and let him live in the other. At this age,
they don't need anyone to bathe them and tuck them
in bed."

"No, I don't suppose they do," she said, "but we
don't know about curfews and homework and pocket
money and school lunches. What if he were to take
drugs or drink alcohol?"

I picked up my purse. "You may feel you have some
degree of moral responsibility for Roy, but you certainly have no legal one. The social services department can provide temporary shelter in a group home
until someone can get in touch with his parents."

Malthea allowed me to make it to her front door before she put her hand on my shoulder. "I noticed an
office at the back of your bookstore. Is there also a
bathroom?"

"Yes, there is," I said, "and no, he can't." I forced
myself to smile at her, noticing for the first time how
pale and anxious she seemed. It was evident that
Nicholas's death had caused her more grief than she
was willing to acknowledge. I softened my tone. "I'll
call Sergeant Jorgeson and ask him to contact social
services."

"These homes cause more damage than good. What's
more, Roy has told me that if he's placed in any kind
of restrictive environment, he'll run away. He claims
he has ample funds to leave the country."

"Why can't he stay with Morning Rose and Sullivan?" I asked. Desperation had added an edge of
shrillness to my voice, but I was no longer concerned

that Malthea was on the verge of collapsing. Her shoulders were rigid, her mouth tight, and her eyes blazing as she tried to stare me into compliance. "I'll go talk to them. After all, they were the ones designated by Roy's parents to look after him. If there was some sort of problem, perhaps we can find a solution so that he can return there."

Malthea closed the door in my face. I toyed with the idea of banging on Fern's door and then clinging to her ankles until she agreed to intervene. It wouldn't have been dignified, I'll admit, but I was not about to allow Roy Tate to sleep in the Book Depot for even one night.

When I got back to the store, I took out the directory and found the Sawyers' address. Walnut Street ran through the Historic District, but it had its origin in a seedier tract development, and their house number seemed suspiciously low. Still, it was likely not to be more than a ten-minute drive away, and if I took no action, I had a pretty good idea who would show up at the door of the store at closing time—with a backpack or overnight bag, as well as black candles, sticks of incense, and whatever other paraphernalia necessary to open lines of communication between Farberville and Hades.

As I'd expected, the Sawyers lived in the south end of town, but I was a bit surprised when I realized the development adjoined Nicholas Chunder's estate. Many of the boxy, semi-identical houses were abandoned, the yards surrounding them overgrown and littered with beer bottles, papers, and the lumps of sodden clothing one sees in such areas, as if pedestrians were unaware as shirts and socks dropped off their bodies. The Sawyers' house was in no better shape. A bicycle had been left in the middle of the yard, along with broken toys and a moldy stuffed animal of an indistinguishable species.

I locked my car and went up onto a splintery porch. A curtain twitched, then fell still. I waited for a moment, shifting uneasily and assessing the distance to my car, then reminded myself of Caron's likely reaction if I took in a foster child who drove a hearse. Coward that I am, I knocked on the door.

I would have preferred to deal with Morning Rose, but the day had been going downhill since well before dawn and I wasn't especially unnerved when Sullivan opened the door.

He stared for a moment, then pulled off discount-store reading glasses and cleaned them with a grayish dish towel, as if this simple ritual would reduce me to nothing more than a twinge of heartburn. He wore a T-shirt and baggy trousers; without a winter coat he was much thinner than I'd remembered. On the other hand, he wasn't any friendlier.

"I'd like to speak to you," I said hesitantly.

"What about?"

"Roy Tate."

Rather than invite me inside, he came out onto the porch and eased the door shut. "Then you've wasted your time and gasoline. I am not going to discuss Roy with you or the police or anyone else. My children and wife are forbidden to so much as say his name. Am I making myself clear?"

"Yes, but that doesn't mean I'm leaving. I drove all the way over here to try to find a place for Roy to stay until his parents can take charge. They left him in your care, didn't they? Do they know you broke whatever promise you made to them?"

"Probably not," he admitted, "but I didn't throw him out on his butt, even though I would have been justified. I found an acceptable place for him to live. Nicholas had him do odd jobs around the estate in exchange for rent, and his parents left money for food and necessities. I'll have to tell the Tates what happened when they get back in ten weeks, but I feel I did the best I could under the circumstances."

Guilt had weakened his certitude, and I deftly moved in. "Why did you make Roy move out of your house?"

Sullivan sat down on the top step and rubbed his temples. "I was opposed to him staying here to begin with, but his father's head of the department and I'm a lowly grad student with a family to feed. Rent's not cheap, even in this slum. One or the other of the kids is always at the doctor's or dentist's office, running up bills. I couldn't afford to jeopardize my assistantship by pissing off Dr. Tate." He paused as I sat down beside him, then continued pleading his case. "Roy's not a normal teenage boy. If I were his father—and thank god I'm not, by the way—I would have packed him off to some sort of adolescent treatment facility. His parents preferred to observe him as they would any aborigine from a diverse culture. They're big on non-judgmental interpretation. That's what they said, but I used to wonder if they were intimidated by him—or even frightened."

"Mr. Sawyer," I said, "I don't want to waste any more of your time than necessary. I've seen enough of Roy to know he won't be elected president of his class. What did he do that upset you?"

"I told him up front that I wouldn't tolerate any hint of satanism in my home. Cosmos and Rainbow are too young to be exposed to practices that might lead them in an unhealthy direction. Roy agreed to this, but within a month I started finding evidence that he was doing as he damn well pleased. What's more, he was using drugs in his room. What if the children were to come across a bag of pretty green capsules? One evening I came home and found them playing poker on the porch. Do you know what they were using for chips?"

"Pringles?"

"Foil-wrapped condoms they'd found in Roy's drawer. Teenagers these days—they're more mature than I was, but maybe I was a hopeless nerd back then. Or maybe it's just Roy. He swaggers around and acts like a jerk, and for some reason it appeals to women. I guess it's kind of a disenfranchised antihero thing. You know, like James Dean in that tight black T-shirt with the sleeves rolled up and a cigarette dangling out of his mouth. It brings out the maternal instinct in women."

"Not this one," I said. "My only instinct was to buy him a bottle of shampoo."

Sullivan looked away. "But the most important thing was the children's well-being. Their mother believes they should have total freedom to explore their world, but I believe they'll thrive in a more structured environment with clearly defined limitations and an awareness of the potential consequences of their behavior. Which means, basically, that Roy was a bad influence."

"Was Morning Rose in agreement when you told Roy to move out?" I asked.

"Hardly. She seems to think she alone can save Roy from his perverted belief that he can empower himself through Satan. She *is* about the only person he says more than the absolute minimum to. All I ever got was a curt response to a question."

"Can she persuade him to obey your rules until his parents get back? He's smart enough to know that his only options are here or in a group home. Surely he can restrain himself for ten weeks."

"I have to think of the children," said Sullivan.

It occurred to me that Druids could be a teensy bit stubborn, too. "What sort of drugs was he doing? I could arrange for Sergeant Jorgeson to warn him about the consequences of getting caught with an illegal substance."

"The drug's not illegal. It's called 'Herbal Ecstasy' and can be bought at any health-food store or New Age record shop. It's supposed to be a stimulant and an aphrodisiac."

"An aphrodisiac?" I said. "Are you positive this is legal?"

"Look at the signs in the store windows along Thurber Street. It's legal for the moment, but the FDA's liable to ban it before too long." He flipped the dish towel back and forth, then added, "Do you understand why Roy can't move back here? My children spend all day being told they can do anything they want in the name of learning. Cosmos has already learned that grass burns quickly in the summer and goldfish can't survive with peroxide in the water. Rainbow obsesses on dead squirrels. I could search Roy's room every night, but I wouldn't be here when he got home after school."

I glumly watched a haggard dog slink across the yard and disappear under the house, wishing Roy Tate could do the same. "I understand your concerns, Mr. Sawyer. Malthea's worried about him being out

there by himself with no supervision whatsoever—
and if she knew about this drug, she'd probably be
hysterical. Do you have any suggestions?"

Sullivan stood up. "No, and I don't care. He's a
nasty piece of work, Mrs. Malloy. I was opposed to allowing him to join our grove, and nothing he's done
has convinced me to change my mind. There are so
few of us who consider ourselves to be pagans that we
have to form some uncomfortable alliances. This one
has proved to be an unholy one as well."

I could think of no rebuttal, so I settled for a nod
and headed for my car. As I opened the door, I heard a
child shriek, "Look, Daddy! I found a dead squirrel in
the backyard! Did he eat poison?"

I opted to pass up the opportunity to conduct a
spontaneous autopsy of the corpse and drove up the
hill, trying to convince myself that someone else
would deal with the Roy Tate problem. So what if he
didn't want to be taken into temporary custody? No
teenager would, especially when savoring the specter
of living alone and doing whatever he wanted day
and night. Caron might not enjoy the isolation, but I
had a feeling it was precisely Roy's cup of Herbal Ecstasy tea.

I intended to go straight back to the store and im-
merse myself in paperwork until it was time to pick
up Luanne. At the fateful moment, however, I failed to
turn on Thurber Street and headed for the road that
led to Nicholas Chunder's estate.

Clearly, the Druids were getting to me.

# CHAPTER 5

This did not constitute meddling, I assured myself. I'd had more experience with teenagers than any of the others; I was the most likely contender to convince Roy that he could survive a few months in a group home without, as Malthea had predicted, becoming warped, bitter, and the victim of unspeakable abuse. I could also make it very clear that he would not be staying in the back of the bookstore or—I shuddered—at my apartment. Afterward, my conscience clear and my hands washed in true Herodian fashion, I could devote my energies to filing invoices, updating sales-tax figures, deciding which books to return to the publishers, and dusting the front window display of calendars and novels with Christmas-related artwork.

This all seemed so admirable that I was smiling as I turned down the driveway to Nicholas's manor house. Earlier in the day I'd failed to spot the brass plaque that identified the property as Primrose Hill. It had a pleasant ring to it, although it may have taken its name from some infamous Druid sacrificial site. Nicholas had hardly evinced a sense of humor, but I'd learned that Druids were a wily lot.

The front door of the house had been sealed by the police, and a cardboard sign threatened would-be trespassers with retribution. The murder was Jorgeson's arena, not mine, I told myself as I parked. The hearse was not in sight, but it might be inside the carriage house beside whatever more conventional vehicle Nicholas had driven.

At one end of the stone building was a flight of stairs. I was a bit breathless by the time I arrived on the landing and knocked on the door without allowing myself to question the shrewdness of my action. If Roy was gone, fine. If he was there and amiable, fine. If he was there but unwilling to talk, fine. The only option that did not fall into the 'fine' category would be if he was so angered by my visit that he shoved me over the railing. That would definitely be un-fine, as well as painful.

I was pondering this ultimate possibility when the door opened and I was met with a blast of noise from unseen speakers. I swallowed a gurgle and said, "I'd like to speak to you for a moment."

Roy was wearing his standard monochromatic apparel: black on black, and his T-shirt for the day was emblazoned with a fire-spitting skull. He scowled at me for a long moment, then said, "I'm kinda busy."

"Aren't we all?" I said as I squeezed past him and went into his living room. The furniture was cheap and utilitarian, the walls adorned with posters of bands with names like "Putrid Stench" and "Ebola." The music, to use the term loosely, was so loud that my skin crawled as if it were being pelted with sleet.

"Turn that off!" I said to my involuntary host.

He picked up a remote control and aimed it at an elaborate stereo system, cutting off a particularly graphic bellow of anguish. "Whatta you want?"

"Well," I said as I sat down and did my best to come

across like a sanctioned social worker, "we need to discuss your plans for the immediate future. Malthea doesn't think you should stay out here by yourself."

"So?"

"I spoke to Sullivan Sawyer. He's not comfortable with the idea of you returning to his house until your parents can make more permanent—"

"You've got a daughter, don't you?" he interrupted. "Red hair, loudmouthed, a real snob."

"My daughter's a sophomore at the high school. Her name is Caron and she's not a snob."

"Right," he drawled, then took a cigarette out of a pack and stuck it in the corner of his mouth. "What'd she say about me?"

"Nothing much," I said.

"She tell you what they call me?"

"I seem to recall something," I said, moistening my lips, "but we need to talk about where you're going to stay. I assume your parents have a house in Farberville. Can you stay there?"

"It's rented out." He scraped a wooden match across the tabletop, lit the cigarette, and sat back, clearly amused by my discomfort. "I don't think the Baptist minister and his wife would want me to move into my old bedroom."

"Do you have any friends you might stay with?"

"What do you think?" he said with a harsh laugh. "I've only been here four months. I used to live with my mom, but she got all freaked and sent me to live with my father and that bitch he married." He blew a stream of smoke at me. "Why's this any of your business?"

"Malthea thinks it's her business and asked for my help. You really shouldn't stay out here by yourself, especially after what happened to Nicholas Chunder. Whoever broke into his house may still be in the vicinity."

"I can take care of myself." ·

Dealing with teenagers can be like building a castle with dry sand. I pretended to consider his response, then said, "Nicholas was shot. Do you have a gun?"

"I can get one."

"It may be more difficult than—" I stopped as someone banged on the door. "Who's that?"

He gave me a contemptuous look as he went across the room and opened the door. Corporal Billsby stood on the landing, his expression leery and one hand resting on his sidearm.

"The sergeant wants you to come back to the station."

Roy flipped his cigarette over the railing. "What for?"

"The statement you gave wasn't adequate. Sergeant Jorgeson wants you to add some details, like what you might have seen and heard in the middle of the night."

"I didn't see a burglar lurking in the shadows outside the study—okay?"

"It's looking less and less like a burglary. Somebody broke the window to try to make it look like one, but the officers on the homicide team didn't just get off the turnip truck. The sergeant wants to know if maybe you heard the glass break and forgot to mention it."

I went to the doorway, nodded politely at Corporal Billsby, and then said to Roy, "You have to cooperate with the police."

Corporal Billsby did not seem to appreciate my well-intentioned support. "What are you doing here?" he demanded. "Is there a body in his kitchen, too?"

"I haven't looked." I put my hand on Roy's arm. "Do you want me to come with you?"

"I don't know," he said, making a weak effort to shrug off my hand. "I've never been in trouble before. Should I get a lawyer?"

Corporal Billsby crossed his arms and sighed as though the rigors of law enforcement were giving him an ulcer. "This is not some idiotic cop show. All the sergeant wants to do is go over your statement and ask a couple more questions like what time you went to sleep and if you saw anything out of the ordinary this morning on your way to that—that orgy or whatever it was. If you'd been more talkative in the first place, you wouldn't have to be doing this."

Instead of looking reassured, Roy turned pale and began to sway unsteadily. "I went to bed at midnight," he said numbly, "and I didn't see anything or anybody before dawn when I cut across the pasture."

"Are you okay?" I asked him.

He shook his head. "I think I'm gonna throw up."

Billsby retreated until he bumped into the railing. "Don't do it on me, punk. I just got my uniform back from the dry cleaner's yesterday."

I was no more inclined than he to be splattered with the dregs of Roy's breakfast, but I was in my maternal mode and unable to loosen my grip on his arm. "Can you make it to the bathroom?"

"Yeah, I think so." As soon as I released him, Roy turned around and stumbled across the room.

My maternal mode did not extend to holding anyone's head over a commode. I waited until a door slammed, then said, "Has Sergeant Jorgeson made any progress in the investigation?"

"No weapon's been found," Billsby said. "We searched the house and the grounds, but it could be anywhere by now."

"Was anything stolen?"

He squinted at me. "Why are you asking?"

I smiled sweetly. "Just passing the time while we wait, Corporal. Nicholas Chunder was obviously a wealthy man, and it seems likely that he had something worthy of being stolen. A coin collection, perhaps, or the family jewels. I guess he'd keep things like that at a bank, though. Was there any indication that any of the rooms had been searched?"

"He's the only one who could answer that. How long is it going to take for the punk to puke? I haven't got all day, fer crissake. I never got any breakfast, and it's getting on toward lunch."

"Feel free to check on him," I said as I stepped out of the doorway and gestured (rather gracefully, I might add) at the interior of the apartment. "I don't know where the bathroom is, but you can follow the sounds of retching. I'm sure a trained police officer can do that easily enough. We civilians lack your proficiency in such matters."

"Yeah, right." He came into the living room, paused to stare at the posters, and then went into a hallway. Seconds later I heard him roar, "Goddamn it! When I catch that kid, I'm gonna bounce him against a wall!"

This seemed to suggest Roy Tate was no longer available for a session at the police department. I picked up my purse and waited for Corporal Billsby to come storming back into the living room. His demeanor was not attractive when he did so; the blotches on his face did not flatter him, nor did the spittle on his chin.

Nor, for that matter, did the glower that he aimed at me. "You're in on this, aren't you?" he said in a voice almost as loud as the music had been when I arrived. "You asked all those questions to give him time to escape out the bathroom window!"

"I did no such thing," I said indignantly. "You were the one who was worried about your uniform and terrified you might have to shine your shoes tonight. I didn't hear you offer to escort him to the bathroom, either. That was really very negligent on your part, wasn't it? I do hope Sergeant Jorgeson's not too cross with you when he hears about this."

"Aw, hell," the corporal said as he collapsed on the sofa. "I've already got one reprimand in my file for roughing up a junkie."

"Then you should consider tracking this witness, shouldn't you?"

"There are at least forty acres surrounding this house. I walked most of them earlier today." Corporal Billsby stood up and slammed his hat back on his head. "Stay here, ma'am. I'm gonna call for backup."

"Roy Tate isn't a suspect," I said.

"Now he is."

Corporal Billsby had a point, I thought as I listened to him call the police department and squirm through an explanation of why he needed additional officers on the scene. He banged down the receiver, gave me a final glower, and hurried down the exterior stairs. I followed at a more decorous pace, wondering if I ought to call Malthea and report the dismal outcome of my mission. Presuming Roy was on foot and eluded the police, he was likely to be sleeping in the woods in the future.

I went onto the porch of the house and peered in the window at the shrouded living room. A strand of tinsel had come loose and hung like a thick silver snake. I tried to envision a blazing fire, tankards of mead, and a rousing rendition of a pagan hymn, but my thoughts kept returning to the bloodied corpse on the kitchen floor. Hardly convivial.

I went to the double doors of the carriage house and dragged them open. Although I'd anticipated the sight of the hearse, it still jolted me. It was long and sleek, with polished chrome accents and fringed curtains in the back windows. I stuck my head in the window in case Roy was hunkered on the floor of the front seat; all I saw were paper cups and crumpled cigarette packs. The key was in the ignition, but I was not tempted to drive around Farberville and drum up a little extra income.

Parked next to it was a burgundy Cadillac, indicative of Nicholas's more conservative taste. I made sure Roy was not hiding under either vehicle, then opened the door of a small room with a tool bench, a headless marble statue draped in cobwebs, and shelves piled with oddments such as flowerpots and wicker baskets.

Satisfied Roy had fled elsewhere, I emerged as a patrol car pulled up. Corporal Billsby came around the corner of the carriage house, unaccompanied by his errant witness.

"How'd the sergeant take it?" he asked the driver.

"About like you think he would, Billsby. Can you say 'school crossing guard'?"

Apparently Billsby couldn't. He waited until his colleagues climbed out of the car, then gave them a rambling account that characterized me as a cross between Ma Barker and Bonnie Parker.

"Look here," I cut in before I was cuffed and thrown into the backseat, "I have no control over Roy's past or present behavior. I came here out of concern for a minor whose parents are on the other side of the world. Sergeant Jorgeson should not have allowed him to continue to live here. Why weren't suitable arrangements made?"

"We aren't in the baby-sitting business," snapped Billsby. "Come on, guys—let's scatter and see if we can find this punk."

No one bothered to commend me for my virtuous motives as they walked between the two buildings. I waited for a moment to see if Corporal Billsby might return to order me to sit in my car or go back upstairs, then decided I'd been dismissed and drove back to the bookstore.

The telephone was ringing as I unlocked the door. In that there were many people with whom I did not wish to converse, including Peter, Jorgeson, and Malthea, I answered it with a guarded acknowledgment that this was indeed the Book Depot.

I'd overlooked Gilda D'Orcher.

"I need to talk to you," she said over the background clamor of voices and machinery. "My shift's over in an hour. Can we meet someplace?"

I was beginning to feel as if I was beset by a parasitic vine that was curling around my limbs. "I'm busy the rest of the day. The person you need to talk to is Sergeant Jorgeson. Would you like the number?"

"No, I need to talk to you, Mrs. Malloy. Can't you please give me a few minutes?"

"I'll be here until six o'clock," I said. "If you want to come by, you can."

She began to snuffle. "My bicycle's out at Primrose Hill. Fern gave me a lift to the police station and then to the hospital so I wouldn't be late. I meant to ask the Sawyers to bring it back to town in their van, but they left before I had a chance." The distasteful snuffling increased in volume, if not sincerity. "There's no way I can get to the bookstore before you leave. This is really important, Mrs. Malloy. I know you think I'm a crackpot, but please hear me out."

The metaphorical vine slithered up my back and twined around my neck. "I might be able to meet you at seven or eight tonight," I said.

"I guess that'll have to do," she said. "One of the orderlies lives in the trailer park, so I can get a ride home with him. It's on Appleby Road, and I live in the last unit on the left. I'll put a candle in the window."

I admitted I could find the trailer park and hung up, all the while cursing myself for being such an easy mark. Lacking the proper Wiccan vocabulary, I employed old-fashioned Anglo-Saxon expletives.

My only sale the rest of the afternoon was to my amiable science-fiction hippie, who was a relic of the sixties and a local institution. He ambled in and out of the store in his typical haze; I considered asking him if he knew anything about the local Druids, but his eyes were so unfocused that I was afraid my question might further bewilder him.

No police officer appeared to drag me to the nearest dungeon for impeding an investigation, and at six o'clock I locked up and drove to Luanne's store. She was waiting on the sidewalk, her hands buried in the pockets of a tatty fur coat.

"Do you think it'll impress him?" she said as she got into my car. "I realize that fur's not politically correct, but neither is a guy who denigrates children's self-esteem by categorizing them as naughty or nice."

"Get a grasp, Luanne," I said as I eased into the stream of cars heading up Thurber Street. "Caron described the previous Santa as an old geezer who didn't require makeup for his cherry-tinted nose. I doubt he'd have cared if your entire body was covered with fur."

"That attitude does not reflect the Christmas spirit of goodwill to men, especially the kind with admirable physical attributes and limitless financial resources. Speaking of which, anything more from Peter?"

"No, and I don't expect him to call anytime soon. Our last conversation did not go well. I suppose he deserves some credit for being concerned about his mother, but he's so blinded with infantile jealousy that he'd object to the pope."

"The pope's pretty old," Luanne said, ogling a pedestrian who met at least one of her criteria. "Pull over, Claire—he winked at me."

I kept going. By the time we arrived at the mall, I'd told her the entire Druid saga, which she found more amusing that daring. It took nearly half an hour to find a parking space, and only then did I succeed by stalking a woman laden with shopping bags.

The mall was jammed with shoppers. The organized ones clutched lists and darted between those with slack-jawed faces. Children were dragged along by grim parents bent on bargains. Strollers competed in an informal version of the Indy 500. The odor of sweat competed with perfume, popcorn, cedar, and recycled air. The worst of it, however, was the clash of carols from inside stores; the Little Drummer Boy was banging away over the warning that Santa was mak-

ing a list and Rudolph was being denied participation
in reindeer frivolities taking place away in a manger.
Cash registers jangled in kiosks in the middle of the
promenade.

"I don't know if I can do this," I said to Luanne as
we elbowed our way through the teeming masses, at
least one of whom was yearning to go home and
spend a quiet, uneventful evening with a novel.

"Don't be ridiculous."

She scooted around a line of swaggering adoles-
cents, forcing me to trot after her. The crowd coagu-
lated as we neared the food court, and our progress
slowed to a maddening crawl. New odors assaulted
us. I was amazed that anyone could eat in such a
raucous environment and not succumb to terminal
indigestion.

Luanne grabbed my wrist. "It's down this way."

After a few more minutes of weaving through a
maze of humanity, we found Santa's Workshop in a
pavilion in front of a department store. It was delin-
eated by a two-foot-high picket fence and festooned
with twinkling lights, faux icicles, and blankets of
cotton strewn with glitter. Plastic elves grinned maniacally from strategic points. On a stage partially surrounded by lattice sat the man himself; below him was
a camera on a tripod and the invincible Mrs. Claus.
There must have been forty or even fifty children in
line, each held in place by a parent. A few of the children were smiling, but most of them were pouting or
whining. Their parents reminded me of soldiers being
briefed on the eve of a critical campaign.

Luanne and I wormed our way closer to the gazebo,
and finally caught a glimpse of the two reindeer in

their tunics and antlers. Both appeared to be exhausted but determined to keep the line moving (and the bonus money flowing). While Inez consulted Mrs. Claus, Caron took a sobbing child by the hand, hauled him up the two steps, and deftly deposited him on Santa's lap. Thirty seconds later, she removed the child and Inez fetched the next victim.

"I can't make out his age," said Luanne, gazing thoughtfully at Santa. "Do you think he's padded or really that pudgy?"

"You'll have to fork over fifteen dollars for the answer to that," I said. "Furthermore, I don't suggest you try to cut in line. Those mothers are probably packing designer pistols in those imported leather handbags."

"I'll ask Caron about him. She and Inez look cute in a goofy way, don't they?"

"Don't tell her that," I said, watching as yet another child was positioned on Santa's lap. Mrs. Claus remained hunched over the camera, raising her head only to announce she was ready to take a photograph. All I could tell about her was that she had white hair (possibly a wig) and an ample rump (probably her own). As Luanne had said, it was impossible to make out Santa's features under the bushy beard, equally bushy white eyebrows, and fur-trimmed hat.

A girl of five or six, dressed in a red velvet party dress, ran up to the head of the line. "I'm next!" she screeched in a voice that imperiled the vases in a nearby jewelry store.

Caron rolled her eyes and said something to the girl, who in response shoved the boy next to her with enough force to send him sprawling onto the cotton. Mrs. Claus straightened up and gave Caron a stern look.

"I want to go now!" the girl repeated, stamping her foot with each word. It sounded as if this were a familiar assertion in her home, whether the issue was a glass of milk, a cartoon show, or a basic demand of nature.

"Wait your turn," said a mother in the middle of the line.

The girl's face was pink and her chin trembling. "I don't want to wait! I hate to wait!"

Luanne nudged me. "Guess who'll be getting coal and switches in her stocking."

Caron seemed nonplussed as angry mutters from those in line grew louder. Santa and the child on his lap stared at the crowd as if it were a mob in the making. The little boy who'd been pushed began to wail as his mother yanked him to his feet and brushed glitter off his knees. Shoppers formed a loose circle around the fence, no doubt intrigued by the diversion of violence.

The girl took advantage of Caron's momentary paralysis and darted through the gate. Inez started to reach for her, then timidly lowered her hand and stepped back.

"Where on earth is that child's mother?" I asked Luanne. "Surely she's not here on her own."

"Maybe the chauffeur's out in the limousine, waiting on her royal highness. As we know, her royal highness does not like to be denied the privileges of rank."

The girl was halfway up the steps when Caron spun around and went after her. She caught the girl around the waist, and to the crowd's enthusiastic approval, carried her to the fence and set her down outside it.

The girl froze for a moment, her eyes rounded, then took a deep breath and ran toward a woman in a fur coat that was in no way tatty. "Inappropriate touching, Mommy!" she screamed. "Inappropriate touching!"

# CHAPTER 6

"Idon't believe it," Caron said as we drove away
from the mall. "There must have been two hundred people who saw what happened. All I did was pick her up, for pity's sake. From the way everybody reacted, you'd have thought I flung her across the mall like a red velvet bowling ball. Which, for the record, I considered doing."

I looked at her in the rearview mirror. "You didn't get fired, and that's the important thing."

"I'm not so sure I won't get fired in the morning. Mrs. Claus really bawled me out in the locker room. She'll stay up all night trying to find something in the manual."

Luanne turned around and leaned over the seat to pat Caron's knee. "She's not going to fire you this close to Christmas. She can't risk not being able to find a replacement."

"That's right," Inez said. "I mean, who else would agree to wear costumes like that and deal with an endless line of drooling babies and bratty kids? The pay's good, but I'll sure be relieved when we're done on Christmas Eve."

Caron flopped back in the seat and closed her eyes. "No kidding."

The ambiance was so oppressive that none of us spoke for the remainder of the trip. I dropped off Luanne and Inez at their respective residences, and a few minutes later parked in the garage beneath the duplex.

"Don't worry about it," I said to Caron, treading a fine line between sage and cheerleader. "The girl was just parroting something she'd been taught to say. She sounded like a robot from some science-fiction movie. There were plenty of witnesses who saw exactly what you did."

"Mrs. Claus said I should call the girl's parents to apologize. I told her I hadn't done anything wrong and I wasn't that much of a hypocrite. I expected to get fired, but she shrugged and left the locker room. I can almost hear her on the hot line to the home office asking for the approved procedure for dealing with rebellious reindeer. I'll probably be transferred to a strip mall in some podunk town where all the shoppers are first cousins."

I offered to fix her something to eat, but she said she wasn't hungry and limped down the hall to her room. Her lack of defiance unsettled me; she's always preferred a vigorous offense, no matter how illogical, and she's never held a smoking gun that couldn't be rationalized away in a nanosecond.

I was pouring a drink when the telephone rang. Its sound reminded me of the earlier call from Gilda D'Orcher and my promise to go to her trailer, and I was not enthusiastic when I picked up the receiver.

"How's it going?" asked Peter in a suspiciously jovial tone. "Have you been out Christmas shopping?"

"Luanne and I went to the mall."

"Anything else going on?"

All systems went on red alert, but I managed a careless chuckle and said, "This and that. Any developments with your mother and the diabolic suitor?"

"No, she keeps babbling about his virtues and he keeps taking her to expensive restaurants. He's been dropping hints about giving her an engagement ring for Christmas, but I made her swear not to do anything rash until . . ."

"Hell freezes over?" I suggested.

There was a profound pause during which I could hear only the rush of his breath on the mouthpiece. Finally he said, "Until Leslie gets here tomorrow and she and my mother can have a long talk about Myron."

"Leslie? Is she an old friend of your mother's? A college roommate or sorority sister?"

"Leslie's my ex-wife."

"Excuse me?"

"You heard me. Leslie and my mother became close friends, and since the divorce they've continued to call and visit each other several times a year. When I told Leslie about Myron, she offered to come as soon as she could. I'm picking her up at the airport at noon."

My hand was trembling as I grabbed the glass and took an unladylike swallow of scotch. "Did your mother call her or did you?"

Peter took his time responding to my extraordinarily reasonable question. "Yes, Claire, I called her. To answer your next question, I didn't know her telephone number off the top of my head. I found it in my mother's address book."

"Did you?" I managed to say with only the slightest trace of frost. "How convenient that she could drop everything and come dashing to your aid. She must be *very* fond of your mother."

He either missed the edge in my voice—or opted to ignore it. "It wasn't convenient. She had to make all kinds of arrangements and wheedle her boss into letting her take some days off. She called a few minutes ago to say her travel agent had scrambled around and found a seat on a flight tomorrow. I offered to pay for it, but she wouldn't hear of it. A ticket at the last moment costs a bundle."

I decided not to point out that Leslie may have believed that martyrdom was the first step to canonization. My knowledge of saints was limited to Saint John of God (booksellers) and Saint Patrick (green beer), but I figured no one had laid claim to the title of patron saint of ex-daughters-in-law. "It must have been difficult for her to find a baby-sitter on such short notice, too," I said, feigning sympathy for the woman who'd been married to Peter for twelve years and had remained intimate with his mother. I'd never even met his mother.

"Baby-sitter? Who said anything about a baby-sitter? The biggest problem was trying to find a kennel for Boris Godunov and Prince Igor, her Russian wolfhounds. Leslie's crazy about Russian opera and goes to St. Petersburg for the season every year."

"Isn't that fascinating?" I said. "I hope this impromptu visit doesn't interfere with her consumption of vodka and caviar."

"I'm sure it won't," he said blandly. "What else have you been up to besides the mall?"

Standing around a gloomy forest while water dripped down my neck lacked the glamour of the St. Petersburg opera season. "Selling books, that sort of thing," I said with matching blandness. "Do you have any idea how much longer you'll be in Newport?"

"It depends on Leslie's plans. Since she's making the effort to come and be supportive, I can't just toss her the car keys at the airport and take the next flight home. I'll be here for at least a few more days."

"No, I don't see how you can leave while Leslie's there," I said, hoping he hadn't caught the slight hiss in my voice when I said her name. Someone with Russian wolfhounds, no doubt pedigreed to the $n$th degree, would never be so vulgar as to hiss. "You must have a lot of catching up to do."

"The only reason she's coming is to talk to my mother," said Peter. "There's nothing more to it than that."

"Oops, someone's at the front door," I said. "I know you'll be busy over the next few days, so I won't expect a call. 'Bye."

I carefully replaced the receiver, freshened my drink, and made it to the sofa without any disasters. Leslie was likely to be a spontaneous woman, I thought as I pulled off my scuffed loafers and propped my feet on the coffee table. I tried to remember if Peter had ever mentioned where she lived or if she'd remarried. Anyone who jetted to St. Petersburg every year was not likely to have a menial, minimum-wage sort of job. She was apt to be a stockbroker or a network news anchor or an editor at a prestigious literary house that publishes the sort of books that everybody buys and nobody actually reads. That, or Anastasia incarnate.

When the telephone rang, I stayed where I was, my fingers crossed that I was not going to be regaled with an addendum to the litany of Leslie's selfless, magnanimous sacrifices, such as donating a kidney to an orphan or single-handedly funding a Kurdish refugee camp. I heard Caron answer it in her room, her initial enthusiasm almost immediately replaced with ill-disguised resentment. Seconds later she came down the hall and said, "It's for you. Would you please keep it short? Inez thinks she saw Marissa at the mall when— well, you know when. I may need her to testify when I'm tried for assault and battery. Is that a felony?"

"I don't know." I picked up the receiver. "Hello?"

"This is Malthea, Claire. You must come over here and explain what's happening. I'd put on the front porch light for you, but I think it's better that you arrive under the cloak of darkness. Park around the corner and watch out for rough spots on the sidewalk. We can't have any scraped knees, can we?"

"Absolutely not!"

"I'm glad you agree with me. I'll see you shortly."

Before I could get in a word, she hung up. I considered throwing the telephone through the nearest window, but the apartment was chilly enough without inviting in the December wind. I could have hurled my glass at the wall, but someone would be obliged to sweep up the broken glass—and odds were not good that it would be Caron. The obvious option was to turn off the light and go to bed; I'd been up since an absurdly early hour.

Wishing I'd never heard of *The Encyclopedia of Pagan Rituals and Initiations* or any of the other oddball titles, I put on my shoes, set the glass in the kitchen sink, and went to Caron's door. She was sitting cross-legged in the middle of the bed, gloomily keeping watch over the telephone in case it attempted to scuttle away.

"I'm going out for a few minutes," I said.

"That's fine. I'll just sit here in the dark while my future gurgles down the drain."

"I truly don't think you have any reason to worry, dear. Luanne was right when she said Mrs. Claus wouldn't dare fire you so close to Christmas. You'll be able to retrieve everything on layaway and humiliate Rhonda on the first day of school."

"The only person who'll ask me to the prom is Mr. Mortician. I can see myself in the front seat of the hearse, dressed in black with a calla lily corsage. I might as well ask him to drop me off at the cemetery, since my life is over anyway."

I could think of nothing else to say, so I left the apartment and drove to Malthea's. I parked in front of the duplex, sat for a moment while I reminded myself how annoyed I was at her, then marched up to the dark porch and rapped on the door.

"It's cold out here!" I called. "If you don't open the door in the next ten seconds, I'm—"

The door opened. Malthea eyed me for a moment, then stepped back and waited until I was inside before saying, "I thought we'd agreed you would arrive under a cloak of darkness, Claire."

"It's plenty dark out there," I said. "What's more, it's getting late and I still haven't had dinner. Here I am. What do you want this time?"

"Goodness," she murmured, "you sound as if you've had a difficult day. Let's do sit down and have some tea while we talk."

I stared at her. "A difficult day? I think that sums it up nicely, although I might have chosen a more forceful adjective—like nightmarish. What do you want, Malthea? If you've decided I should adopt Roy Tate, you can forget it. I went out there to help, and it backfired. Now I quit."

"Some of us have forgotten our manners, haven't we?" She sat down on the sofa, crossed her arms, and waited until I'd reluctantly joined her. "I thought it might be better if I tell you what took place last night while we were decorating Nicholas's front room. Then, if you feel strongly that I ought to tell the police, I will do so—although I cannot see why it should have any bearing on the tragic accident that befell Nicholas."

"Okay," I said neutrally.

The telephone began to ring, but as she'd done previously, Malthea ignored it. "As of late there has been growing dissension in our grove. Each of us brings an individual philosophy, and eclecticism and tolerance are important tenets of contemporary Druidism. There are Orthodox Jewish Druids, Catholic Druids—"

"Malthea," I said. "It's eight o'clock. I'm tired and I'm hungry—and I'm not predisposed to listen to a lecture. My daughter is at home preplanning her funeral. The significant man in my life is picking up his ex-wife at an airport tomorrow." I bit down on my lip, took a calming breath, and added, "Just tell me what happened last night."

"All I was trying to do was present the situation so that you can grasp the—"

"What happened?" I growled.

"Nicholas owned many of the residences along this street, as well as apartment buildings and houses in other neighborhoods. He was so very kind about helping his fellow Druids find affordable, if not luxurious, housing. Fern has been paying the same rent for ten years, and the Sawyers pay almost nothing. That's why they were upset."

"Well, of course. I myself would be heartbroken if my landlord threatened to reduce the rent." I paused so that she could hear my stomach rumble. "Who wouldn't be?"

"Sarcasm does not become you," she said with a sniff. "To return to the point, Nicholas was vehemently opposed to any practices that fell outside his interpretation of unadulterated meso-Druidic tradition. He was forever grumbling about our two Wiccans and their somewhat quaint notions about matters of ritual. He observed Roy's drift into satanism with horror. He went so far as to object to the little herbal remedies that Fern concocts when someone is feeling unwell." She stood up. "This is all so difficult. I must have a cup of tea to give me the strength to continue."

She was out of the room before I could protest, which would have been a waste of perfectly good breath. I used up most of it with a drawn-out sigh, tucked a pillow behind my back, and resigned myself to incipient starvation. I was wondering how Leslie would have handled the situation when Malthea returned with a tray laden with the necessary accessories.

"Last night," she said as she sat down and poured the tea, "the room was thick with tension. Gilda and Morning Rose were sulking because of our decision to disallow them to perform the solstice ritual while sky-clad. Sullivan was pacing about like a caged animal, shooting dark looks at the rest of us. Fern was complaining about the placement of the greenery and tinsel, the smoke from the fire in the fireplace, the effect of the dampness on her rheumatism, and Roy's lack of

participation. I had to agree with her about Roy. He refused to so much as climb the ladder or tack a clump
of mistletoe to the wall. It wasn't like him at all."

"That's not how you described it this afternoon," I
said. "What happened to the pagan songs and tankards of mead?"

"I did everything I could to create a festive air, but it
was almost impossible. I'd just proposed a toast to the
rebirth of the Earth Goddess when Nicholas made his
announcement. After that, I'm sorry to say, there was
no hope that any of us could maintain even a facade of
gaiety. Harsh words were exchanged. Fern was in
tears as I helped her out to the car, and Sullivan drove
away with so much fury that we were left in a cloud of
dust. It was very inconsiderate of him."

"What did Nicholas say to upset your happy little
grove?" I asked.

Malthea took a tissue out of her pocket and touched
it to the corner of her eye. "Nicholas told us that he'd
made arrangements to put all of his property, including Primrose Hill and his rental holdings, on the mar-
ket. He'd decided to move to Wales and continue his
genealogical efforts to trace his lineage back to the
Celtic Druids at the dawning of the Christian era."

I thought for a minute. "You, Fern, and the Sulli-
vans were renters. What about Gilda and Roy's
family?"

"Gilda rents her trailer from the man who manages
the park. I'm not sure about the Tates, but I suspect
not. Their home is in a lovely neighborhood. Nicholas's properties are of a lesser quality and rented primarily to students, with the exception of a few retirees
such as myself and Fern."

"I can understand why those of you paying minimal rent might be perturbed, but surely not to the extent of harsh words, tears, and abrupt departures," I said. "Farberville has a goodly number of low-income rental properties. Moving might be inconvenient and the rent might increase, but still . . ."

Malthea rose and crossed the room to look out the window at the dark street. "The Sacred Grove of Keltria is very dear to me, as are its members. I've always considered us to be a spiritual family, and assumed Nicholas felt the same way. He was so brusque last night, so uncaring. He refused to discuss it further and said we had thirty days to vacate the property. When Fern tried to convince him to reconsider, he ordered all of us to leave."

"Even Roy?"

"He said that suitable arrangements would be made," she said, not turning.

I could see her face reflected in the windowpane. Rather than sad or even distressed, she seemed to be battling to suppress an anger that might have rivaled Nicholas's purported display the previous evening. Her eyes were narrowed, her lips squeezed together, and her cheeks flushed. I could easily imagine her at the stone altar in the grove, intoning an ancient prayer as she raised a dagger above a sacrificial victim.

Neither of us had moved when Fern opened the front door and came into the room. She stared at me for a paralytic moment, then swallowed and said, "I didn't realize you had company, Malthea."

Malthea's shoulders relaxed, and her expression was cordial as she turned around. "Claire came by to discuss how best to deal with the problem."

"She did?" said Fern. She put her hand on her face

to conceal her mouth from my view and mutely communicated something.

"Frankly," Malthea said as she came to the sofa and took my cup and saucer out of my hand, "there's nothing any of us can do. The police are searching for Roy. He can't go too far without transportation, and I should think he'll turn himself in rather than sleep outside."

Fern began to twist her bony hands, squeezing the blood out of her fingers. "Don't let us detain you, Claire."

"Thank you for dropping by," added Malthea, conveniently forgetting who'd issued the directive.

Five minutes earlier I would have chewed off my leg to escape, but the scenario had taken a peculiar direction and I was tempted to resist being dismissed like a chastised child. However, I picked up my purse, nodded, and went out onto the porch. I hesitated, but when no one opened the door and begged me to come back inside, I continued out to my car. Curiosity may have been gnawing at me, but I told myself it was more likely to be the combined effects of inadequate sleep and an empty stomach.

As I pulled away from the curb, two figures emerged from Malthea's side of the duplex. By the time I'd turned the corner, they had scurried into Fern's side. I slowed down, then caved in and parked the car. Mindful of the irregularities in the sidewalk, I cautiously approached the duplex and went across the yard in hopes I could see Malthea and Fern in the living room.

The drapes were drawn, and there were no telltale shadows. From one of the nearby houses I could hear a television blaring, and in the distance, a baby crying. There was no indication of any kind of activity, nefarious or innocuous, in Fern's apartment. She'd been agitated, though, and dismayed by my presence. Why?

I eased into the side yard and found yet another set of closed drapes. A thorny branch raked my hand as I tried to move closer to the window, underscoring the folly of allowing my overly active imagination to stifle my common sense.

I resisted the impulse to dive into the rosebushes as a car drove by, and instead dropped to my knees and turned my face away from the glare of the headlights. Once the car had passed, I arose and continued toward the back of the duplex, hoping to see them through a kitchen window.

Away from the glow of the streetlight, the only illumination came from a curtained window in the house next door. I felt my way toward a particularly impenetrable shadow that proved to be a high wooden fence. I was groping for a gate when I heard a door open and Malthea say, "How did he get here?"

"I have no idea," answered Fern, "and I must say I was not pleased to find him under the potting table. I like to keep everything arranged in a logical order so that I can easily put my hands on whatever I need. He's moved several stacks of flowerpots and pushed the bag of sphagnum moss against the wall. I do not look forward to having to crawl under the table to retrieve it."

I had a fairly good idea who was under the potting table, but I wasn't sure what to do. If I returned to my car and drove to a telephone to call the police, Roy might be long gone before they arrived. And turning him in wasn't necessarily the right thing to do. He'd been frightened when Corporal Billsby appeared at his door, and he'd certainly behaved suspiciously by climbing out the bathroom window, but as far as I knew he hadn't been charged with anything. If in fact he had, Fern and Malthea could be charged with harboring a fugitive. I had no desire to find myself in a courtroom, testifying against elderly ladies. Peter would not be amused when he saw the headline: BOOKSELLER IMPLICATED IN DRUID CRIME SPREE.

Perhaps I could persuade Roy to turn himself in, I thought as I gave up trying to find a gate and headed toward the front of the house to determine if I could go through Fern's apartment. I'd reached the edge of the porch when I saw two dark figures advancing toward me.

"Hold it right there!" one of them said in a decidedly unfriendly voice.

"Keep your hands where we can see them," said the other. His voice, although no doubt meant to sound equally menacing, ended with a squeak.

I noted the light glinting off both their weapons and their badges, so rather than swoon or bolt for the bushes, I said, "Do we have a problem, officers?"

"I don't know what you have, lady, but we had a call about a burglary in progress."

"In this neighborhood?" I said skeptically. "Is someone stealing beer cans out of garbage bags?"

The officers considered this for a moment, then lowered their weapons and gestured for me to move into the light. Neither was familiar, which I found heartening; I'd experienced entirely too much of Corporal Billsby's charm at various moments during the day—and it was feasible he would seize upon the most feeble of excuses to shoot me.

"Let's see some ID," Squeaky demanded.

"My purse is in my car," I said. "I'd like to add that I came here at a friend's behest. She lives in there."

"So why are you prowling around in the yard?" he countered.

"I am not prowling," I said.

"Look," said his partner, "the lady who lives in the next house saw you go by her window. According to her, you were prowling. Maybe you'd better explain why you went to visit your friend who lives there"— he jabbed his finger at Malthea's door—"and ended up out here in the dark. Maybe you were checking to see if the windows were locked in case you wanted to come back later."

I plucked a dried leaf off my jacket while I tried to decide how much of the truth I was willing to relate. "As I was driving away, I realized I had something else to tell my friend. She was not in her half of the duplex, so I assumed she and her next-door neighbor were in the greenhouse in the backyard."

Squeaky leaped on this tidbit as though it were a morsel of ripe cheese. "And you thought you'd break in and make off with her grocery money! I think we'd better take you down to the station and hear more of your fascinating story."

"Sergeant Jorgeson isn't going to like that," I said.

"Why not?"

It was time for a brief moment in the confessional before I was faced with a long moment in a cell. "He's eager to interview a possible witness in a murder that took place early this morning. The witness, Roy Tate, is in the greenhouse, too. Why don't I wait here while you fetch him, and then we'll all go to the station together? If you'd like to stop for doughnuts on the way, I'll pay for them. Better yet, let's order a pizza."

The officers looked at each other. "I guess it can't hurt to see who's out there," Squeaky said at last. "You aren't gonna wait here, though. Show us how to get to this greenhouse."

I led the way to Fern's front door. It was not locked, so we proceeded through the cluttered living room. As we went into the kitchen, I nearly tripped over the sill as I saw Malthea seated at a small table and Fern taking porcelain cups out of a cabinet.

"Goodness gracious!" said Malthea, although her performance was less than convincing. "I thought you'd gone home, Claire."

"Who are those men?" asked Fern. "Did you let them into my house? Why would you . . . ? Oh dear, Malthea, they're policemen."

Malthea cocked her head and gave them a beady look. "You really must explain this, gentlemen. This is a private residence, and unless you have a search warrant, you have no right to barge in like this."

"She," Squeaky said, pointing at me, "claims there's a fugitive hiding in the greenhouse out back. You'd better show me where it is."

"A fugitive?" repeated Malthea. "What a quaint notion. Fern and I were out there only minutes ago, and we saw no one."

I shook my head. "Sorry, but I heard you and Fern talking about Roy Tate's unauthorized presence in the greenhouse. He needs to stop being foolish and cooperate with the police. If it turns out that he needs a lawyer, I'll make sure he gets one who's had some experience."

Malthea stood up and gestured dramatically at the back door. "Officers, go see for yourselves that there is no one in the greenhouse. Fern discovered a stray dog earlier in the evening, and asked me to accompany her to make sure the creature had not returned."

The two policemen dutifully went through the door. Malthea, Fern, and I waited in stony silence. I mentally reviewed the snippet of conversation I'd overheard and concluded that Roy—or someone else, albeit unlikely—had been in the greenhouse. It was clear from their demeanor that whoever it had been was gone by now.

"No sign of anybody," Squeaky said as he and his partner came back into the kitchen. "We're going. Lady, stay out of other people's yards—okay?"

Fern managed to step on my toes as she went past me to escort the policemen to the front door. I looked down at Malthea, who was celebrating her minor victory with a contented smile.

"Roy was here," I said coldly.

"Only if he's reverted to a past life and taken the form of a large yellow dog," she said. "I was an eagle once, and what a lovely life it was. Soaring in the sky, swooping down on unsuspecting rodents and sinking my talons into warm flesh—"

"Did you give Roy money?"

Malthea's smile widened. "To buy dog biscuits?"

"If you know where he is, you need to convince him to call Sergeant Jorgeson at the police station and arrange to be picked up. Otherwise, Jorgeson will have no difficulty obtaining an arrest warrant and putting out an APB."

"Roy is a child."

"No, he's not," I replied levelly. "He's old enough to be tried as an adult and sentenced accordingly—if he killed Nicholas. His behavior certainly suggests it."

Fern came back into the kitchen. "Claire, in the future I'd appreciate it if you do not bring men into my home without my permission. It endangers my reputation in the community."

I threw up my hands, literally as well as figuratively, and stomped out of the duplex and down the sidewalk to my car. I knew what I'd heard, and it wasn't a discussion about a yellow dog. Roy Tate had taken refuge in Fern's greenhouse. My exchange with Officers Unfriendly and Squeaky must have carried to the backyard and sent Roy over the fence.

Scowling, I yanked open the car door and settled myself behind the wheel. As I reached for my purse to retrieve the car key, a male voice (neither squeaky nor unfriendly) said, "I gotta talk to you."

# CHAPTER 7

"Talk to me about what, Roy?" I said, annoyed with myself for not checking the backseat before I got in the car. It was something I always did, except, of course, when I'd been jerked around by a couple of gray-haired Druids.

"Start driving."

"Driving where?"

Roy breathed heavily for a moment. "I don't know. Just drive around and keep both hands on the steering wheel."

"And if I don't?" I said.

"I have a gun, Mrs. Malloy. I don't want to use it, but I'm in such deep shit already that it probably doesn't matter what I do." He thumped the back of my seat hard enough to rattle my teeth. "Let's go!"

I couldn't see him in the rearview mirror, so I had no idea if he was bluffing or not. It did not seem wise to press the issue. I pulled away from the curb and drove in the general direction of Thurber Street, where there might be a few cars and pedestrians. Roy had said he'd moved to Farberville only a few months earlier, so he might not have been aware that we were also headed in the direction of the police station.

"About last night," Roy began, cleared his throat,

and tried again. "You seem to have some inside edge with the cops. If I tell you what really happened, maybe you can explain it to them. I could tell from the way they were looking at me this morning that they think I'm some kind of psychopath who'd decapitate his grandmother for the price of a hamburger. I wouldn't be surprised if they dug up the flower beds at my father's house today in search of graves."

His supposition was likely to be accurate, but I saw no advantage in saying so. "Tell me what happened, Roy."

"Nicholas got pissed and yelled at everybody to get out of his house. Everybody did. I went up to my apartment, stuck a frozen dinner in the oven, and turned on some music. Around midnight, Nicholas knocked on my door and asked me to go back to the house with him. He was acting real odd, grinning at me and patting me on the back like I had colic. I could smell booze on his breath. I should have refused, but I was hoping maybe he'd changed his mind about selling all his properties. Living in the carriage house was a lot better than sharing a crappy little bedroom at the Sawyers' dump. Sullivan's a tight-ass, and Morning Rose fixes these weird vegetarian casseroles. Their kids give me the creeps."

"I'm sure it was an improvement," I said as I turned onto Thurber Street. Cars were scarce, pedestrians nonexistent. In the dark, the Book Depot looked more like an abandoned warehouse than a haven of intellectual enlightenment. I made a note to buy a few strands of Christmas lights—presuming the passenger in the backseat was not a psychopath who'd shoot a mild-mannered bookseller on a whim.

"So I was thinking I might not have to move out af-

ter all," Roy went on, "as long as I didn't do anything
to set him off again. We went into the kitchen. He
poured himself a glass of brandy and asked me if I
wanted some. I said I didn't. He got all huffy and kept
insisting until I finally said okay. Then he said for me
to sit down at the kitchen table because there was
something he needed to share with me. I was—well, I
was getting really nervous at this point."

"Had he ever offered you alcohol before?"

"Never. He hardly spoke to me unless there was
something he wanted me to do, like go down to the
end of the driveway to get the mail or do minor re-
pairs on his rental stuff." He tapped my shoulder.
"Don't turn here, Mrs. Malloy. I'm not ready for the
cops."

I abandoned my less-than-subtle subterfuge and
drove toward the campus. "Okay, last night Nicholas
was behaving strangely. You sat down as ordered—
and then what?"

"Maybe I shouldn't tell you," he said in a voice that
reminded me he was only sixteen years old. "You'll
probably think it was all my fault. It wasn't like I was
handcuffed to the table or anything. I could have gotten up and left. I wish I had."

"Why?" I asked softly.

"He started putting moves on me. You know what I
mean? He put his hand on my knee, and then, before I
could figure out what the hell was going on, he—you
know—he was saying things and grabbing at my
crotch. This never happened to me before. Girls,
maybe, but not some guy older than my father! A guy,
fer chrissake!"

All I could hope at that moment was Roy would not

be so overwhelmed with raw memories that he inadvertently squeezed the trigger. I heard the anguish in his voice, the adolescent uncertainty that he might have dropped a hint, might have done or said something to suggest that his true sexual identity was being suppressed. Whether or not it was did not concern me, and I certainly had not spent enough time with Nicholas Chunder to have formed an opinion about his.

I pulled into the football stadium parking lot, selected one of five hundred empty spaces, and turned off the engine. "What did you do?"

"I hit him. He sat there for a minute, then took a gun out of his pocket. I told him that all I wanted to do was go back to my apartment and go to bed. He started making this grotesque noise, like he was laughing but not really. I was so scared, Mrs. Malloy. You've got to believe me."

"Why didn't you run out the door at this point?" I asked.

Roy's fist bounced against the top of the front seat. "I should have, but I was petrified. He had a gun. It flashed across my mind that all he had to say was that I'd attacked him and he shot me in self-defense. I only hit him to make him leave me alone."

"Then what happened?"

"I went after the gun, and we sorta fell on the floor. The next thing I realized, the gun went off and he was breathing funny. I figured he could call himself an ambulance, so I went back to my apartment and tried to stay awake until somebody showed up. The brandy must have gotten to me, because I fell asleep on the couch. When my alarm went off at six, I walked across the pasture to the grove. I was praying like I'd never prayed before that Nicholas would come. You know the rest."

"I'll do what I can to help you," I said, easily imagining his version but not completely buying it. Nicholas Chunder had been an elderly single man, but I was not ready to stereotype him so neatly. Roy seemed distressed; however, he'd had time to rehearse. "If you're telling the truth, Sergeant Jorgeson can steer you through the maze of legal problems. He'll certainly sympathize with your reaction to Nicholas's advances."

"I should have pushed him down and run," he said glumly. "I know that."

"You're young. No one will fault you for what you *should* have done. Why don't we go to the police station now? I'll stay with you and do whatever I can until your parents get back from Borneo."

He began to whimper. "Would you do that for me, Mrs. Malloy? Like, nobody's ever done that before. My parents got divorced when I was ten, and my mother's an alcoholic and hooked on prescription drugs. My father married that bitch with all her dysfunctional relatives, so he's too busy to deal with me. Malthea's about the only person who cares about me."

"I'm sure other people care about you, too," I said, hoping he wouldn't demand a list of names.

"Look, why don't you talk to the police and see what they say? Let Malthea know, and I'll get in touch with her."

The car door opened and then slammed shut. Roy sprinted across the parking lot and vanished into the trees surrounding the admissions building at the top of the hill. As I sat, pondering his story, a campus cop pulled into the lot and stopped next to me.

"The lot's closed," he said. "Is something wrong?"

"I'm not sure," I replied truthfully.

I drove to my duplex, rerunning Roy's story in my mind. I reminded myself that I didn't know him well enough to judge his sincerity. I'd heard derogatory comments from Caron and Sullivan Sawyer, but for all I knew, Roy could have qualified for the title of patron saint of abused postpubescents—or at least those whose parents were on sabbatical in Borneo.

I was thinking all these muddled thoughts when I arrived at home and found a uniformed officer waiting for me on the doorstep. He was yet another member of the Farberville Police Department; I seemed to be going through the roster at an alarming rate.

"Yes?" I said.

"Where's Roy Tate?"

"I don't know. Maybe he's applying for admission to the college. That's where he was going when I last saw him."

"This isn't a joke," said the officer. "There's a warrant for his arrest."

I gave the officer a sketchy account of what had taken place at the duplex and in my car, omitting any mention of the gun Roy'd claimed he had. I would have to bear full responsibility if he used it on a rookie campus cop, but I didn't want that same cop to be so jittery that he shot Roy on sight. The phrase "armed and dangerous" can lead to such a result.

"I doubt he'll go back to Malthea's," I added, "but you might send someone to the Sawyers' house and Gilda D'Orcher's trailer. He doesn't seem to know any other people. Please let Sergeant Jorgeson know that I'll come by the station tomorrow morning."

The officer wrote down the names and left. I went

inside, kicked off my shoes, and punched buttons on the microwave to reheat that which had had nearly two hours to congeal into gelatinous glop. Caron's door was closed and her lights were off. I eased open the door to make sure that she was under the covers (as opposed to having gone undercover—an entirely different concept), then returned to the kitchen and retrieved the entrée.

At least, I thought as I mindlessly shoveled food into my mouth, my day had been anything but dull.

So there, Peter Rosen.

Jorgeson put down the stubby pencil and looked at me. "Do you believe his story?"

"Hard to say." I took a sip of coffee, shuddered, and set the Styrofoam cup on the corner of his desk. "That sort of thing does happen. Roy put on quite a show, but he's still just a kid and he certainly could have panicked when Nicholas molested him. Teenagers can be painfully self-conscious about their bodies. Every time Caron gets a pimple, she plunges into despair and spends hours staring at it in the mirror. That isn't to say she doesn't spend hours in front of the mirror when her skin is clear. If I'd let her, she'd put a mirror on the ceiling of her bedroom."

"Forensics didn't turn up anything useful," Jorgeson said, apparently inured to the toxic sludge that passed for coffee at the PD. "There were fingerprints all over the house, but that's usually the case. We'll match what we can to persons known to have been there that evening. The rest of them will be sent to the FBI, but I don't think they're going to come back with a serial killer. I can't see asking for prints from the membership of the genealogical society."

"I suppose not," I said, sighing. "I feel sorry for Roy. He's clearly unhappy and seems to go out of his way to be a misfit and a loner. Problems with both of his parents, a stepmother, a new school—those things can corrode any teenager's sense of worth. What'll happen to him, Jorgeson?"

"Nothing at the moment, since we don't have him in custody. It's a shame you didn't deliver him to us, Mrs. Malloy. He'd be talking to a lawyer instead of hiding in the basement of almost any building on campus."

"He *said* he had a gun; I wasn't inclined to find out if he did by daring him to put a bullet in my back. None of the other Druids have seen him?"

"They say not, but who knows? I can't figure out any of them. My wife and I go to church where there are pews and stained-glass windows, not bushes and squirrels." Jorgeson shuffled through a pile of reports, snuffling and wheezing like a bulldog. "Here's what we've got on the victim. Nicholas Chunder was sixty-eight, a retired doctor, an upstanding member of a couple of civic clubs. He was born and raised in Indianapolis, went to medical school in Chicago, and opened a private practice here after twenty-five years in a group practice back in Indianapolis. Not so much as a hint of scandal back there. His wife, an heiress with a considerable trust fund, died of cancer when she was in her early thirties. There were no children."

"Did he have family in this area?"

"We didn't come across anything in his files to suggest it. I spoke to his lawyer on the phone. He said the heir is a nephew in Terre Haute. Don't start wiggling your nose like that, Mrs. Malloy—the nephew was wounded in Vietnam and is a paraplegic. Besides, I thought we'd just agreed that Roy confessed to the homicide. Why would he do that if it wasn't the truth?"

"I have no idea," I admitted.

Jorgeson said he'd assure Malthea that Roy would be treated gently if he turned himself in. I drove to the Book Depot, made sure Roy wasn't hiding behind the boiler, and then started a pot of coffee and sat down at my desk while the Mr. Coffee machine groaned in what sounded like terminal agony. It was slightly after nine, which meant Peter would be drinking coffee, reading a newspaper, and no doubt keeping an eye on the time so he wouldn't be late picking up Leslie at the airport. I battled back an irrational urge to break into his house and search for a photograph of the blissful couple on their wedding day.

When the coffee was ready, I filled a mug and went up front to read the newspaper. A short article about Nicholas Chunder's murder had made the second page, but there was no mention of the Druid connection. It was only a matter of time before reporters heard rumors and started nosing around. Malthea might decide it would be diverting to be interviewed on the local news so she could proselytize to the non-tree-huggers. My name would surface. Despite my efforts to downplay my involvement in previous cases, I'd had a bit of publicity in the past. I could anticipate a good deal more than fifteen minutes in the limelight this time.

I spent the remainder of the morning wishing that Jorgeson would call to say they'd taken Roy into custody and arranged for a lawyer. At eleven o'clock (aka noon EST), I snatched up the feather duster and attacked the racks with heretofore unseen diligence. When my science-fiction hippie came into the store, I went for the dandruff on his shoulders. He retreated out the door and scurried up the sidewalk.

I was inking out pearly white teeth on the bridal page of the newspaper when the bell jingled and Malthea came into the store. "Claire," she said, "may I speak to you for a moment?"

I added a mole to a brunette's nose, then put the page and the pen in a drawer. "Have you heard from Roy?"

She shook her head. "No, and I'm terribly worried. That police officer who called this morning said only that Roy confessed to you. I'm at a loss to understand why he would do such a thing, and I was hoping you might tell me more about what he said."

"I'm afraid I can't go into detail," I said. "They were in the kitchen and got into an argument. The gun went off accidentally. Roy was too panicked to call an ambulance, so he . . ." I faltered as I realized what I'd just said. For starters, Roy hadn't been too panicked to break the window in Nicholas's study in order to make it look as though a burglary had taken place. Furthermore, the brandy bottle and glasses had been removed before our arrival. As had the gun. I doubted I would have been so coolheaded in a situation of that nature. Caron would have been on the roof in a matter of seconds, screaming for an ambulance.

"You're looking pale," Malthea murmured. "Why don't we sit down in the back?"

I followed her into the office and cleared off a chair for her. "Would you like a cup of coffee?"

"That would be nice. It's rather chilly back here. Could you turn up the thermostat?"

"Certainly," I said mendaciously, since I'd yet to find a way to influence the boiler. I made decisive motions with a gizmo on the wall, then poured two cups of coffee and sank back down behind my desk, still puzzling over the discrepancies in Roy's story.

Malthea gave me a concerned frown. "Is something vexing you, Claire?"

"A couple of the things Roy said don't support his version of what happened. I guess I'd better call Sergeant Jorgeson and make sure he's aware of them." I reached for the telephone, then noticed her birdlike expression and said, "After we've finished our conversation, of course."

"Well, there is one little thing I believe I should tell you. If you think it's important, you can pass it on to your friend on the police force. I failed to mention in my statement that I returned to Nicholas's house shortly after midnight."

I choked on a mouthful of coffee, nearly spewing it across the desk. "You did what?"

"After Fern and I arrived at the duplex, we said good-night and went into our respective sides. I made tea and was trying to distract myself with my tarot cards when I heard her back door open. I peeked out my kitchen window. Fern was inside her greenhouse, sobbing uncontrollably. I wanted to rush to her side to offer comfort, but I knew she would be appalled to be discovered in such an emotional display. Oh, if only Nicholas had been there to see her misery."

"Because she was going to lose her greenhouse," I said.

"Her plants and the Sacred Grove of Keltria are all she has," Malthea said, taking a tissue out of her satchel to wipe the corner of her eye. "She's tried other hobbies, but nothing fascinates her more than puttering around the greenhouse, misting and repotting and pinching off dead blossoms. She'd sleep out there if it were feasible."

"There's no way she could have it moved?"

"She has very limited financial resources, and will most likely have to settle for a subsidized apartment complex for senior citizens. She can take a few of her leafy friends with her, but not the special ones that require a carefully regulated climate." She took another swipe at her eyes. "Nicholas did a terrible thing when he told her she had to move within thirty days. What's more, he was overreacting to the disagreement between himself and the Wiccan faction. The ultimate decision as to what's allowed during our rituals is up to the Arch Druid, and I assured him that I would not vacillate from my stated position."

I jumped in before she could lapse into a discourse on the variations in pagan practices. "So you went back to Nicholas's house to talk to him, right?"

"I knocked, then repeatedly rang the bell. Nicholas enjoyed doing things on his computer. I never quite understood what he did, but he always said what satisfaction it gave him. I assumed he was too immersed to hear me, so I went around to the back of the house, planning to tap on his study window. To my surprise, the kitchen door was wide open. When I saw his body, I almost swooned, but I pulled myself together at the last second and took a more careful look at the scene. I felt exactly like Sherlock Holmes as I deduced what had taken place."

"And what did you deduce?"

Malthea stared grimly at me. "I knew no burglar had been responsible for Nicholas's death, since neither of them would have sat down and enjoyed a bit of brandy. Mumsy did that once and came close to being arrested." She waggled her finger at me to prevent me from interrupting. "Therefore, whoever had been there was someone Nicholas knew well enough to offer hospitality. A chair was overturned, indicating there'd been a scuffle. It was obvious that the police and paramedics had not been alerted or it would have been very crowded in the kitchen." Her eyes shifted away from me and her hand fell to her lap. "Roy came to mind."

I was beginning to suspect where this was going. "Malthea, did you decide to make it look like a burglary in order to protect him?"

"How clever of you, Claire. I washed the glasses and put them away, wiped fingerprints off the brandy bottle and returned it to its cabinet, and broke the window in the study. After a final inspection to make sure I'd missed nothing, I locked the door behind me and went home. It was rather late by then, and I wanted as much rest as possible before our celebration at dawn."

"And said nothing to the police, of course," I said wearily. "Don't you know it's wrong to remove evidence from a crime scene?"

"I have a duty to protect Roy, and I was convinced that whatever had taken place was not his fault. He's a good boy at heart. When he matures, he'll forget about this satanic nonsense and become a productive member of society. I did what was necessary for him to have that opportunity. It was the least I could do."

I had a flash of insight into Peter's reaction whenever I made assertions of a similar nature. I was always proved correct, of course, which made it all the worse. Perhaps after Leslie counseled his mother, she could counsel him, too.

"I think we're finished," Malthea said as she stood

up and headed for the door. "You might want to clean your coffeepot on a more regular basis. It will decrease the bitterness."

I trotted after her. "You absolutely must go straight to the police department and tell all this to Sergeant Jorgeson. He's not going to be happy, but he may handle it better if it comes from you instead of me."

"Do you think so?" she asked. "I was under the impression you and he are good friends."

"Not that good," I said coldly. "Will you promise to go there now?"

"I'd planned to go out to the grove and meditate. It's very peaceful out there, with the wind rustling the leaves and the shadows creating a lovely quilt."

"It won't be peaceful when the cops arrive to drag you to the police department."

"My, you are in a cantankerous mood, aren't you? Do take my advice about cleaning the coffeepot. It might improve your disposition."

She gave me a bright little smile and left. I considered chasing after her with the feather duster, then took a couple of breaths and refilled my cup with perfectly decent coffee. I decided to wait fifteen minutes before calling Jorgeson in order to give Malthea a chance to do the honorable thing. I would not have bet on it.

While I waited, I thought about her story. Like Roy's, it was plausible; she certainly could have taken it upon herself to lecture Nicholas. That she'd gone there at twelve-thirty at night would have seemed unremarkable to her. Neither, apparently, did tidying up the scene to suggest a burglary. I wondered if all Arch Druids were as protective of their underlings as she.

I finally called the police department and asked to

speak to Jorgeson. He came on the line with a martyred, "Yes, Mrs. Malloy?"

"Has Malthea Hendlerson arrived there yet?"

"The one who insisted on singing some song about holly and ivy when she gave a statement yesterday? The one who claimed her mother'd had an affair with Archduke Francis Ferdinand just prior to his assassination? Her?"

" 'Fraid so," I said, then related what she'd said.

He was silent for a long moment. "Jeez, what with all the cop shows on television these days, I'd like to think civilians have some idea of the word 'tampering.' Which planet has that woman been living on for the last fifty years? How could she calmly wash the damn glasses and wipe prints off the bottle? Gad, we're lucky she didn't haul the body upstairs and tuck it in bed!"

"Or bury it in the woods," I said, grimacing as I realized how effortlessly I could envision her doing it. "In any case, she's admitted what she did, and it explains a lot of inconsistencies with Roy's description of what went on in the kitchen . . . with one exception. She never mentioned the gun."

"So the kid took it with him. As it happens, there's a major inconsistency you haven't heard yet. I checked with the medical examiner and there was virtually no alcohol in the victim's blood. He hadn't been drinking brandy when he was shot."

"What do you think that means?"

"I'd like to ask Roy Tate that very same question," Jorgeson said with a trace of acerbity. "Everybody on patrol is keeping an eye out for him. The campus security guys are checking the buildings, but it's gonna take them all week because so many of them are off duty when the college is closed. We'll find him sooner or later, and he'd better have an explanation."

I told him where Malthea might be, then hung up. Malthea and Roy had both attested to the presence of the brandy bottle and glasses in the kitchen, and Roy had said he smelled alcohol on Nicholas's breath. But unless the lab report was wrong, Nicholas hadn't been drinking. He could have been pretending to be drunk, I supposed, and hoping to bully Roy into joining him.

Or Roy and Malthea were lying about this one particular detail. Was everything else they'd said lies, too? There were more than enough members of the grove for a full-fledged conspiracy, presuming three Druids (Malthea, Fern, and Sullivan), two Wiccans (Morning Rose and Gilda), and one satanist (Roy) could collaborate without coming to blows. Based on what I'd seen and heard, it did not seem likely.

I felt sorry for Jorgeson. He clearly had no clue how to deal with his less than conventional witnesses. Standard police procedure was no match for someone who'd casually stepped over a corpse to put away a brandy decanter—and hadn't thought it was worthy of mention until the following day.

When the phone rang, I eyed it unhappily. Malthea calling to say the gun was in the dishwasher? Jorgeson calling to report that Roy'd been killed in a shootout with the campus cops? Gilda calling to berate me for not going to her trailer? Peter calling to announce that he and Leslie were getting remarried in the Winter Palace, with canine attendants?

Scolding myself for this ultimate petty thought, I picked up the receiver and chirped, "Book Depot."

"Mother," said Caron, her voice low and hoarse, "can you pick me up at the mall?"

"Sure. At eight o'clock—right? Which entrance?"

"Now, in front of Sears."

"What's wrong?" I said. "Did you get fired?"

"It's a lot worse than that. Please hurry."

She hung up. I did the same, locked the store, and drove to the mall, speculating about what she'd find worse than getting fired and having to sacrifice her layaway purchases.

I navigated through the crowded parking lot and pulled up in front of the appointed entrance. Caron was leaning against the wall, her arms wrapped around herself and her face lowered as if she could will herself into invisibility. She seemed to be having a degree of success; none of the shoppers streaming in and out the doors so much as glanced at her.

I rolled down the window and called, "Caron?"

She jerked her head up as though a bullet had hit the pseudo-stuccoed wall, then focused in on me and darted to the car. As soon as she'd slammed the door, she said, "Drive!"

I glanced at her, but she'd bent over and her face was hidden. "Okay," I said with a great deal more composure than I felt. I worked my way back to the stoplight and eventually escaped from the parking lot.

"You can sit up now," I said.

"What's the point in doing that?" she said, her voice muffled.

"Well, we're not being pursued by a car packed with heavily armed gangsters. Should I be watching for a police car?"

"No." She sat up, ran her fingers through her hair, and let out a grandiose sigh. "You're not going to like this."

"Did you get fired?"

"I think you can safely assume I will be within a matter of hours. Before I go on, you have to promise not to start yelling at me—okay?"

I turned into the bowling alley lot and stopped. "I promise not to yell at you. It's only a part-time job, dear, and you hated it. Some of the stores will hire temps after Christmas to help handle returns. You can find something."

"What I need to find, Mother, is a lawyer."

# CHAPTER 8

I sat on the sofa, reading the document that Caron had taken out of her purse. "What's MultiPackaging, Incorporated, in Dallas?"

Caron was draped across a chair opposite me, her fingertips brushing the floor and her eyes closed for maximum effect. "That's the all-powerful home office, and it's more likely to be in Oz than Texas. They run Santa's Workshops in malls all over the South and Midwest. They also do this kind of crap with the Easter Bunny, as well as studio portraits and videotaping of everything from birthday parties and weddings to class reunions. You can hire them to come into the delivery room. That's the grossest thing I've ever heard."

"North Hills Mall is down as a defendant, too. Who's Winifred Portmeyer?"

"Mrs. Claus. I'm surprised they didn't go after Santa himself, although the only thing he did was watch."

"That's all I did," I pointed out, "and I made the defendants' list as your guardian." I began to read aloud. " 'Comes now Morgan G. Connolly, by and through her guardians, Suzanne and Eric L. Connolly, and for their complaint, state and allege the following, to-wit: that the parties are—' "

"Residents of the county, blah, blah, blah," Caron said, sagging further into the chair until she resembled an afghan. "What matters is they're saying that I committed assault and battery, that Morgan was bruised so badly and in such a state of hysteria that she had to be treated by a doctor. Can you believe this?"

I continued reading. " 'The plaintiff suffered various bruises and lacerations and other injuries to her person for which she is entitled to a judgment against the defendants herein in the amount of ...' " My throat squeezed up so tightly that I couldn't say the figure.

"One million dollars," Caron said for me. "Go on to the next page, Mother."

I forced myself to turn the page. " 'That, also, the plaintiff suffered great emotional distress and has been unable to sleep or attend school, which was intentionally inflicted upon her by the defendants, for which she is entitled to unspecified punitive damages in an amount to be determined by a jury.' This happened less than twenty-four hours ago! So she had a bad night and wasn't in the mood this morning for whatever fancy private school she attends. How can they claim she's been permanently traumatized? I'll bet right now she's contentedly eating ice cream and watching Disney videos."

"Or ripping limbs off her dolls."

I tossed the complaint on the coffee table. "What about Inez?"

"She is such a wimp. She wanted to leave with me, but Mrs. Claus went ballistic and made her promise to work through Christmas Eve."

"What did Mrs. Claus say to you?"

Caron's lip inched out. "Well, after the guy shoved the papers at us and left, she grabbed my arm, dragged

me into the employee lounge, and started in on me
about how it was all my fault. I reminded her that
she'd just stood there like a tick on a reindeer's rump
when the brat slipped by me. The conversation went
downhill after that. I tore off my antlers and said I was
leaving, and she said not to come back until she's
talked to her supervisor."

"I'd better call a lawyer," I said, gloomily wondering about prevailing legal fees. Although Caron had
come perilously close to the brink of criminal charges,
she'd never before taken a plunge into the abyss. The
summons and complaint stated that we had thirty
days to respond, and I doubted an articulate, artfully
composed letter from me would suffice.

"Is there anything to eat?" asked Caron, sounding
like the last orphan in line at the workhouse.

I took some money out of my billfold. "Why don't
you go pick up Chinese? The car key's on the kitchen
counter."

"Yeah, okay." She curled her lip at the document,
then went through the kitchen and out the back door.

I fixed myself a cup of tea, and then looked up the
telephone number of the only lawyer I knew in Farberville. It was hardly my lucky day, but Franklin Adamson was in his office and unencumbered with a
client.

"Merry Christmas, Claire," he said. "How's everything? Business brisk?"

"I suppose," I said, then told him about the summons and complaint. "The whole thing is absurd," I
added. "The child may have a bruise or two, but she
definitely didn't suffer lacerations. Okay, so she skinned
her knee when she fell down while running to her

mother. They're making it sound as if Caron chased her around the mall with a carving knife."

"Welcome to the wacky world of litigation. Who's their attorney?"

I flipped to the second page. "The child's father, Eric L. Connolly. I suppose that's why this was filed at the approximate speed of light."

"The holiday season's usually slow for us. I'm trying to think if I've met Connolly. The name's familiar. I'll see what I can find out about him. I'm going to switch you back to my receptionist so you can make an appointment. Bring Caron and the papers."

"Franklin, damn it," I said, "are you saying there's a grain of validity in this? I can't believe it. The child threw a tantrum because she didn't get her way—and we're being sued? If anyone deserves to be sued, it's Suzanne and Eric L. for raising an ill-mannered, egotistical monster!"

"Vent if you must, but make an appointment," he said, "and whatever you do, don't initiate any contact with the child or her parents."

I made an appointment for the next morning at ten o'clock, then decided tea was inadequate for the occasion. I poured a stiff drink, returned to the sofa, and retrieved the complaint. I could have gone to the store and reopened for an hour, but my mood was vile enough to frighten potential customers, who would then sue me for "great emotional distress" and future bouts of insomnia brought on by the lack of mystery novels on the bedside table. Heaven help me if one stubbed a toe while fetching a magazine.

Caron returned with an array of cardboard cartons and very little change. "I'm not hungry right now," she said as she unloaded the bags. "Inez said she'll call me as soon as she gets home. I don't know how she's supposed to deal with the kids by herself, but you know what? I don't care. I don't even care if a pointy-headed elf topples off the roof of the gazebo and embeds itself in Mrs. Claus's skull. It would be an improvement."

I was heartened to hear a more characteristic edge in her voice, but she'd not spoken in capital letters in two days. I smiled and said, "I'll put the food away and you can warm it up later."

"The prisoner had a last meal of moo goo gai pan and sesame beef," she intoned, then retreated to her room. The door closed with a tiny click.

I reread the complaint until I could recite every word of it, from the header to the date the notary public's commission expired. I wanted to call Franklin back and say, "You were kidding—right? No judge is going to even tolerate this nonsense in his courtroom—right? Oh, you had me going there for a minute, but we both know you were teasing me—right?"

Wrong.

An hour later, the telephone rang. I waited, assuming Caron would answer it, but it continued to ring. I picked up the receiver and said, "Hello."

"Mrs. Malloy, it's Jorgeson. We've got a problem."

"You have a problem, and I have a problem. However, we do not have the *same* problem unless you're being sued for a million dollars."

"Huh?"

"What do you want?" I asked.

"First, we found Malthea Hendlerson where you said and brought her in. She told me the same thing she told you. When I asked her about the brandy bottle, she insisted it had been on the table with one glass and the other glass was on the floor. She couldn't explain why the lab didn't find alcohol in the victim's blood and stuck to her story. There wasn't anything to do but let her leave."

"Is that your problem, Jorgeson? I could have told you that's what would happen."

"No, I was just telling you. The problem is another of those dadburned Druids. I put a man out at Nicholas Chunder's place to watch for Roy Tate in case he went to his apartment or tried to get the hearse. The officer caught Gilda D'Orcher trying to break into the main house. We've got her in custody, but she won't say anything except that she wants to talk to you. She's kept it up for a couple of hours. Doesn't want a lawyer, doesn't want to make a call, doesn't want coffee or anything to eat."

"Perhaps she'll change her mind after spending the night in a cell," I said without sympathy. "Your amenities are not on par with a luxury hotel. Give her a couple of prostitutes and drug addicts for cellmates."

He was silent for a minute. "I thought you'd want to talk to her, find out why she was breaking into the house. Listen, I've kept my end of the bargain. Lieutenant Rosen called this afternoon and I didn't mention your name when I gave him a synopsis of the case. I can't say what I would have done if he demanded particulars, but he seemed kinda distracted and didn't press me. This business with his mother must be getting him down."

"That would explain it," I said through clenched teeth. "I have an appointment in the morning. If Gilda hasn't capitulated by noon or so, call me at the bookstore and I'll think about it. Right now I have a headache and entirely too many other things to worry about—and not one of them is Lieutenant Rosen's mother."

I nibbled at the Chinese food and tried to finish a novel, but I found myself searching the complaint for fine print that would expose it as an idle threat or an unamusing practical joke. Lawyers were not notorious for that sort of thing, I told myself.

By eight o'clock I'd made little headway with the food or the fine print. My headache had eased, but I suspected it would rekindle itself in Franklin's office in the morning. I was considering a long, steamy bath when the doorbell rang.

I opened the front door and found myself looking at an unfamiliar woman. She was in her thirties, with short dark hair, a slender body clothed in a gray silk suit, and the resolute demeanor of someone intent on selling beauty products. "Yes?" I said.

"Mrs. Malloy, I'm Winifred Portmeyer. We need to talk. May I come in?"

She was already inside before she'd finished the question, rendering it moot. She sat down, crossed her legs, and opened a briefcase. "Is Caron home? She needs to be included in this discussion since it affects her, too."

"I'll get her." As I went down the hallway, I recalled my brief impression of Mrs. Claus bent over the camera and then straightening up to glare at Caron. I'd been right about the white wig—and wrong about the ample rump. I tapped on Caron's door, then opened it and in a low voice, said, "Mrs. Claus is in the living room."

"That's not funny," Caron said without looking up from the magazine spread across her lap.

"Sorry, dear, but she really is and she wants to talk to you."

"Tell her you came in here and found me hanging from the light fixture, my eyes bulging and my tongue blue. Threaten to sue her if she doesn't leave."

"Please come into the living room so we can get this over," I said. "I assure you I'm not any more delighted at the opportunity than you are, but she seems like the sort who will sit there all night."

"Let her."

After a few more exchanges of this nature, Caron threw down the magazine and trailed me back to the living room.

"Hello, Caron," the woman said smoothly. "Why don't you and your mother sit there on the sofa? Shall we get started?"

I sat down, but Caron remained standing behind the sofa, her arms crossed and her lower lip trembling. "Has Caron been fired?" I asked, attempting to regain some control of the situation, since we were in my apartment and not the corporate boardroom in Dallas.

Ms. Portmeyer nodded. "Yes, she has. I'll calculate her pay and she can pick up the check tomorrow. The cost of the hood will be deducted, as well as having the tunic dry-cleaned for the next reindeer."

"Good luck finding one," muttered Caron. "Talk about a stupid, demeaning—"

"And the lawsuit?" I cut in quickly. "That *is* why you're here, isn't it?"

"Yes, indeed," she said. She rummaged through papers in her briefcase, but as far as I could tell, she was doing so only to impress us with her professionalism. "I spoke with Mr. Longsterger in the Dallas office about this. He'll have to consult the legal department, but in previous cases of a like nature, MultiPack has settled with the plaintiff in order to avoid negative publicity. We wouldn't want the media to pounce on a story about someone suing Santa, would we? It could have a devastating effect on children too young to make the distinction."

Despite her slick presentation, I got the message. "MultiPack, as you call it, is going to pay off the Connolly family to keep them quiet?"

"I should think that will be the ultimate decision. Our insurance carries a liability clause. North Hills Mall has a similar policy and will most likely choose to settle, too. They prefer a reputation as a place where children are safe from physical injury and emotional distress."

"What about you?" asked Caron.

She flashed small white teeth. "As a MultiPack employee, the liability covers me from any lawsuit resulting from my assignment. I've been with them for fifteen years. I started out just as you did, then did a degree in business law, and went on to become an assistant regional season events director. We've used the same Mrs. Claus in Farberville for several years, but she was taken ill at the last moment and I stepped in as a replacement. Sacrifices must be made for the good of the corporation."

I gave her a cold look. "Caron was an employee at the time. Is she covered?"

"I'm afraid she isn't, since she was a part-time employee and therefore not entitled to any benefits. It's made quite clear in the contract she signed. I believe it's paragraph eleven, subsection four, item eight." Ms. Portmeyer closed her briefcase and stood up. "I'm glad to have met you, Mrs. Malloy. Caron, I enjoyed working with you while it lasted. I hope you'll remember us fondly."

"Wait a minute!" I said as I stood up. "Let me make sure I have this straight. You, MultiPack, and the mall are bailing out of the lawsuit, leaving Caron and me to face the possibility of a million-dollar judgment. Is that correct?"

She held out a business card. "This has the telephone and fax numbers of our legal department should your attorneys wish to be in communication with them. If Caron has misplaced her copy of her contract, I have the original which can be placed in evidence. I can also provide the manual given to her; it contains very precise guidelines on the policy of handling difficult customers. Physical roughness is explicitly forbidden."

Caron moved in front of the door, blocking Ms. Portmeyer's withdrawal. "What was I supposed to do, then? Let her go up on the stage and knock other kids off Santa's lap?"

Ms. Portmeyer blinked. "Oh, no, that would have resulted in a lawsuit, too. It's unfortunate that you didn't take time to study the manual, Caron. You would have made a fine senior reindeer in years to come. Because of what happened, MultiPack cannot continue any association that might taint our image as a family-focused organization."

Caron looked as though she was ready to punch her ex-boss in the nose, which no doubt would have resulted in yet another lawsuit. I hastily clutched her elbow and pulled her away from the door. "Good night, Ms. Portmeyer," I said. "You'll be hearing from my attorney within a matter of days."

"Good night," she said, then went through the doorway and down the stairs.

I released Caron's arm and told her about the appointment in the morning with Franklin Adamson. "Why don't you sleep in? I have a few things to do at the store, and then I'll come by and pick you up at a quarter till ten."

"I feel like I'm on drugs. I mean, this has to be a hallucination, doesn't it? One minute I'm a dorky reindeer, the next minute a defendant in a million-dollar lawsuit. Maybe we should just hop in the car like you said and take off—and never come back. Is there some kind of booksellers' underground railroad?"

"Good night, dear."

The session in the law office was more painful than an equivalent amount of time on a rack in a dungeon. Franklin emphasized the severity of the situation and the very real possibility of a judgment in favor of the plaintiffs. MultiPackaging and North Hills Mall were within their respective corporate rights to settle out of court for whatever amount was necessary to be detached from the complaint. What's more, we'd never find out how much they'd paid.

I'd brightened a bit when Franklin had said Caron was entitled—perhaps—to indemnification from MultiPackaging. The crumb having been offered, he'd then snatched it away by adding that our lawsuit against them could drag on into the next century.

Caron was atypically subdued during the session, and was no more animated as we got into the car. "I'm sorry about this, Mother. Maybe I should have read the manual like she said."

"Don't be silly," I said, squeezing her shoulder. "I would have done the same thing, as would anyone. The manual is apt to contain nothing more than vague policies so that MultiPack can claim to have provided sufficient training for new employees. When you point-blank asked Ms. Portmeyer what you should have done, she didn't have an answer." I started the car. "Do you want me to take you to the mall so you can pick up your check?"

Caron sniffled rather endearingly. "No, Inez said she'd get it and come by tonight. Drop me off at Luanne's store. I think I'd better get used to wearing secondhand clothes."

I did as she asked, then continued to the Book Depot and took the "closed" sign off the door. This did not result in a mad rush of customers, alas, but eventually a professor I knew from the English department ambled in and we spent a pleasant hour deconstructing Dickens's *A Christmas Carol* over coffee. He bought a couple of sugary romance novels, claiming they were for his wife, but I knew her taste ran more to erotic time-travel fantasies.

No man is a hero to his valet—or to his bookseller.

Franklin had made it clear that there was nothing Caron and I could do except wait to see what developed. He would file our response (presumably, just legalese jargon for "did not!") and request copies of reports from the child's physician and whoever performed the psychological evaluation. Pacing and tearing out my hair were counterproductive.

"It could be worse," I said out loud, testing the level of conviction I could achieve without sounding completely deranged. Not much, I concluded, and I had a feeling I was going to be spouting that particular cliché many times over the next thirty days.

I needed a distraction. Although I'd lost all interest in the Druids, including Roy's current whereabouts and Malthea's motive for lying about the brandy decanter, I decided I might as well come to Jorgeson's aid and find out what Gilda wanted.

I dialed the station, and when put through to Jorgeson, said, "Do you still want me to talk to Gilda?"

"No, that's all right," he said. "She's not gonna be talking to anybody today."

"You said she specifically mentioned me."

"I went ahead and had her in a cell overnight. She got hold of a sharp object, maybe a piece of glass or something, and carved up her wrists. We took her to the hospital for a brief stop in the emergency room and at least twenty-four hours in the psych ward."

"Good grief," I said, stunned.

"There was another prisoner in there with her—just a woman who'd had too much to drink and broke a beer bottle over her boyfriend's head. The woman was still woozy, but she said Gilda was acting really weird and weaving around the cell, calling out long foreign-sounding names. It scared the woman so badly that she put the blanket over her head."

"Not an unreasonable response," I said. "Has anybody heard from Roy Tate?"

"Not yet, and I'm catching some hell from the captain. We've got around-the-clock surveillance at the victim's place, and patrolmen cruising past the Druids' houses every half hour or so. He's probably holed up at a friend's house."

"What about Gilda's trailer?"

"We've been there, and the manager promised to keep an eye on it. You know, Mrs. Malloy, I liked it better when you had other things on your mind. Why don't you go shopping or make a fruitcake?"

I didn't need to make a fruitcake; I was acquainted

with several of them, and in the middle of the afternoon, one entered the store, accompanied by her two well-bundled offspring.

"What's going on with Roy?" Morning Rose demanded as she came to the counter. "The police came to our house last night looking for him, and they've been driving by all day. Do they have evidence he had something to do with Nicholas's death?"

"They seem to think they do," I said. "Have you heard from him since yesterday morning?"

She shoved her children toward a display of cookbooks. "Go look at all the yummy food," she said, then turned back to me. "I called him yesterday afternoon to make sure he was all right. He's much more sensitive than anyone suspects, and prone to depression. It's a result of his studies in the realm of evil forces that are capable of toying with our individual destinies. He's seen things most of us have never imagined could exist, and is periodically overwhelmed with an agonizing sense of impotence and—"

"What did he say when you called?"

She took off her gloves and aligned them on the counter. "Not much, really. He wasn't especially fond of Nicholas, and in·fact, a month ago he told me that there was something about Nicholas that made him uneasy. Nicholas affected others of us the same way. He was very private about his business and personal affairs. We saw him only on major holidays."

"He was your landlord, wasn't he?" I asked, straining to hear noises from behind the rack. "Didn't he come by to collect the rent every month?"

"Sullivan mailed him the check. No, Nicholas had a side of him that was every bit as sinister as Roy's demons. Who knows what might have gone on inside his house? He chose it for its isolation, he once told me. I intuitively realized that he didn't want anyone to see who visited him at night."

"Don't you think you ought to see what your children are doing?"

"They always like to explore a new environment on their own terms. Do you have any idea where Roy is?"

"No more than I do of what"—I braced myself to say the names—"Cosmos and Rainbow have found so fascinating. Please make sure they aren't damaging any books."

"They would never do anything like that. When I talked to Roy, he was terribly worried that he wouldn't be allowed to stay in the carriage house. He knew Sullivan wouldn't let him move back in with us. Because of his mother's substance problems, he was placed in foster homes several times, and he hated them."

"Where's his mother now?" I asked, increasingly concerned about the future salability of the cookbooks.

Morning Rose shrugged. "Roy doesn't know. When he first moved in with his father, he talked to her on the phone every week. Then, without warning, the phone was disconnected. Roy called a neighbor, who said his mother had packed her belongings and left town with a man she met at a nightclub."

"A tragic story," I said. "Will you please check on your children?"

"Oh, all right," she said sulkily, "although you seem to have an unhealthy obsession with their behavior." She disappeared around the rack, then returned with a smug smile. "They're sitting quietly, looking at photographs in cookbooks. A perfectly innocent activity, wouldn't you say?"

I was growing rather tired of being accused of sub-standard attributes. What's more, her children were quite capable of *licking* photographs instead of looking at them. I waited a moment to allow my irritation to subside, then said, "Has Roy ever mentioned any friends or fellow satanists in Farberville?"

"He doesn't make friends easily. His mother moved so often over the last six years that I doubt he has friends anywhere. I've never heard him mention any names."

"How did he become a member of the grove?"

Morning Rose made a vague gesture. "That was Malthea's doing, and I don't remember the details. She struck up a conversation with him and he attended our Samhain celebration at Halloween. No, that wasn't the first. He was with us for the autumnal equinox, which was about the time his father was informed that the grant was approved. They wanted him to accompany them to Borneo, but he refused." She picked up her gloves and twisted them. "I wish Sullivan hadn't made Roy move out of our house. None of this would have happened."

"Are you sure?" I asked. "Wouldn't Nicholas still have been upset by the intrusion of Wiccan and satanic practices?"

She gave me a cross look. "Oh, I suppose, but Roy would have been asleep in the upper bunk in Cosmos's room and therefore have had an alibi. Do the police suspect him just because he was conveniently nearby—or are they being prejudiced against him because of his religious beliefs?"

"You'll have to ask them. Look, Morning Rose, I think it would be better if you collected your children and left before one of them starts ripping out pages for souvenirs."

She leaned forward. "Do you swear you don't know where Roy is?"

As I stared at her, the rack of paperback fiction came crashing down on her back. I was amazed at the number of books that went flying through the air.

Simply amazed.

# CHAPTER 9

It took the remainder of the afternoon to replace the paperbacks in a semblance of order. Morning Rose had hustled away her children without offering to help undo their damage. It was just as well, since I might have said something that would stifle the cognitive development of her ignoble little savages.

I was locking up when Luanne came into the store. "Caron told me what happened," she said in the breathy gush of a forties' actress. "Are you okay?"

"I'm not worried. All I have to do is make it out to the mall and ask Santa to bring me a million dollars for Christmas. Maybe I'd better ask for an extra couple of thousand to cover legal fees. Franklin dropped his rate to seventy-five dollars an hour, but he warned me it could add up, especially if we go to court. Start thinking about what you'll wear on the witness stand."

"Something modest, I suppose, with a high neckline and white cuffs. I've always fancied myself in a hat with a veil. Is that too British?"

I grinned at her, but it must not have been convincing because she gave me a hug and said, "Don't worry about it, Claire."

"Don't worry about it?" I laughed, perhaps a bit maniacally. I moved away from her and stared at the racks and shelves of books, all begging to be bought, savored, lovingly tucked on a shelf, and brought out again on occasion to be reread. "What if I lose the store?"

"You can marry Peter for his money and lead a life of self-indulgence. Breakfasts in bed, lunches at trendy cafés, candlelight dinners at romantic country inns. I got in a consignment last week that included a floor-length beaded dress. It's red, but you can still borrow it for the wedding. I know—we'll go for a theme! Peter can rent a Santa Claus suit and hire three-foot-tall groomsmen. I don't think we can persuade Caron to don a reindeer outfit, though. She's inordinately hostile toward the species."

I tried to hide the sudden pain that seemed to char my internal organs like a flamethrower. "No mistletoe in the bridal bouquet, okay?"

"Do you want to have a beer across the street?" asked Luanne. "Better yet, we can pick up tacos and a bottle of cheap wine, then go to my place to start working on the guest list. I've always regretted paying my daughter to elope and thus depriving myself of the opportunity to play bridal consultant. I adore bossing people around."

"Not tonight," I said, struggling to hold back tears. Like Fern, I have an aversion to being caught in a public display of emotion, and the last thing I needed was puffy eyelids in the morning. Puffy eyelids do not become me. "Where's Caron?"

"I offered her a ride, but she said she had some last-minute shopping to do."

"I hope she buys me the biggest bottle of aspirin in the drugstore," I said with a grimace.

After Luanne left, I took a last look at the paperbacks to make sure that lusty barbarian princesses had not crept among teapots and cats, then went home. Caron had come and gone; a note on the kitchen table announced that she was stopping by Rhonda Maguire's and then spending the night at Inez's house.

I had no appetite, but I forced down a few bites of moo goo gai pan while I watched the local news. A woman with stiff hair and capped teeth appeared on the screen, with the Primrose Hill house in the background. I was relieved when she said only that a local doctor had been brutally slain in his home and the police were investigating possible leads. The next segment featured kindergarten children belting out an adenoidal version of "The Twelve Days of Christmas."

Fearing an encore, I switched off the television. The complaint lay on the coffee table in all its accusatory glory, but I ordered myself to ignore it. Perhaps I should have had dinner with Luanne, I thought as I roamed around the apartment, picking up books and then putting them down, taking a load of fuzz-encrusted dishes from Caron's room to the kitchen sink, rearranging tinsel on the Christmas tree, and basically doing everything I could in order not to imagine Peter and Leslie in an intimate setting. They were much more likely to be seated in his mother's formal living room, chaperoning the couple. Unless, of course, Myron had whisked away his beloved to a restaurant, and Peter and Leslie were in a less formal room.

With no chaperons.

A major distraction was needed. In that I had no background in economics, balancing the federal budget was out of the question. It was too late to dash out for a dozen rolls of wallpaper and a bucket of paste.

I'd promised Franklin that I wouldn't so much as drive by the residence of Morgan, Suzanne, and Eric L., much less deposit a gaily wrapped box of manure on their porch. If I relented and went to Luanne's, eventually I'd tell her about Peter and Leslie, and then embarrass both of us with an unattractive bout of wailing and gnashing of teeth.

I found a notebook and sat down at the kitchen table to contemplate the cast of characters from the Sacred Grove of Keltria. I wrote down what I knew of Roy's background; none of it seemed very positive, from his splintered family to his alleged use of drugs. Fern's husband had died ten years ago, leaving her with a minimal income and a passion for all things botanical. I added what Jorgeson had told me about Nicholas Chunder. The fact that he'd been married did not have significant impact on Roy's credibility. The lack of alcohol in his blood, on the other hand, did.

I moved along. Sullivan Sawyer was a grad student in anthropology. Morning Rose home-schooled her children and prepared vegetarian casseroles. Gilda D'Orcher worked at the hospital, lived in a trailer, and traveled by bicycle (and broom, possibly). I drew a question mark beside her name as I tried to come up with an explanation for her peculiar behavior.

When nothing suggested itself, I wrote Malthea's name at the bottom of the page. I didn't need any more space, since I knew nothing about her except her address for the last two years. Had she lived in another state or in another part of town? Was she widowed, divorced, or steadfastly single? She'd spent more than a hundred dollars on books, so she had some discretionary income. From a pension or from selling nosegays of holly and mistletoe on the street?

I turned to a clean page and wrote down a timetable that began with the arrival of the group at Nicholas's house to decorate and concluded with Malthea's return after midnight. I wondered where the others had been during that period. Despite their indisputable idiosyncrasies, they were liable to have been performing commonplace rituals, such as watching television, reading, and sleeping. In Fern's case, misting plants; in Nicholas's, cruising the Internet. The Sawyers had children to be bathed, disarmed, and put to bed. Gilda might have been poring through dusty old volumes of curses for something suitably malevolent for Nicholas.

I kept coming back to Roy's confession. He'd taken a risk by hiding in my car so that he could tell me his story. His reluctance to do so at the police station was understandable. It just didn't quite play.

I was staring at my notes, my chin resting on a fist, when the telephone rang. It seemed as though every call lately had been disastrous, and it was tempting to let it go unanswered. However, Caron was not safely ensconced in her bedroom, so there was the possibility she might be calling about bail.

As soon as I'd said hello, Peter said, "Good, I caught you at home."

"Where did you think I'd be—down at the gym playing basketball with the college boys?"

"I thought you might be out shopping or having dinner with Luanne."

"I couldn't handle that much excitement. What do you want?"

He gave a rueful chuckle. "I was wrong when I said Myron was after my mother's money. He's rolling in it. He has a lodge in a ski resort in Vermont, and has invited all of us to go up there for Christmas."

"All of us?" I echoed.

"Yes, all of us. Leslie doesn't need to be back in her office until after New Year's Day, and the kennel's agreed to keep Boris and Igor. She's a serious skier. I, on the other hand, will undoubtedly break a leg and have to be brought down the mountain on one of those silly-looking sleds."

"I'm sure you're an excellent skier," I said.

"It's been a while. Anyway, I wanted to let you know not to expect me for nine or ten days. I'm sorry I won't be there for Christmas or New Year's Eve, but this will be a good opportunity to get to know Myron."

"I guess you already know Leslie—or has she changed since the divorce?"

I was hoping to hear how she'd gained a hundred pounds and lost her teeth, so I was disappointed when Peter said, "Not that I've noticed, but she only arrived this afternoon. Everybody's waiting in the limo for me, so I'd better say good-bye."

"Have a lovely time in Vermont, Peter." I hung up and sat back down at the kitchen table, ashamed of my acerbic remarks. He'd had the decency to pretend not to notice, but neither of us was fooling the other.

I was in the terminal stage of the Sour Grape Syndrome, and it was not pretty.

I debated calling Luanne and spilling out my pitiful plight, but decided against it. What I needed to do, I told myself resolutely, was to put all of this out of my mind and recover a modicum of self-respect by resolving Nicholas Chunder's murder to my own satisfaction. If Roy had committed it, then all I needed was an explanation for the enigmatic brandy decanter and glasses. This would require me to question him, which was a bit of a problem since no one knew where he was.

He'd taken refuge in Fern's greenhouse the previous evening and might have returned; it was not a night for camping out under a bush. Anyone dressed in black would have no problems avoiding being spotted by a cruising patrol car.

I put on my coat and went down the steps to the garage. I made sure Roy wasn't there, either, then drove to Fern's and Malthea's duplex and parked. Lights were on in both sides, but drapes were drawn. I approached with admirable stealth and found a slit that gave me a limited view of Malthea's living room.

She was talking on the telephone while toying with what I recognized as tarot cards on the table in front of her. Her expression was so absorbed that I was reluctant to interrupt her.

Fern did not respond to my repeated knocks. I went around the side yard to the gate. This time I found a latch, let myself into the backyard, and was pleased to see a glow inside the greenhouse.

The glass panels were milky with condensed humidity, but there was a hint of movement. I wasn't sure of the etiquette for barging into a greenhouse and startling its occupant into overmisting. I finally tapped and let myself inside.

Fern looked up at me. "Claire?"

My lungs were clogged with air so warm and wet that I could barely breathe. "Steamy, isn't it?" I croaked.

"Some of the tropical species require it," she said without inflection. "Is there a reason why you're here?"

Most of my resolve was leaking through my pores and forming beads of sweat on my surfaces. "I'm concerned about Roy. No one's heard from him all day. Did Malthea tell you what happened?"

"Some of it, yes."

"He needs to turn himself in," I said, fanning my face with one hand. The heat and humidity were more like an equatorial rain forest than a sunny island. Admittedly, the plants were thriving. Everywhere I looked I saw brilliant oranges, pinks, yellows, and reds. Leaves were dark green, tendrils thick and hardy enough to strangle a small dog.

Or a bookseller.

"I haven't seen Roy," Fern said.

"He didn't come back here?"

She gave me a pinched smile. "Wouldn't I have seen him if he did?"

Time for a new tactic, I told myself. "These are all so lovely, Fern. You must have a green thumb."

"They do thrive here, don't they? I used the last of the insurance money to have this built, and it's been a pleasure and sanctuary for me ever since." She put down a trowel and came around the edge of a table. "What will happen now? Will Nicholas's heirs sell the property?"

"I don't know, but probate takes a long time and you may not have to move anytime soon. Malthea said you were distressed about giving up your greenhouse." I waited a moment, then added, "I can see why. This is a different world, isn't it?"

"It's different," she said as if speaking to a particularly dim child. "Do you see these yellow berries? One of them can kill an adult in a matter of minutes. I find it odd that they're so attractive and yet so fatal. Mother Nature can be naughty." She pointed at a plant with spiky orange pods. "This is a castor-oil plant. The seeds are very poisonous."

I eyed it, then edged back toward the door in case it was exuding fumes. "Did Malthea tell you that she returned to Nicholas's house after the brouhaha?"

"I don't believe that," Fern said as she began to dig into the soil surrounding a feathery fern. "I would have seen her."

"You would have seen her drive away?"

"Is your hearing defective? I would have seen her at Nicholas's house, or at least passed her car on the road." She yanked the plant out of the pot and grimly thrust it into a larger one, seemingly oblivious of the soil spilling on her shoes. "I am more than capable of recognizing her car. It's dreadfully noisy and emits billows of black smoke. I don't know how many times I've told her to have the oil changed, but she's too stubborn. My husband stressed the importance of proper automobile maintenance. I have my oil changed every two thousand miles."

I frowned at her. "You went back to Nicholas's house the night he was murdered?"

"I just said so, didn't I?" She took the newly repotted plant to a sink and turned on the tap. "Setting the roots is a vital step in the process. It packs down the dirt and compresses air pockets. Air pockets can lead to bacteria."

I felt as though I had more than one such pocket in my brain. "Let's talk some more about this, Fern. When did you go back—and why?"

"I went back at eleven, and obviously in hopes that I might persuade Nicholas to change his mind. This business about the Wiccans was ridiculous, and he no more would have enjoyed living in Wales than he

would in a dwelling made of mud and wattle. He was
not friendly, but he invited me inside and allowed me
to sit at the kitchen table. I suggested we talk over
brandy. I could sense that he was uneasy, but I had little sympathy since he'd brought this crisis on himself
with his childishness. He brought out the decanter
and glasses and poured a bit for both of us."

"And drank it?"

Fern began rearranging a tray of seedlings in tiny
pots. "I wasted no time in telling him what I thought
of his petty display earlier in the evening. He spat out
a mouthful of brandy and threatened to throw me out
of his house. It was clear that he was beyond reason,
so I returned to my car and sat until I felt calm enough
to drive home. I am not accustomed to being treated
that way. My deceased husband, rest his soul, was always solicitous of my feelings and never so much as
raised his voice. Not, of course, that he ever had reason to do so."

I wasn't interested in the late Mr. Lewis, no matter
how he died. "How long did you sit in your car?"

"Until I realized I was shivering not from shock but
from cold. Ten minutes, I'd say."

"Did you see lights on in Roy's apartment?"

"I believe so, and I could hear the caterwauling that
passes as music with today's youth. It's disgraceful. I
don't know why their parents allow them to listen to
such garbage. Music should have a melody and lyrics
that contain no obscenities." She looked down at the
rows and smiled to herself. "I'm finished for the evening, Claire. I suggest we walk through my apartment
so you can leave through the front door like a proper
guest."

Her rebuke was hard to miss, but I merely said, "It

is rather dark in the yard. There's something I don't understand. If you arrived at eleven, it sounds as though you left no later than eleven-thirty. Malthea claims she was there after midnight."

Fern shoved me out the door and flipped off the lights in the greenhouse. I thought she might ignore my question, but after a moment, she said, "Then my previous statement was in error. I was confused about the time. This has been so dreadfully upsetting that it's a wonder I can remember anything that's happened. The winter solstice is meant to be a glorious celebration, not a nightmare of rage and violence. You must excuse this lapse on my part."

She continued to apologize as she propelled me through the apartment, and I found myself on the front porch before I could get in another word. "Good night," she said, then closed the door. Seconds later, the lights in the living room went off.

Good night, Fern.

Malthea was still holding the receiver to her ear, but the tarot cards had been replaced with standard ones and she appeared to be playing solitaire. She spoke steadily for a few moments, paused to shift a card, and then resumed.

Gilda was not available and it was too late to drop by the Sawyers' house. I drove home, thinking about Fern's account of her visit. It explained the presence of the bottle and glasses, and also Roy's assertion that he'd smelled booze on Nicholas's breath. There was no alcohol in Nicholas's blood because he'd spat it out. It was all falling into place so neatly that I wouldn't have been surprised to find Morning Rose in my garage, ready to tell me how she'd gone back to Primrose Hill at precisely twelve-fifteen and taken away the murder weapon.

As I went inside, the telephone started to ring. It was not apt to be Peter, who was in a limo headed for a lodge in Vermont. Would he be sharing a bedroom with Myron, while his mother and Leslie shared the other one and stayed up all night, giggling and giving each other pedicures? If there were lots of bedrooms, how much tiptoeing might take place in dark hallways? Myron might be rolling in money, but what would Peter be rolling in?

I realized the telephone was still ringing. I picked up the receiver and waited silently.

"Mrs. Malloy?" said Jorgeson. "Are you there?"

I exhaled. "Yes, I'm here. It's eight o'clock, Jorgeson. Don't you ever go home?"

"I went home at five, and as soon as I got there, my wife dragged me out to the mall. It's how I imagine the Black Hole of Calcutta would be if everyone had American Express and Visa. Haggard faces, dazed eyes, twitchy fingers, bad tempers. Not a healthy place."

"Are you calling me to pass along your sociological insights into a great American tradition, Jorgeson? Couldn't you have waited until tomorrow?"

"Thing is, I got beeped in the middle of Sears. The murder weapon's been found, and I thought you'd want to know. It's registered to Randall Tate."

"Roy's father?"

"Randall ain't his dog, Mrs. Malloy. He's owned the gun for ten years."

"And you're sure it's the murder weapon?"

"The only thing I'm *sure* of is that my wife's still at the mall, buying everything that's left to teach me a lesson. You need any sheets? She's real fond of sheets."

I sat down and rubbed my eyes. "Where was the gun found?"

"In the hearse, which is appropriate in a screwball way. There's a compartment under the carpet in the back part. I dunno why, unless the funeral director needed a place for his wallet during the cemetery service—or he plucked watches and jewelry off his customers during the ride. Anyway, you see the problem, don't you?"

If I'd rubbed any harder, I would have peeled off a layer of cells. "Yes, Jorgeson, I see it. Nicholas didn't pull a gun on Roy. Roy took the gun with him when he went into the house. This seems a tad premeditated, doesn't it? He either sensed what might happen and armed himself, or he had an entirely different agenda."

"The real reason I called was to warn you, Mrs. Malloy. Randall Tate owns another handgun. All of his furniture and personal belongings are in storage, and it'll be a couple of days before we can determine if it's there. You need to be careful. Roy lied to you."

"That doesn't mean he's going to stalk me," I said, glancing uneasily at the kitchen window. "All I know is what these Druids insist on telling me. By the way, I listened to yet another casual confession this evening." I repeated the gist of Fern's story. "Tidy, isn't it?"

"That's what my wife puts in the toilet bowl," Jorgeson said without amusement. "I wish the lieutenant was here to figure these people out. I don't think even one of them is telling the truth."

"As in the whole truth, and nothing but the truth? I

don't think we've heard a pitiful fraction of the truth," I said. "What are you going to do about Roy?"

Jorgeson grumbled under his breath. "Same thing we've been doing, which is hoping to catch him on campus or walking down the street. We know where he's not—and that's about it. If he approaches you, Mrs. Malloy, don't offer him eggnog and cookies. Get hold of me or whoever's on duty. The boy could be dangerous."

I replaced the receiver and went into the living room. Roy's version of what had happened in Nicholas's kitchen might inspire an R-rated Disney film, but not a documentary. It had been holding up rather well until now; Malthea and Fern had covered a few glitches, and Morning Rose had volunteered several comments about Nicholas's questionable motive for living in isolation.

Only two more shopping days till Christmas, I thought as I gazed at the packages under the tree. I'd planned to give Peter a hefty book about the history of some football organization; for reasons unfathomable to me, he seemed enamored of bearish men knocking each other to the ground.

The book was among the other packages, meticulously wrapped and adorned with a big silver bow. Clearly he would not open it Christmas morning— or any other morning until January was under way. Leaving it there would only serve as a reminder of where he was.

I considered putting the book on a closet shelf, but even its unseen presence in the apartment would wear away at me like an endlessly dripping faucet.

I decided to take the book back to the store, and

then see if I could persuade Luanne to watch a movie rather than plan a wedding. If she persisted in harping on the subject (and she could be very persistent after a few glasses of wine), I would feign the onset of flu symptoms and allow myself to be ejected.

The wind was colder than it had been earlier, and gusting imperiously. Brittle leaves scratched across the floor of the garage. I quickly got in the car, started it, and gave it a moment to warm up. As I waited, I tried to recall the last time I'd had the oil changed. It was definitely more than two thousand miles ago.

The streets were almost empty as I drove alongside the campus and turned on Thurber Street. Anybody playing with a full deck (tarot or conventional) was at home, wearing warm bedroom slippers and munching popcorn.

I parked behind the Book Depot, grabbed the package, and hurried to the back door. My teeth were chattering by the time I managed to get the key in the lock and push open the protesting door. I stomped my feet to announce my presence to the nighttime denizens, some with six legs and some with brown fur, long tails, and an irksome habit of leaving traces of their presence along the baseboards.

It was tempting to unwrap the book and return it to its rightful rack, but that would be an admission of abject defeat by lovely, capricious, athletic, wealthy Leslie.

"Stop this!" I said loudly. "You are being more immature than Nicholas and Peter combined."

I dropped the book on my desk and went outside. I stood for a moment to let the wind batter me, hoping its frigidity would bring me to my senses.

When all it did was sting my face, I got in the car and reached for the ignition switch.

"Good evening," said a voice from the backseat.

This was getting old.

# CHAPTER 10

"Where do you want to go tonight, Roy?" I said without bothering to return his greeting. "The lot by the stadium is closed, so we can't go back there. How about the police station?"

"What did the guy say when you told him?"

"He said that you ought to turn yourself in."

Roy grabbed my shoulder. "So he believes me? I mean, he understands that it wasn't my fault because Nicholas said he was going to kill me. All I was doing was protecting myself. You told him that, didn't you, Mrs. Malloy?"

"I repeated exactly what you told me. Why didn't you mention all the traffic in front of the house that night? It must have rivaled the parking lot at the mall."

I could hear him sucking on his lip as he thought about it. "I guess I had the music pretty loud. Once I thought I saw headlights, but I didn't bother to look out the window."

"Why would you?" I said comfortingly, if inanely. "Let's go to the station. Sergeant Jorgeson's off duty at the moment, but I can call him at home and ask him to join us. He'll want to question you tonight, and tomorrow he'll arrange for a lawyer from legal services.

Everything will be okay, Roy, and you'll have a place to sleep and hot meals."

"I don't need a lawyer. I already told you why it was self-defense. Any guy my age would have done the same thing. The kids at the high school may think I'm weird, but they sure as hell don't think I'm gay. I had a girlfriend while I was living with my mother. We had sex every weekend—and nothing kinky, either. You want her name and phone number? As long as her parents aren't in the room she'll tell you the same thing."

He was more agitated than I would have preferred. The whereabouts of the handgun used on Nicholas was known, but Jorgeson had made a point of mentioning the possibility of a second one. Roy's jacket had deep pockets.

"What's the matter, Mrs. Malloy?" he continued, thumping the seat. "I'll bet you don't believe me! Is that it? What's wrong with what I told you last night? You got problems with it?"

"Nothing major," I said, wishing I sounded more sincere. I am not adept at lying; normally, it's a praiseworthy attribute, but under the current circumstances, it was a distinct disadvantage. "I'm sure you can easily explain a couple of things that are a teensy bit confusing. You just now said why you didn't hear the cars drive up, and I believe you. The autopsy report said that there was no alcohol in Nicholas's blood, but one of your fellow Druids admitted that she was there before midnight and saw him take a mouthful of brandy." I realized I was babbling, but I couldn't seem to stop—even though I knew the most credible fabrications are unadorned. "We know who broke the window in Nicholas's study, and who put away the decanter and glasses. Most of the inconsistencies have been dealt with, Roy. You shouldn't worry about talking to the police. It'll be nothing more than a formality. You'll be released on your own recognizance tomorrow or the next day."

And the archbishop of Canterbury would elope with Princess Margaret.

This time his fingers dug into my shoulder and I could feel hot breath on my neck. "Who broke the window and put away the decanter?" he growled.

"Malthea. Fern was there earlier, when Nicholas got out the brandy and glasses. That was when he took a drink of brandy and then spat it out."

"They told you that?"

"Yes, they did. Do you mind if I start the car so we can get some heat?"

He released my shoulder and fell back against the seat. "Don't so much as move a finger, Mrs. Malloy. I've got to think here for a minute. I don't like this."

Neither did I, but I refrained from saying so and waited passively as the wind found ways to sneak in through the floorboard. I could see him in the rear-view mirror, but it was too dark to discern his expression. His hisses and muttered curses indicated he was not in the best of moods.

I was on the verge of repeating my suggestion about heat when he said, "After I went out the bathroom window, they searched my place, didn't they?"

"They might have looked for some tips about where they could find you. If they did, it was because they were concerned about your welfare."

"Did they find the gun?"

"I couldn't say," I said, struggling to sound casual. Alas, even I heard a faint tremor in my voice.

He slammed his fist on the seat. "That's it, isn't it? That's the detail that's 'a teensy bit confusing,' as you put it. Damn! I knew I should have buried it in the woods! How could I have been so friggin' stupid!" He hit the seat again. I did not interpret it as a request for consensus with the assessment of his mental faculties.

"All of us make mistakes," I said. "I can think of several I've made lately."

"Shut up."

I shut up as he resumed hissing and cursing. Having never spent a significant amount of time in my car behind the Book Depot at night, I had no idea if patrol cars ever ventured into the parking lot. If I'd believed for one second that my forty-year-old reflexes were at all quicker than his sixteen-year-old ones, I would have attempted to scramble out of the car and run down the railroad tracks. However, I had no desire to be shot in the back or even tackled in the gravel.

"Okay," he said abruptly, startling me to the point I nearly yelped. "I'm gonna tell you the truth about what happened. I stole my father's gun back in the fall because some guys at school were giving me grief, and I used it to shoot Nicholas Chunder. First I hit him a couple of times, then I stepped back, aimed, and pulled the trigger. I would have shot him more than once if I hadn't freaked when I saw the blood. I rolled him over, thinking I'd take his wallet so the cops would jump on the burglary story, but I guess he'd left it in his bedroom."

"Why did you do it, Roy? He overlooked his personal dislike of your . . . ah, religious practices and allowed you to live on his estate. If you were short on cash, I'd think he or someone else would have loaned you enough to get by until your parents returned."

"I didn't kill him for spending money, fer chrissake! I killed him because of her. She made me do it, and there wasn't any way I could refuse. She's had this power over me since the moment we met. She took me out to the grove, just the two of us, and she drew a pentagram on my forehead with her finger. It burned so fiercely that I thought I was gonna pass out. You can't see it, but I can every damn time I look in the mirror. When I do something that she doesn't like, it turns bright red and begins to smolder. The pain's unbearable, like someone's pressing an ember against my skin."

I felt as though he'd knocked me on the head with a rock. "Who are you talking about," I asked.

"Malthea, of course. I know nobody will believe me, but I swear it's the truth. I'll swear on a bible if you want me to, or a whole stack of them. Malthea ordered me to kill Nicholas, so I did."

He began to whimper, and when I looked back at him, I saw him wiping away what I presumed were tears. I waited until he'd calmed down, then said, "Why would Malthea have done that, Roy? I haven't heard her say anything that implied she hated Nicholas so vehemently that she wanted him dead."

"You haven't been around her that much. Sure, she can come off like somebody's grandmother when it suits her, and she puts on a really good pretense of being scatterbrained and helpless. She's not, though. She may be the Arch Druid, but she's also a member of a secret cult called the Sisters of Illumination that goes all the way back to ancient Egypt and Babylon. Once a year they have a Black Sabbath and perform a human sacrifice."

"Malthea Hendlerson?" I said. "That's . . . hard to believe."

"I know it is," he said dispiritedly. "What happened was, when I first moved to Farberville, I spent a lot of time in that used bookstore up the street, just poking around for funky old stuff. I saw her there a couple of times, then one afternoon she came up to me and said we had to talk. She looked pretty harmless and I didn't have anything better to do, so I said okay. We drove out to the grove in her car. That's where she told me she worshiped Satan and could sense that I would make a perfect servant after she finished training me."

"Were you wearing a black T-shirt in the bookstore?" I asked.

He nodded. "I buy them at rock concerts because they're cool."

"What about the hearse? How long have you owned it?"

"The guy who lived down the street ran a funeral home. When he died last summer, I talked his wife into selling it to me real cheap. I get a buzz when people on the street stare at me. It wasn't like I was into satanism."

"Why don't you tell me more about what happened at the grove?" I suggested politely, as if we were discussing the merits of a movie.

"She pulled out a little pair of scissors and cut off a lock of my hair. She said she could use it to send this demon called Ambesek whenever I needed to be disciplined. I didn't believe her, but one night at the carriage house I was awakened by the stench of sulfur. I sat up and saw this—this eight-foot-tall creature with a hideous face, fiery red eyes, and huge hands. Its skin was covered with black scales that glinted like armor.

It dragged me out of bed, ripped off my shirt, and raked my back with its claws. I passed out on the floor. The next morning I thought maybe it had just been a really bad nightmare. I changed my mind when I saw the bloody marks on my back."

"Come on, Roy," I said, "you fell out of bed and somehow scratched yourself on the bedside table."

"I wish that was true, but she sends the demon whenever she's angry at me. Once she ordered me to steal a dog and bring it to the grove so she could slaughter it and drink its blood. I refused. That night the demon came and practically disemboweled me. She told me later that its formal title was Ambesek the Eater of Intestines."

It didn't matter whether or not he believed what he was saying; I was getting nauseated—and nervous. "Did you go to the hospital?"

"She said the demon could find me no matter where I was and not to get medical help. I bandaged myself as best I could. I was scared the wound would get infected, but she gave me this salve and it worked so well you can barely see a scar."

"When did Malthea order you to kill Nicholas?" I asked.

"She's been saying nasty things about him ever since the Samhain celebration at Halloween. He wanted everything to be done his way, and he and Malthea had an argument. I wasn't there, but she said he was hateful. You should have seen the look on her face the night before the solstice when he said he was selling his properties and moving to Wales. While the others were pleading with him, she took me out to the patio and told me what to do. I didn't want to, Mrs. Malloy, but she gave me a gruesome description of what Ambesek would do if I disobeyed her. You want to hear what she said?"

"I don't think so," I said. "If Malthea has this demon at her beck and call, why didn't she sic him on Nicholas instead of getting you involved?"

"She said I had to kill someone so I could participate in the next Black Sabbath. I knew I wouldn't live that long if I didn't do it. I went to my apartment, popped some pills to give myself the guts to go through with it, then went to the house and knocked on the door till Nicholas let me inside. You know the rest."

I still couldn't see Malthea as an evil dominatrix, and Roy had already proved himself to be a much more adept liar than I. "If you're so terrified of another visit from the demon, why are you telling me now?"

"I deserve to suffer for what I did. I've been trying to find spells that can protect me. If they work, they work. If they don't, then I'll be tortured until I beg to die. Let's go to the police station and get it over with."

I wasted no time starting the car. Although his story of demonic retribution was preposterous, I was not about to sit there in the dark and wait for an eight-foot-tall creature with fiery eyes to come ambling down the railroad tracks, swooping down from the sky, or popping up from the sewer drain in front of the Book Depot.

I was exhausted the next morning, having not been able to fall asleep until almost dawn. Jorgeson had permitted me to be present at the interrogation, but it hadn't lasted long. Roy's descriptions became increasingly graphic and filled with repugnant details; he'd shouted and cried and stormed around the room until Jorgeson gave up and packed him off to the psych

ward for sedation and a seventy-two-hour evaluation.
Gilda was already there in a padded room. I rather
longed for one, myself.

After Roy'd been taken away, Jorgeson had asked
me what I thought, and I'd told him that for the first
time I could remember, I was out of opinions. He'd almost smiled.

Now, at nine in the morning, the sun was shining,
but this was not enough to lure in the occasional
pedestrian. I was hunting through the racks in hopes of
finding a book about satanism when the telephone
rang. The sound was not as harsh as a fiendish screech,
but it had a comparable effect on me. There were a few
people I was willing to talk to, but the converse list was
very long and multiplying steadily.

Then again, it could have been Franklin with good
news. I numbly picked up the receiver.

"Claire, this is Inez's mother."

Goose bumps rose on my flesh, but I managed a
calm, "Is anything wrong?"

"I think the girls are up to something. They were
acting odd last night, and her father and I agreed you
ought to know about it."

This was a very forceful decision on Mrs. Thornton's part. She's as mousy as Inez and usually only
faintly bewildered by the girls' escapades, but I never
knew quite how much of the truth she heard from
Inez. At this moment, I could almost hear her twisting
her hands, which was alarming. I waited for a moment, then said, "What did they do?"

"Nothing, and that's what worries me. Last night
when I picked up Inez at the mall, she told me about
this ridiculous lawsuit and said she was going to quit
her job, no matter how desperate Mrs. Claus was. I

told her that she'd made the right decision. Well, Caron came over and the two locked themselves in Inez's bedroom for a long while. I could hear them talking and arguing. Then Inez came out and said she'd changed her mind about quitting. I was flabbergasted that Caron would want her to continue at Santa's Workshop, but it's obvious that she does."

"Hmmm," I said eloquently, in that I was in complete agreement with Mrs. Thornton's assessment. If in some way Caron could make a profit from unplugging someone's respirator, she would at least consider it. Not necessarily do it, mind you, but weigh the possibilities. Making life easier for Mrs. Claus, aka Ms. Portmeyer, would not have merited even fleeting consideration. And Inez, for all her meekness, has a streak of stubbornness that runs as deep as a vein of coal.

"It was odd," Mrs. Thornton continued, "and when they begin to behave oddly, they tend to end up in trouble. Inez will be applying for scholarships next year. She won't have much luck with a felony conviction on her transcript."

I could only commiserate, which I did for a few minutes. Once Mrs. Thornton was somewhat pacified, I said, "So where are they?"

"Inez had me drop her off at the mall. Caron said she was going to walk home. It all seemed so innocent, Claire, and I truly wish I thought it was."

We speculated aimlessly for a few minutes, then I replaced the receiver and sat down at the counter. I stayed there for most of an hour, making unattractive faces and finding myself unable to come up with a plausible explanation for Caron's behavior. I had little hope that she'd tell me the truth—unless she found it convenient. This rarely happened. She'd gone to Rhonda Maguire's house the previous evening, which in and of itself was worthy of a headline in the local newspaper. But why?

I was lost in thought when Jorgeson came into the store. He gave me a sour smile and said, "We interviewed Malthea Hendlerson. You ever seen a marble statue, Mrs. Malloy? She's a little less talkative than one of them."

"I can't see her summoning a demon and commanding it to disembowel a boy," I said. "You've met her, Jorgeson. I grant she's not your ordinary person, but she hasn't ever indicated she's that ... well, wicked. Did you ask the doctors to check Roy's back and abdomen for scars?"

"He's got scars," said Jorgeson as he went into the office and poured himself a cup of coffee. "But," he added from the doorway, "that doesn't mean they were inflicted by some fiend from hell. Could be an indication of past abuse from one of his parents, or even self-mutilation. He's a sick one."

"I won't argue with that. Is Malthea in custody?"

"She's been told to remain available until the shrinks evaluate the kid. I was expecting her to laugh at us, but she got real grim and said, 'So he told you that, did he?' No denials, no nothing. If somebody accused me of that, I'd be cussing up a storm and swearing I was innocent. We couldn't get another sentence out of her."

I shook my head. "It's impossible to figure her out, but that doesn't mean she's diabolic. She may be as sane as anyone else. Who's entitled to define what our senses take in and how we ought to process it? Look at this, Jorgeson." I poked a publisher's catalog on the counter. "You see what you call red, and you assume I see the same shade. We'll never know if we see something entirely different because we have no way to compare our input. We both agree that what we see is red, but who can say if we're actually receiving the same response in our brains? My red may be your green. We simply use the same term for what may be entirely opposite."

"What does this have to do with anything?" Jorgeson asked gently.

"Demons," I said. "My bout of indigestion may be Roy's fiend from hell ripping at his bowels. It's a matter of interpretation, of translation between his mind and his own concept of reality. He's disturbed; neither of us can argue with that. Is he genuinely disturbed? Who knows?"

Jorgeson seemed to sense he was dealing with a madwoman. He patted my hand for a moment, his face puckered, and then said, "You talked to the lieutenant lately?"

I tried for a stiff upper lip and a glib response, then poured out everything. I did not allow a tear to escape, but my demeanor was at best quavery and I resorted, albeit briefly, to a tissue in order to blow my nose in a ladylike manner.

"Leslie, huh?" said Jorgeson. "The lieutenant's never said much about her."

"What *has* he said?"

"Jeez, it's hard to remember." He stared into space and scratched his stubbly gray scalp. "She's a stockbroker, I think, and she breeds some kind of fancy dogs that are worth a bundle and win ribbons at competitions. One night when we were drinking beer, he showed me a picture of her. Blond, all the equipment— but not nearly as nice looking as you, Mrs. Malloy. You shouldn't fret over the lieutenant. His only concern right now is his mother and this guy named Myron. As soon as he gets it resolved, he'll come home."

"Unless the skiing is good," I said, not at all comforted by Jorgeson's sad gaze.

After he left, I called home to speak to Caron, but she was either in the shower or elsewhere. I hesitated to call Rhonda and try to get information out of her; she had the ability to spread gossip as easily as the rest of us spread peanut butter on bread.

Or caviar on toast.

I ordered myself to put aside self-pity and do something useful. If Caron spent the morning holding up banks, I'd hear about it eventually. I couldn't bring myself to confront Malthea until the images Roy had implanted in my mind faded to black and white. If I went to Fern's duplex, Malthea would spot me. It might be enlightening to talk to Morning Rose, but I didn't want her children doing further exploration and I couldn't close the store two days before Christmas.

My circumspection was rewarded when a few shoppers came in and browsed. One woman wanted a paperback for her daughter. Since she knew neither the title nor the author, but only that it featured a woman archeologist in Victorian times, we studied covers and discussed possibilities until I found one that met her criteria. A man needed a handyman's guide to replacing circuit boxes, having put up one too many strings of Christmas lights. Another wanted "anything a middle-aged woman like yourself would like." Three giggly junior high girls found a romance novel and paid me in dimes and quarters. They reminded me of Caron and Inez when they'd been in their Azalea Twilight phase, and this, of course, reminded me that an unknown game was afoot.

During lulls, and there were many of them, I pondered Roy's bizarre story. Was there any way at all that ditzy, kind-hearted Malthea could have ordered Roy to kill someone? She seemed to be genuinely concerned about him, but she was the one who'd introduced him into the Sacred Grove. It seemed logical that she'd feel some responsibility in loco parentis, with an emphasis on the *loco*.

I was calling home when my science-fiction hippie came into the store. He eyed me cautiously, then satisfied himself that I was unarmed. Despite his scruffy, crumb-encrusted beard, discolored bandanna around his forehead, and glazed eyes, he had a certain charm. As had, I supposed, Rasputin.

"Last-minute Christmas shopping?" I said.

"Yeah, I met this chick in a chat room and I want to get her something. From what she said, she sounds like a dead ringer for the woman on the cover of *Galactica Galore: Transvestite Empress of Andromeda*."

"You met her, but you don't know what she looks like?" I said, perplexed. "Were you blindfolded at the time."

"I don't think I was, but I may have missed something." He went behind the rack, and a subsequent thud informed me that he'd opted to sit on the floor. As long as a prissy matron didn't come in for an updated edition of Emily Post, it didn't matter all that much.

"Did you find a copy?" I called.

"Yeah, I'm just trying to decide if I want to lay out five dollars. For all I know, she could be a twelve-year-old boy. They do that kind of thing for kicks."

"What kind of thing?"

"It's hard to describe," he said vaguely.

I went to the end of the rack and looked down at

him. He was, as I'd expected, sitting cross-legged on the floor with paperbacks fanned around him. "Do you have a name?"

"Yeah, do you?"

"Yeah, I guess I do. May I ask you about a drug?"

He looked up at me. "I never thought you'd want to score. You're always so . . . well, I dunno . . . centered, like an earth mother. Things swirl around you, but you don't like even flinch. You ever read *Sidhartha*?"

So now I was reduced to a reincarnation of Buddha; I really needed to work on my image. "What do you know about a drug called Herbal Ecstasy?"

"It's legal, which is good. Twenty years ago I got picked up with less than a quarter of an ounce of pot, and you'd have thought I had bullion from Fort Knox the way everybody got fired up. All I was doing was—"

"Herbal Ecstasy?" I said.

"The main ingredient is mahuang. It's this organic stimulant that's supposed to work like ephedrine, but all it did was make me itch. I thought I was going to scratch off my skin."

"Does it cause hallucinations or psychoses?"

"Not that I've ever heard. It mainly fires up your central nervous system. The problem with the stuff is that you don't know what's in it besides the mahuang or how much you can take. A kid died of an overdose at a rock concert in Florida or one of those places, but the FDA still hasn't banned it. Makes you wonder what the world's coming to, doesn't it?"

"It surely does," I said dryly. "The book's my Christmas present to you. May it cement this relationship with the dead ringer."

He thanked me amidst a profusion of flying crumbs, then left before I could change my mind. He may have had another paperback or two in his army surplus jacket pockets, but 'twas the season. I might not have been blessed with lords a-leaping and swans a-swimming, but at least I had a hippie in a fuzzy fog.

Ho, ho.

Caron showed up in the middle of the afternoon. I was glad to see her, in that it indicated she was not in custody. She studied me appraisingly, then said, "Can I have the car?"

"To do what?"

"Nothing, really. I told Inez I'd pick her up after she gets off work at eight."

"Which will be in approximately six hours."

"Well," she said, studying the floor for inspiration, "I haven't bought a present for Peter, so I thought I'd go out to the mall and look around for something. Do you think he'd like a tie?"

I told her that Peter wouldn't be back until after New Year's Day, but did not elaborate on his present whereabouts and companions. "I'll make a deal with you," I added. "If you take over here for an hour while I run an errand, then you can have the car for the rest of the day."

"Are you going to pay me?"

"Only with the use of the car. Feel free to walk home and call the Department of Labor if you prefer. There's bound to be a toll-free number to report violations of this heinous nature."

"Oh, all right," she said with a sigh, "as long as nobody bothers me. We have to read some utterly suffocating book next semester for English. I might as well get started on it instead of watching the cockroach races in the back room."

"Good idea." I carried a pile of paperwork to said

racetrack, got my purse and coat, and came back to the front room. Caron was standing in front of the classics rack, looking as though she were on a scaffold awaiting the arrival of a hooded man. "By the way," I said ever so casually, "I was a little surprised that you went to Rhonda's last night. I thought you'd still be seething over her reindeer remark."

"I got over it."

"Was she having a party?"

Caron glanced at me. "If you must know, I needed to borrow something from her."

"Oh, really?"

"I wish you'd go run your errand so I can get to the mall before the parking lot is full. It's bad enough during the day, but after five everybody in the county descends like turkey vultures. You can almost hear the flapping of wings."

Having made no progress in unraveling this latest scheme, I went out to the car and drove toward the south part of town.

# CHAPTER 11

Morning Rose must have seen me coming up the sidewalk, because she flung open the door before I reached the top step of the porch. "Has something happened to Roy?"

"Several things," I said. "May I come inside?"

"I guess so, but only for a few minutes. Sullivan went to the co-op to pick up mung bean sprouts and cheese. Do you know that the cheese sold in regular grocery stores contains animal by-products? Most of the yogurt does, too. Isn't that disgusting?"

Unable to respond with any sincerity, I nodded and went into the living room. No Druid touches were evident in the decor, which could be described as later-American thrift shop. Graduate assistantships appeared to be no more remunerative than they'd been in my day, when scavenged lumber, concrete blocks, and beanbag chairs had been our rejoinder to Martha Stewart.

"Sit down." Morning Rose gestured at a sofa with lumpy cushions and stained plaid upholstery. "I need to send Cosmos and Rainbow outside before we talk. They saw an old spy movie on television, and they've been eavesdropping like CIA agents ever since."

She left the room. I removed a headless Barbie doll and several potentially lethal slivers of plastic from the sofa, then sat down and listened to the muted sounds of her voice, interspersed with whining. Eavesdropping was not required.

"They always act as if they're being exiled to Siberia," she said as she came back and sat down on a wooden chair. "I insist they have at least two hours a day of fresh air and sunshine."

If I was obliged to stay home with Dennis and Menace all day, I would have opted for eight, maybe ten. "Roy turned himself in to the police last night," I began. "While he was being questioned, he became so upset that he was taken to the hospital."

Morning Rose stared at me. "I don't understand, Mrs. Malloy. Was he beaten?"

"I was there, and I can assure you that he was treated with kindness and concern. No rubber hoses or thumbscrews, just bad coffee and stale doughnuts. All Sergeant Jorgeson did was try to get a coherent story that explained why Roy shot Nicholas Chunder."

"Are you saying that Roy has confessed?"

"He claims that Malthea forced him to do it. It's hard to believe, though."

She was still staring at me as if I'd materialized from one of the numerous dust balls under the furniture and introduced myself as Farberville's resident Eater of Intestines and Disagreeable Children. "Malthea denies it, of course?"

"She refused to admit or deny the allegation. Sergeant Jorgeson is waiting for the psychiatric evaluation before he decides how to proceed. The allegation has some grotesque elements, but if she has that degree of influence on his behavior, she's in serious trouble."

Her gaze shifted away from me. "I've been afraid

something like this would happen ever since Sullivan and I joined the grove two years ago."

"How did that come about?" I asked, desperately hoping that Sullivan was mesmerized by an array of fresh, frozen, and for all I knew, pickled bean sprouts.

"Sullivan had a teaching position at a college run by a conservative religious denomination. We had no friends because we knew that one slip about our personal beliefs would lead to his dismissal. Cosmos and Rainbow weren't allowed to play with other children for the same reason. Everybody in the town was a potential enemy. Sullivan finally decided to get a doctorate so he could try for a job at a larger college where we might find a more enlightened community. When Nicholas came by with our copy of the lease, he noticed the titles on the bookshelves and invited us to attend a ritual. We were not pleased with the bickering and rigidity within the grove, but we ended up joining."

"How many were there of you two years ago?"

"About the same number, I suppose. Fern, Malthea, Gilda, Nicholas, and a middle-aged couple from California who moved to a commune in Oregon last summer. A newspaper reporter tried to infiltrate the grove, but Nicholas did a background check and we refused to allow her to participate. He was very adept at using his computer for that sort of thing. I prefer divination."

"You mentioned yesterday that Roy had joined the grove in September of this year," I said.

"Initially, Sullivan and I had reservations about Roy. He seemed to be so very ill at ease. I spoke to Malthea about it, and she assured me that he was merely intimidated by his lack of knowledge. She planned to instruct him herself so that he could be formally initiated when the time was right. Our celebrations are open to everyone, but admission into the higher ranks takes study and dedication."

Higher ranks—or lower circles?

"I gather that Roy got along better with you than with your husband," I said.

She went to a front window and pulled aside a curtain. "It usually takes him only half an hour to go by the co-op. Maybe he went by his office to pick up something." She let the curtain fall back. "Sullivan can be as prudish as Nicholas was. He is well suited for Druidism, the patriarchal bastion of rationalism. Wicca is intuitive and more feminist. He wants the sterility of sunlight; I prefer the caress of moonlight."

"But you and he reached a compromise?"

"In regards to the children, we have. I do many of my rituals in the backyard while he baby-sits. It's worked out thus far."

"Is that what you were doing on the eve of the solstice?" I glanced at my watch. How many varieties of sprouts could there be?

Morning Rose sat back down and smiled at me. "I gather you want alibis rather than a description of the Wiccan ritual. We arrived home a little after nine. I put the children to bed, then went into the backyard for a private welcoming of the birth of Horned God. He will mate with the Goddess in spring, be sacrificed and die in the autumn, and be reborn in the form of himself at the next winter solstice. The Mother Goddess receives her strength from this, her power over all that exists in both the physical and mystical realities. Union and reunion are divine."

"Of course," I said lamely. "Why did you say that

you'd been worried that something like this might happen? Did you have a reason to think Malthea might have . . ."

"Gained control of Roy? Manipulated him into doing something dreadful? I encouraged him to confide in me. He wasn't very forthcoming, but I could tell that he was in the grips of a tremendous internal struggle. Terror doesn't begin to describe what I sensed. I don't know whose demons he was facing—but he was haunted by images so horrific that he was being driven crazy. From what little he said, I suspected Malthea was behind it." She took a shuddery breath, then stood up and began to pace across from me, her chin quivering as she struggled to maintain her composure. "I'm frightened, too. Sullivan refuses to acknowledge the possibility of demons, but I saw Roy's wound. I *saw* it, Mrs. Malloy, mopped away the blood, and put bandages on it. The physical scars are gone, but the spiritual ones will never go away. He needs help. I'm just not sure that doctors and shrinks can battle forces from the bowels of hell."

Stephen King, please pick up the white courtesy phone.

I tightened my grip on my purse and asked myself— not for the first time—why I'd voluntarily embroiled myself in these people's problems, when what they needed were soft-spoken therapists and mind-dulling drugs. In industrial strength doses.

"But what about Malthea?" I persisted. "Do you honestly believe she has control over Roy?"

Morning Rose let her curled fingers relax, and to my relief, sat down, saving me from a pinched nerve in my neck. She pushed her hair out of her face and leaned forward to peer earnestly at me. "Roy *believes* it, and that's all that matters. I've never met a demon, but he has. My time may come, and so may yours. Is reality what you accept—or what you deny because of your own primal fear?"

Having never had this conversation before, I was at a loss for a reply, glib or otherwise. I was reduced to looking at the floor when the door opened and Sullivan came into the room.

"What's going on?" he demanded.

Morning Rose clamped down on her lower lip, making it clear that she wasn't going to respond. I said, "Roy has confessed to killing Nicholas. He's in custody."

Sullivan dropped a grocery sack, presumably made from recycled paper, and leaned against the wall. "Roy confessed? I thought it was a burglar."

"The authorities have the weapon," I said. "It was registered to Roy's father. Did he ever mention owning a handgun?"

Sullivan's complexion was beginning to take on the cast of the dull beige sack on the floor, and he was reacting as though Roy were his firstborn son and successor to the throne. "Dr. Tate said he bought a gun when he did a stint on a reservation in Arizona back in the eighties. He wasn't into artifacts, but treasure hunters kept digging up sacred sites to get things to sell to tourists. It's often a battlefield to preserve certain cultures from so-called progress. Then again, maybe the only reason we preserve them is so that academics like Dr. Tate can write papers about them. Publish or piss off, as the saying goes."

"Sullivan!" said Morning Rose. "Have you been drinking?"

"Me?"

She glared at him, then made a quasi-successful attempt to soften her expression as she turned to me. "Mrs. Malloy, if you don't mind, I think I need to have a word in private with my husband."

"Don't mind me," I said with my customary grace and charm. "I was once married to someone who was known to detour by a bar on occasion. Go right ahead."

"Dada is blotto," sang a high-pitched voice from around the corner. "Dada is blotto."

"Can I have a pet demon?" asked another, somewhat deeper voice.

Morning Rose grabbed my arm and pulled me to my feet. "Thank you for coming by. Please let me know if there's anything we can do to help. Now, if you don't mind . . . ?"

I was on the porch by this time, and the grip she had on me made it clear I wasn't going back inside the house unless I was versed in sumo wrestling. I pulled myself free and said, "If there's anything else you want to tell me, call or drop by the bookstore."

She pulled the door closed behind her. "I would like an update on Roy. He's been through so much, and I don't believe that he realized what he was doing when he shot Nicholas. He doesn't need to go to prison, where he'll be abused by hardened inmates and tormented by his guilt. He's only sixteen. He can be saved, turned around, aimed in the right direction. At the moment, he's into drugs and some unhealthy philosophies, but he and I used to talk about poetry and light and goodness. Is there anything you can do for him?"

"I'll certainly try." I heard Sullivan bellowing at the children. "I guess I'd better go."

Morning Rose looked at me for an uncomfortably long moment, and then went back inside and shut the door.

As I drove toward Thurber Street, it occurred to me that by now Roy had proffered three versions of what had taken place on the eve of the winter solstice. The burglary version had held up only until Corporal Billsby had said there'd been no forcible entry into Nicholas's house. That evening, Roy had come up with the purported sexual-advances version. Malthea and Fern had conveniently stuck wadding in the cracks, and Morning Rose had dropped dark hints about Nicholas's secretive personal life.

The current version was a real doozy. I didn't know whether it would play in Peoria, but I doubted it would in Farberville, USA.

Caron would still have time to beat the crowd to the mall if I made a small detour, I decided as I turned onto a side street and made my way to the police station for the third time in less than a week. At this rate, I'd merit my own parking space in the lot next to the innocuous brick building. Lieutenant Rosen had one; the stenciled lettering on the sign was faded, but still legible. I considered yanking it up and tossing it in a Dumpster, then hurried inside before I gave way to the impulse.

"Is Sergeant Jorgeson here?" I asked the shiny-faced rookie at the reception desk.

"No, he's out at a crime scene right now. You want to leave a message?"

"Is he at Nicholas Chunder's house?"

"I'm not allowed to say, ma'am," the rookie murmured, his ears turning as red as geraniums.

"Please let him know that I'll be there shortly." I

went back out to my car before I could be detained on some fictitious violation.

Fifteen minutes later I parked next to a patrol car and a rather dismal car that was likely to belong to Jorgeson. After a brief argument, the uniformed officer at the door went inside to consult his superior, returned with a chagrined expression, and gestured for me to go inside. I found Jorgeson in the hallway, gazing pensively at an oil painting of one of Nicholas's long-departed ancestors. If the artist had accurately captured his subject, this ancestor had died of bad hair.

"Jorgeson," I said in the resolute tone of a brolly-wielding spinster, "I've had a thought."

"I'm sure you have, Mrs. Malloy. Oddly enough, so have I."

I overlooked this less-than-warm reception. "If Gilda D'Orcher was willing to risk breaking in, she must have been looking for something. It could be a pentagram drawn in chalk on Nicholas's bedroom floor, or proof that she's his illegitimate daughter and therefore entitled to inherit Primrose Hill and all the rental properties."

"Could be," Jorgeson said. "But I think we'd have noticed a pentagram the first time we searched. At the moment, we're going through all the papers in the desk. I'm more inclined to expect to find a bunch of boring letters to county courthouses and genealogical libraries than a birth certificate, but what do I know? I'm just a cop."

I glanced at the door of the study. "What about computer files?"

"We're not having much luck. Apparently, there's a way to put secret passwords on files, and no easy way to determine what they are. Maybe Chunder was an agent for a foreign power and was sending classified documents about military breakthroughs, or maybe he was into pornography and weird sex, or maybe he just liked to play games. Hard to know until my guy gets into the files. It could take days, even weeks."

"Was he really going to sell everything?" I asked.

"Now that we do know. He'd listed his property with a real estate agency, and was corresponding with a company in Cardiff. One of our college-educated boys says that's in Wales. I wouldn't know, myself. The most exotic place my wife and I have ever been is New Orleans. She didn't like it because of all the topless bars and drunks urinating in alleys."

"I don't blame her," I said, disappointed that nothing startling had been uncovered. I went to the doorway of the living room and looked at the artificial winter wonderland. A few strands of tinsel had fallen, and the greenery was turning brittle and brown. Two pewter tankards had been left on a shelf near the fireplace. It looked like the aftermath of a party awaiting the attention of a hungover host.

Jorgeson joined me. "Depressing, isn't it?"

"This entire mess is depressing," I said. "Roy's the same age as Caron. He's either psychotic or the most polished liar I've ever encountered. He must have done it, though. He's confessed twice now, and the weapon's damning."

"There's no doubt it was the weapon, and his prints were on it. There were a couple of smudges, but they've been identified as belonging to his father, who's been gone for three months."

"What about the brandy decanter?"

"We thought of that, too, Mrs. Malloy. It was in a cabinet over there, and covered with dust. No one, in-

cluding your friends, moved it or wiped off prints or
did anything with it before the murder. These people
are giving me a helluvan ulcer. They're all lying, and
I don't know why. We've got a perp, we've got a
weapon, and we've got a confession, which is enough
proof to dump on the district attorney's desk. The doctors and the prosecutors can determine if the boy's
competent to stand trial."

"What about Malthea?"

"The jury may have sympathy for the boy, but I
don't think they'll feel anything but revulsion for her.
Most people who serve on juries are parents or grand-
parents. They're not going to let her go free to find another messed-up teenager."

"Particularly if she won't defend herself," I said.

Jorgeson stepped into the hallway. "She may have
something to say if and when she's charged with first-
degree homicide, as well as impeding an investigation, perjury, contributing to the delinquency, and
whatever else the DA can find. His hemorrhoids flare
up during the winter."

I asked Jorgeson for permission to go to the grove.
He thought it over, shrugged, and told me to watch
out for snakes. I assured him I would, then drove back
to the main road and found the narrow lane that I'd
taken the morning of the solstice. If only I'd missed it
in the dark, I thought as my car slid from rut to rut like
an inept ice-skater. Or better yet, if I'd flatout told
Malthea that I was unable to get her encyclopedia and
other books. Aspirin, scotch, and gasoline would eat
up the profits from that transaction."

The pasture was no more appealing in the daylight
than it had been previously, although it was easier to
transverse. I found the tree where Gilda had waited

for me, ducked under a branch, and headed into what appeared to be the primeval forest.

I took a few false turns, but eventually floundered through a line of firs and found myself at the edge of the grove. Much of the greenery had fallen off the stone altar or been dragged away by rabbits to decorate their burrows.

I sat down on a stump and tried to picture the scene Roy had described. Had Malthea really brought him here and convinced him that she possessed the power to summon a demon? That she belonged to a secret cult that performed human sacrifices? Twinkly Malthea?

If Roy stuck with his story, he was apt to be sent away to a mental hospital until the doctors found the right balance of therapy and drugs. Malthea would spend the rest of her life in a prison. Fern might, too, since she'd implicated herself when she lied to me about the brandy decanter. She, like Malthea, had been familiar with Roy's initial confession and done her part to substantiate it.

Could that have also been Gilda's motive when she foolishly tried to break into the house? Had she intended to dust off the decanter and contribute a smeared fingerprint or two?

A shadow fell across the altar, reminding me that it was getting late. I stood up and brushed off my derriere, took a last look at the somber circle of oak trees, and was about to leave when I heard a crackling noise from somewhere behind the firs. Not the rustling of a small animal, mind you, or the fluttering of dried leaves in the branches, or even the blazing of a satanic furnace as something slipped out for a field trip.

At this time of year, bears were in caves and cows

were in barns. I'd noticed in the local paper that deer-hunting season had passed. Not at all pleased, I took refuge behind a somewhat inadequate tree trunk (I am svelte, but not so that I can be toppled in a light breeze).

Malthea stepped into the grove. In a heavy overcoat, gloves, and a scarf, she looked like an ordinary house-wife on her way to the grocery store for frozen peas and a can of cat food. This, however, was not a grocery store, and she was far from ordinary.

"I must speak to you," she said to whatever of my anatomy was visible.

I emerged, my face warm with embarrassment. "Have you been following me, Malthea?"

"Earlier this afternoon I parked across from your store, but each time I started to get out of the car, someone would go inside. I was ready to give up when you drove away. You've been as busy as a squir-rel in autumn, haven't you? First to the Sawyers' house, then the police station, Nicholas's house, and now here. Was it the desire for solitude that brought you to the Sacred Grove?"

"Something like that," I said.

She sat down on the stump I'd vacated and settled her satchel in her lap. "I'd like to hear exactly what Roy told you last night."

"You've been told the gist of it, and I don't see any reason to go into detail." I began to sidle around the perimeter of the grove, keeping an eye on her satchel. "If you want to discuss Roy's allegation, I'm sure Sergeant Jorgeson will be happy to oblige you. My daughter's waiting for me to get back to the bookstore so that she can have the car."

"I cannot discuss this with the sergeant until you

tell me what Roy told you," she said. "I was under the
assumption that you wanted to help. This is your opportunity, if I am correct."

"I do, which is why I'm advising you to go to
Sergeant Jorgeson."

"I can't do that," she said mulishly.

"Why not? Roy's told his side of the story, and you
should be eager to tell yours. He wouldn't be under-
going a psychiatric evaluation if he were stable. Trust
me when I say he's not. He may have started taking
mind-altering drugs when he moved to Farberville, or
he may have been experiencing schizophrenic epi-
sodes for years. How did he seem to you when you
and Fern found him in the greenhouse?"

"Cold and hungry. He'd hoped he could sleep there
for at least one night, but you ruined that when you
returned with the police officers, didn't you? He
barely had time to stuff a roll in his coat pocket before
fleeing into the night."

Or into the backseat of my car, anyway. "Did he call
you from a pay phone the next morning?" I asked her,
still concerned about the contents of her satchel. Ambesek could not have fit inside, but a handgun scarcely
would have created a bulge.

"What makes you think he called me?"

"I know he called you, Malthea. He told you what
he'd told me, and you spotted his mistakes immediately. You came to the bookstore to do damage control.
Later, after Jorgeson mentioned the lack of alcohol in
Nicholas's blood, you and Fern hatched up another
fabrication to cover it. You and she ought to be writing
screenplays in Hollywood. She could have a greenhouse with every species of plant known to science,

and you could buy several thousand acres with a grove in the middle."

Malthea picked up her satchel and rose to her feet. "All that is irrelevant. You must tell me what Roy said to you and the sergeant last night."

"And if I refuse?" I said, easing backward until my back hit a tree trunk. Forests would be more hospitable with fewer trees. "Will you summon a demon to coerce me?"

"When I first met you, Claire, you seemed like a calm, agreeable person. Lately you've been doing and saying the strangest things. Does the holiday season always disturb you this way? Mumsy had the same problem, which is why she took to opium so fervently. She claimed it was medicinal. To her surprise, the gentlemen from Interpol felt differently."

"I'm leaving, Malthea. We can walk back to the lane together, or you can stay here and meditate until you're blue in the face, which will be well before dawn."

Without waiting for her reply, I plunged back through the firs.

# CHAPTER 12

When I got back to the Book Depot, Caron thrust out her hand and waited until I dropped the car key in it before saying, "Did you forget to mention that this errand of yours involved a trip to Another State? That's probably where the only empty parking place at the mall is by now. Is it in Montana or West Virginia? Is there a shuttle?"

"Did you have any customers?" I asked as I went in the office to hang up my coat.

"Yeah, a few. Is there any gas in the car?"

"Not enough to cross state lines, but ample to get to the mall and back. That *is* where you're going, isn't it?"

"That's what I said," she said, suddenly finding the need to align the pens and pencils on the counter like neatly toppled (and nutritionally challenged) toy soldiers. "We'll shop until nine when the mall closes, and then maybe get a pizza."

"I would have thought you and Inez were sick of the mall by now, particularly after what happened the other day."

She shrugged ever so innocently. "I'm not going to invite Mrs. Claus to share a pizza with us, if that's what you're implying. I don't ever want to set eyes on her or her manual again. Inez is going to meet me a little after eight by the fountain at the opposite end of the mall."

"Be home by eleven," I said, then stood by the window and watched her get into the car, twist the rearview mirror to inspect her makeup, and drive away. I was convinced she was up to something more insidious than wandering around the mall, but I couldn't begin to think what it might be.

I had a partial answer when an unfamiliar teenage girl with frizzy blond hair and unfortunately tight jeans came into the store an hour later. After a brief bout of stammering, she asked to speak to Caron.

"She's at the mall," I said.

"Drat! Even if I knew what she looked like, there's no way I could find her in that madhouse and we're leaving at five-thirty."

"You and Caron?"

"No," the girl said, wringing her hands like a heroine steeling herself to go up the dark, creaky staircase to the attic where things did not bode well for her. "I told her she could come over after supper, but now my mother's decided she wants to leave for my grandma's house as soon as she gets off work instead of waiting until tomorrow. I can ask my grandma's permission to make a long-distance call, but she'll most likely say no. She's so cheap that she unplugs all the lamps and appliances at night so they can't leak electricity."

"Would you like to leave Caron a note?" I said, pushing a piece of paper and a pencil across the counter and hoping I didn't seem overly eager.

Or rabid.

"It's kinda complicated for that. Can I just tell you?" I nodded with commendable restraint. "Darla Jean and I didn't up and quit, although we sure wanted to after Miz Portmeyer started nagging us all the time and bawling us out over nothing. I mean, it wasn't easy to keep the line moving, collect the money, and jam the photographs in the cardboard frames—all with mothers squawking because they didn't like the stiff smiles on their kids' faces and Santa getting lost every time he went to the rest room. Darla Jean said she'd work on her uncle's hog farm afore she'd put up with that again."

"You were fired?" I asked before she could launch into a discourse on the merits of a career in porcine husbandry.

"Miz Portmeyer said we took money from the cash-box when her back was turned. How could we have done that? It's not like the costumes have pockets, and our purses were in our lockers. She just frowned and said that we must have passed the money to some-one outside the fence. I was so mad I wanted to tell her to put one of those elves in a place where the sun don't shine, but Darla Jean started crying and I had to take her to the lounge before she made fools out of both of us."

"Was there money missing?"

"If there was, Miz Portmeyer took it herself. I don't see why she would, though. She always wore real ex-pensive clothes and jewelry, and once she sent me to get something out of the trunk of her fancy sports car. Thirty dollars is nothing but lunch money to her. Any-way, that's what Caron wanted to talk about. Tell her I'm sorry, but I won't be back home until three or four days after Christmas, depending on how long my mother can put up with my grandma. It's usually not very long."

"Wait a minute," I said as the girl headed for the door. "How did Caron find you?"

"I don't know, and even if she'd found out our names, Darla Jean and I live in a little town about twenty miles from here called Maggody."

"I've never heard of it," I said apologetically.

"Nobody has," she said with a lugubrious sigh. "We had to write down our addresses and telephone numbers when we applied for the job, but I can't see Miz Portmeyer letting Caron copy down the information."

"Will Darla Jean be home tonight?"

"No, her family left yesterday to spend Christmas in St. Louis. I'll bet her grandma doesn't have a five-pound ball of rubber bands."

The girl, whose name I'd never ascertained, left the bookstore under her personal cloud of melancholy. No customers appeared after that, and at six o'clock I hung the "closed" sign on the door, locked up, and walked home to an empty apartment, an increasingly mangy Christmas tree, and a newscast that underscored the hazards of public transportation in underdeveloped countries. Vermont was not mentioned.

The following evening would be Christmas Eve. I'd promised the downstairs tenant, a retired professor who'd found himself divorced only recently and for reasons he'd not yet assimilated, that I would drop by his party, but I doubted I would any more than I would drag myself to Luanne's for an evening of cocktail-party chatter and squares of cheese on toothpicks.

The only thing that had any appeal was hearing what Caron had to say when she came home at eleven. It would require a healthy amount of inventiveness on her part to explain—without admitting to any misdemeanors, that is—how she'd found the names and telephone numbers of the previous two assistants at Santa's Workshop.

I wasn't sure what to make of the girl's story of being wrongly accused of theft. She'd sounded sincere (and didn't everybody these days?), but Ms. Portmeyer must have been aware of the risk when she fired them a week before Christmas. Without jingling reindeer to facilitate the operation, profits would plummet and the home office might reexamine her position on the heretofore ascending corporate escalator.

I was trying to decide on the best approach to persuade Caron to tell me what she was up to when the telephone rang. I picked up the receiver with the same eagerness I would a dollop of raw meat and said, "Hello."

"Claire, this is Fern Lewis. I'm so upset I don't know what to do. A woman from the hospital called to tell me that Malthea's in the emergency room. I don't trust myself to drive. Can you please take me there?"

I told her I'd pick her up in ten minutes, then grabbed my coat and was halfway down the steps when I realized the garage was empty. My half, anyway. I went back through the apartment and down the interior front stairs to knock on the door of my nearest, and at the moment, dearest neighbor.

He answered the door in his bathrobe and slippers. "What a surprise, Claire, but I'm afraid you're early. My little get-together is tomorrow. However, if you'd like to come inside, I can offer you a tasty concoction of cranberry juice, vodka, and crème de menthe. I like to call it a 'Jingle Bell Bazooka.' "

"I need to borrow your car," I said. "Caron has mine, and I don't know how to get in touch with her. A friend is at the emergency room." When he hesitated, I added, "The poor thing's quite elderly and frail, and she's never mentioned having any relatives in the area."

I may have been piling it on when I described her as frail, but he must have already had a Jingle Bell Bazooka or two because he blinked tearily, left the doorway, and returned a moment later with a key ring. I thanked him and hurried around the yard to the garage.

When I pulled up in front of the duplex, Fern was waiting on the porch. She wrinkled her nose as she climbed into the passenger's side of the VW Beetle. "Is it cigarette smoke I smell? I do hope you haven't picked up that filthy habit. My late husband used to sneak outside for an occasional cigar, and I always told him afterward that he reeked like an incinerator."

"I had to borrow the car," I said. "What happened to Malthea?"

"I wish I knew. The woman called me because my name and address are on a next-of-kin card in Malthea's wallet. It was just a precaution, and I never expected to be careening through dark streets like this."

I glanced at the speedometer. "I'm going twenty-three miles an hour, Fern. That does not qualify as 'careening.' "

"Perhaps you should step on it. Malthea may die before we get there."

I clenched my teeth and concentrated on shifting rather than stripping gears. As I parked in front of the emergency room, I saw two police cars at the end of the curb. A car that resembled Jorgeson's was in the shadows beyond them.

A succinct expletive entered my mind, in that it did not seem likely that Malthea had fallen off a curb or been stricken with a heart attack. I let Fern out of the car, parked, and joined her at the door. "It's going to be fine," I said, squeezing her shoulder.

"I've been fretting all day. Malthea refused to answer the door or her telephone. The curtains were drawn. I called over and over again. I was beside myself."

"I'm sure you were." I led her into the blindingly antiseptic environment of the emergency room. A multigenerational Hispanic family was grouped on two sofas; even the youngest child watched me solemnly. Beyond them was a woman holding a baby wrapped in a thin blanket. The only other person in sight was a young nurse with a clipboard and a harried expression.

"Malthea Hendlerson?" I said to her.

"She's been taken upstairs," the nurse said, flinching as an elevator opened behind us. "Are you relatives? We need some information about her insurance coverage."

"What happened to her?"

"I can't say. She suffered injuries, and once they stabilized her, she was transferred to ICU. We have her Medicare card, but we must know if she has a private insurer."

"Or what?" I demanded in what even I realized was an unnecessarily high voice. "Are you going to turn off the life-support system if she doesn't have insurance?"

Jorgeson appeared at my side, discreetly hustled me over to a soda machine, and hunted through his pockets for change. "Calm down, Mrs. Malloy," he murmured. "None of us needs to deal with hospital security just now. Why don't you sit and we'll talk?"

I sat. Jorgeson handed me a can and sat down beside me. "Here's all we know so far. Malthea went to

Nicholas Chunder's house sometime after we left at five o'clock. We haven't had anybody on duty out there since we took the boy into custody last night, but I did arrange for a patrol car to cruise by on a regular basis. The officers saw a light, went inside, and found her unconscious on the floor. Blow to the head. She's still out."

Fern, who'd given up badgering the nurse and was hovering nearby, made a gurgly noise. "Is she in a coma?"

"At the moment, she's merely unconscious," said Jorgeson. "We haven't ruled out the possibility that one of our local degenerates heard about the murder and showed up, thinking the house would be unoccupied. The light should have warned him off, though. These weasels are more scared of their shadows than your average groundhog."

I lowered my voice. "Then you think that it has to do with Nicholas's murder?"

"Hold on." He beckoned to a uniformed officer and asked him to escort Fern to the ICU waiting room. Once she was gone, he said, "Nothing was taken, and there're expensive objects everywhere you look. Anyone who'd gone there with the explicit intent to commit theft would have at least stuffed a piece of silver or crystal in his pocket."

I gazed at a greenish expanse of linoleum that brought to mind a stagnant pond. "Look on the bright side, Jorgeson—at least two suspects have been eliminated. Gilda and Roy are somewhere upstairs."

"If only they were. It seems that on this very afternoon, a Brownie troop came to sing Christmas carols and pass out cookies. The nurses and aides on the sixth floor decided that all their patients should be included in the festivities. A very kind-hearted gesture on everyone's part, to be sure. The door was left unlocked, certain patients became overtly emotional, two dozen Brownies started screaming, and Roy and Gilda managed to disappear. Nobody noticed their absence until supper trays were being distributed."

"I'd have thought security on that particular ward would be tight."

"Not as tight as it should be, obviously. Patients walk off the psych ward more often than the public's aware of, since the hospital administrators don't want negative publicity. Gilda and Roy aren't the only ones who slipped away this afternoon. We have APBs out on a convicted rapist and a guy who wears an aluminum-foil skullcap. Gilda works here, so she may have had help. Or maybe the Brownies were in on it."

I told him about my conversation with Malthea in the grove. "She must have lingered in the vicinity until you left, then entered the house to look for something. Could Gilda have gone back, too?"

"Yeah, or Malthea conjured up that demon with the foreign name and bad attitude."

"Have you located the weapon?"

He nodded. "Chunder had a marble replica of Stonehenge in his study. One of the chunks was found near her body. It'd been wiped off, but there was a trace of blood in a crack. Ironic, huh?"

"Very," I said dryly. "So Malthea was in the study when she was attacked? Was she searching the desk?"

"There's a cabinet in the corner. We'd already been through it and found nothing of interest, but she wouldn't have known that. Evidence suggests that she was kneeling in front of it and working on the lock with a hairpin, which would explain why she didn't hear this other person come into the room. Picking a lock requires a lot of concentration."

"So I've heard," I murmured. "What were they looking for, Jorgeson? No one could expect to find clues scattered about after your team went over the scene."

"No one in his or her right mind, anyway. The guy with the shiny cap would fit right in with this group."

"Thanks for the soda," I said as I stood up. "I guess I'd better find Fern and make sure she's not driving the ICU staff crazy." I took the elevator to the appropriate floor and followed stenciled arrows to the glass doors of the unit. A sign sternly forbade unauthorized visitors.

That being precisely what I was, I went into the waiting room across the hall. Fern was perched on the edge of a chair, her face grim with either concern or disapproval of the two androgynous teenagers sprawled across a couch in a corner. The latter was more likely, since they had nose rings and creatively styled purple hair.

I touched Fern's arm. "Have you spoken to anyone?"

"Only long enough to be told I'm not allowed to see Malthea. I'm of a mind to report that woman to her supervisor. Impertinence should not be tolerated."

"Give 'em hell, granny," said one of the teenagers. The other brayed in appreciation.

I stepped in front of Fern before she could launch an attack, verbal or otherwise. "Is she still unconscious?"

"They said that I would be informed of any changes in her condition. I couldn't tell which cubicle she's in or what sort of attention she's receiving. I really should be permitted to sit by her bed. She'll be frightened if she wakes up in a strange room and finds herself clad only in a flimsy gown. There are moments I wish I could cast an effective spell—or a curse that would teach that nurse a thing or two."

I sensed the stirring interest of the pair of eggplant heads in the corner. "There's a coffee machine by the elevator," I said. "I think you'll find a hot drink comforting."

"I only drink decaf after ten o'clock in the morning."

"There will be decaf," I said, tugging at her arm. "Afterward, I'll try to get information from the nurse."

Fern allowed me to guide her to the vending machines. I punched a button, waited while a stream of brown liquid dribbled into the cup, and then thrust it at Fern's trembling hand.

She stared at it. "I can't drink this. It's liable to upset my stomach."

I put the cup on top of the machine. "I can see how worried you are. Have you and Malthea been friends for a long time?"

"We met while we were in college. We both planned to teach secondary English, but my fiancé returned from Germany and wanted to get married immediately. He stayed in the army for the next fifteen years, and was stationed everywhere from Omaha to Manila. It was hard to remain in touch, but Malthea and I did our best with greeting cards and letters."

"What did she do?"

"Taught, of course. How else could she have supported herself?"

"She never married?"

"At one time, she was engaged, but the wedding did not take place. That's all I shall say concerning the matter."

I noted the rigidity of her expression and abandoned the intriguing topic. "How long has she lived in Farberville?"

"Twelve, perhaps thirteen years. She bought a small house and did volunteer work to keep herself busy. We rarely saw each other while my husband was alive. He was a deacon in the Baptist church and disapproved of her eccentricities. When he passed away, Malthea urged me to consider Druidism as an alternative to the orthodox traditions I'd followed since childhood. I attended a ritual and met Nicholas, who offered me economical housing and loaned me money from time to time until I straightened out my financial affairs. He went so far as to help with the paperwork that was required for me to receive a widow's pension from the military. How could he have been so compassionate back then, and so cruel the evening before the solstice?"

I wasn't sure how much further I could go without reducing her to tears, but anxiety had made her garrulous and I was not above taking advantage of it. Amateur sleuths cannot be slaves to scrupulosity. "Can you tell me exactly what happened that evening? Were you and Malthea among the first or the last to arrive?"

"Let me think," she said. "I do my best to be prompt, but we were a bit late because Malthea was so dithery. First, she forgot her sweater and had to go back inside. Nicholas's house can be drafty this time of year. We were all set to start off, and then she remembered a sack of holly she'd left in her kitchen. I was so annoyed that I refused to speak to her until we got there."

"The others were already there, then?"

"Roy and Morning Rose were in the living room,

acting as though they were at a funeral. While we were hanging up our coats, Nicholas and Gilda came out of the study. When I later asked her what they'd been discussing that had so distressed her, she mumbled something about needing to find another place to live. In my day, we were taught to speak clearly."

I did a mental review of the roster. "What about Sullivan?"

"He was a full half hour late. Apparently there'd been a problem with the children, and Morning Rose insisted that he put them to bed by himself. I believe she walked to Primrose Hill. She must have regretted her decision, because she seemed very unhappy."

"It must have been a tense evening," I prompted her.

"Oh, it was that. My annoyance with Malthea soon spread to all the members of the grove. Everyone seemed sullen and disinclined to participate. I had to speak sharply to Roy when he failed to fetch a step-ladder at my request. Morning Rose and Sullivan had a whispered argument in the kitchen, and when they came back into the room, her eyes were red. Nicholas spent most of the evening in a chair by the fireplace, watching us as though we had designs on his knickknacks. I was deeply offended by his implicit accusation."

I spotted the teenagers sauntering down the hall toward us and nudged her around the corner and into a storage room filled with odoriferous cleaning supplies. "Did something specific happen that caused him to make his unexpected announcement?"

Fern clutched her purse on the off chance I was about to mug her with an ammonia bottle. "We'd finished putting up the decorations, and were seated around the fire, drinking that dreadful beverage Nicholas insisted on serving. Malthea did her best to lead us in song, but even I was infected with their gloom. I was about to suggest we leave when Gilda stood up and said that she intended to perform the solstice ritual as she pleased. As she *damn* well pleased is what she actually said. Nicholas came close to spilling his tankard. He began sputtering, but she told him that it didn't matter if she was kicked out of the grove since this would be her final celebration. Morning Rose laughed bitterly and said she might as well join Gilda. Sullivan grabbed her arm, and then Roy grabbed *his* arm, and the two began to grapple. That was when Nicholas exploded with rage. It was quite terrible."

"Why did Gilda say it would be her final celebration?" I demanded, my fingers crossed that the teenagers would not find us and make remarks that would send Fern off on a tangential tirade.

"I don't know. Shouldn't you find out about Malthea?"

"I'll try," I said. We went back to the doors of the ICU and waited until we were noticed.

The nurse who opened the door did not seem pleased to see Fern behind me. "I've already told you that I cannot discuss the patient's condition. That is the attending physician's prerogative."

"Not even with the patient's sister?" I said, hoping Fern was paying attention.

"She didn't say that earlier."

I tried to sound moderately smug. "Did you ask her?"

"She should have said so."

Fern cleared her throat, and in a voice well suited to a displeased schoolteacher, said, "You should have asked me. I was too distraught to respond to your

coldhearted refusal to allow me to sit beside my only
sister. If she should die before I have an opportunity to
hold her hand and reminisce about how we used to
make daisy chains in the meadow on summer after-
noons, I may contact our youngest brother. He's an
attorney."

The nurse paled, then invited Fern to accompany her
into a curtained cubicle. I considered tagging along,
then decided not to complicate the ruse and returned
to the waiting room. I was relieved to have it to myself.

At least I had a better picture of what had taken
place between seven and nine o'clock on the evening
of the murder, I thought as I tried to make myself comfortable on the plastic upholstery. Gilda's threat to
turn up wearing nothing but an amulet may have trig-
gered Nicholas's outburst, but he'd already listed his
property with a real estate agency and contacted a
similar agency in Wales. It seemed likely that he'd
planned to delay his announcement until after the
solstice celebration for the same reason one doesn't
tell children about an imminent divorce on Christmas Eve.

But according to Fern, the Druids were already upset when she and Malthea arrived. Roy and Morning
Rose had been brooding in the living room, and Gilda
had heard something not to her liking in the study.
Sullivan had argued with his wife. The host himself
had been less than genial.

And why hadn't Malthea denied Roy's ridiculous
accusation? She could have been so taken aback that
she was momentarily speechless, but I'd practically
begged her in the grove hours later. Morning Rose had
seemed convinced that Roy had blindly obeyed Malthea's command to kill Nicholas. I wasn't.

I was not likely to find a listing for Sisters of Illumination in the telephone directory so that I could inquire
into their membership role and annual observances.
Surely law-enforcement agencies would have heard
rumors if sacrifices, human or otherwise, were being
performed in the area. There had been one such case
concerning cattle mutilations in the county, attributed
to almond-eyed alien vivisectionists, but the ensuing
investigation had determined that a pack of feral dogs
had been responsible.

I was still juggling ideas when a woman in baggy
blue scrubs and plastic slippers came into the waiting
room. Her hair was hidden under the sort of cap favored by surgical teams, but her sallow complexion
could not be so easily disguised.

"Gilda?" I said. "What are you doing here?"

"It's as good a place as any. I'm waiting for someone
I know to get off duty so he can give me a ride out to
the trailer park. I'd be conspicuous dressed like this if
I was walking down the road, but here I'm invisible.
I was hanging around the emergency room when
Malthea was wheeled in. What happened to her?"

I tried not to stare at the discreet bandages on her
wrists. "She was attacked in Nicholas's study. Patrolmen noticed a light and investigated. Otherwise, she
might have lain there for several days."

"What was she doing there?"

"The same thing you were," I said, "although you
and she may have been looking for different things.
What were you hoping to find?"

"Money," she said quickly. "He was a real miser, so I
figured he'd have a lockbox in a desk drawer. If I'd
known they had the house staked out because of Roy, I
wouldn't have tried it."

"And that's why you wanted to talk to me the other evening? You wanted to ask me if I could suggest the most likely places to find a hypothetical lockbox? Then, after you'd been arrested, you thought my nonexistent license to practice law would facilitate your release? When I failed to bail you out, you attempted suicide? At the worst you would have been charged with criminal trespass, since you never made it into the house. I don't buy this, Gilda."

She sat down on the couch vacated by the teenagers, pulled off the cloth cap, and placed it carefully on the armrest. "You seemed like such good buddies with the cops that I thought you could tell me what was going on. It's only been three hundred years since the Salem witch trials. Wicca is something entirely different, but we're still lumped in with medieval practitioners with their black cats and evil eyes."

"Three hundred years is not the same as last summer," I said. "The Puritans are no longer monopolizing the city council and the school board, and no one except a lifeguard cares if you float or sink. You're not stupid enough to break into Nicholas's house for money. What did he have?"

She went to the doorway and stuck her head out, then sat down next to me. "Will you promise not to tell anyone?"

"I can't do that, Gilda. It's against the law to withhold evidence, and in any case, I'm not going to do anything that will muddy the waters. Did Roy tell you that he confessed?"

"Twice, he said," she said with a momentary smile. "Yes, we talked in the dayroom this morning. He killed Nicholas, Mrs. Malloy. He's ashamed of it, but he did it and he's willing to accept his punishment."

"Not so eager that he didn't escape this afternoon," I pointed out.

"There are things he must do before he turns himself in again," she said somberly. "He must conduct a final ritual in an attempt to protect himself from Ambesek. If it doesn't work, his body will never be found."

"Would you people stop this!" I waited until I'd simmered down, but whiffs of steam may have still been drifting out of my ears. "This is nothing but self-indulgent nonsense. Oh, I'm sure everyone who works here has heard rumors of your Wiccan practices, and therefore thinks you're terribly romantic. Salem witch trials? Ambesek? Demon-repellant rituals? Buy him a can of Raid and give me a break!"

"You're a skeptic," she said, pronouncing judgment from her plastic-covered bench.

"You can bet the farm on it. Now either tell me why you insisted on speaking to me, or see how far you can get after I call hospital security. Odds are not good that you can make it to an exit, but you may know of a door in the basement. Cast a spell and make yourself invisible. I don't care. A week ago I was minding my own business, and now I'm embroiled with a gang of delusional pagans. The man I care about is snuggled up in front of a fire with his ex–significant other. I'm being sued for a million dollars. My daughter's off committing a felony. Malthea's in ICU, Nicholas is in the morgue, Roy's in battle with a demon, and the best you can do is label me a skeptic?"

"Gracious, Mrs. Malloy," Gilda said, again checking the doorway for lurkers, "I'd no idea you were this upset. Shall I cast a spell to envelope you in a protective glow of love and warmth from the Mother Goddess?"

"That's it." I stood up and grabbed my purse. "I'm alerting security that you're in the building. Good-bye and good luck."

She caught my arm. "Okay, I'll tell the truth."

Not only would the archbishop and the princess elope, the pope would conduct the ceremony.

# CHAPTER 13

"Then tell me the truth," I said as I allowed myself to be led back to the couch. This is not to say that I wasn't keenly aware of the distance to a bright red telephone in the hallway. No more than a whoop and a holler, so to speak.

Gilda's face puckered like a bulldog's. "Can this stay between us, Mrs. Malloy?"

"I've already said that I won't keep secrets from the police. If what you tell me is relevant, then I will certainly tell them."

"It's *not* relevant," she said. "It's nothing more than a rumor and it's not true. All the same, if it got out, it would cause problems. You can't believe the amount of gossiping that goes on in hospitals. The only person who'll keep a confidence is in a drawer in the morgue. Nurses, doctors, orderlies, secretaries, aides, cafeteria workers—everybody gossips."

"What's the rumor?"

"Oh, all right. A few years back, I was working at a hospital in Kansas City. I'm a pediatric nurse, so I deal with a lot of neonatal patients. Most of them are healthy and pink, but some are in bad shape and . . . well, not destined to lead happy lives. They're born with AIDS, or they're addicted to crack, or they have deformities to their spinal columns and brains." She moved away from me, her hands clenched and her sallow skin now almost colorless. When she finally spoke, her voice was tight. "Some of these babies die, Mrs. Malloy. We keep them on respirators, we feed them intravenously, we drain fluids from their cranial cavities, we do everything we can to keep them alive." She spun around and looked down at me with strobelike intensity. "But sometimes they die—and sometimes it's for the best. Can you understand that?"

I held up my palms. "Sit down, Gilda. No one's accused you of anything."

"Nicholas did," she said bitterly. "He persuaded someone in personnel to let him read my application, and then used his computer to start a dialogue with his colleagues at the hospital in Kansas City. They were happy to pass along rumors about why I resigned. That's all I did. I wasn't fired, and there were no charges brought against me. All he heard were lies. If there had been any proof that I'd done something wrong, I would have been charged."

I tried to keep my voice even. "If you were never charged, then how could these rumors affect you?"

"That night in his study Nicholas told me that he'd decided to 'clean off his desk,' as he called it, before he left for Wales. He was not only going to inform the head of nursing that I'd made no mention of the reason for my resignation on my application, he was also going to put the word out all over the Internet that I was . . . well, you know. A premature baby, not even three pounds at birth, died last month. I wasn't assigned to that patient, but Nicholas said he was going to retrieve the records and make sure I hadn't been alone in the nursery on that night."

"And had you?" I asked softly.

"I was working the ward, but so were other staff. It's not uncommon for babies born with those kinds of complications to stop breathing. It happens, Mrs. Malloy. I had nothing to do with it. Nicholas said he was going to prevent me from ever again finding work as a registered nurse in any accredited hospital in the country. It's what I'm trained to do. It's all that matters to me."

Saliva was bubbling on her lips and her eyes were overly bright. I glanced at the doorway, hoping Fern would come to the rescue. I would have even welcomed the aberrant teenagers. As it was, I cast about for a soothing comment, and finally said, albeit with monumental inanity, "I understand, Gilda."

"No, you don't, and neither did Nicholas. I did everything I could to dissuade him, but he said that he would contact every state licensing board in the country. Boards administer a slap on the wrist to nurses who steal drugs. They issue a three-month suspension to nurses who expedite terminal cancer patients. But nurses who are rumored to have . . ."

To my astonishment, she collapsed across my lap and began to sob like a heartbroken toddler, her gulps and snorts loud enough to be heard on every floor in the hospital. I was torn between patting her on the back and rolling her onto the floor. I was not unsympathetic, but I'd learned by this time that if one of the members of the Sacred Grove of Keltria announced that the sun would rise in the east, I'd do better to be looking west at dawn.

I was still vacillating when Fern came into the room and stared disapprovingly at me.

"What ever is going on?" she demanded. "Have

you entered into an intimate relationship with an orderly, Claire? It is most inappropriate."

Gilda sat up and wiped her drippy nose on her wrist. "It's me, Fern."

"Oh, dear," she said. "I simply saw your . . . buttocks, and leapt to . . . oh, dear."

I stood up, effectively sending Gilda into an ungraceful tangle on the linoleum. "How's Malthea?" I asked Fern, ignoring the mutters from the region of my feet.

"She awoke some minutes ago, and although she was unable to speak, she was heartened by my presence. She'll be moved to a standard room in the morning, presuming she continues to show improvement. Why is Gilda rolling about like that?"

"She's upset," I said.

"We are all upset," Fern said sternly. "That is no excuse."

Gilda extricated herself up and crawled onto the couch like an intoxicated crab. "Malthea's vitals are stable?"

"A good deal more stable than yours," Fern retorted, then turned to me. "I should like to go home, if you don't mind. It's really quite late. I won't be surprised to find Malthea's cat on my doorstep, mewing piteously for her supper. She can make do with milk until I have a chance to pick up some cat food at the grocery store. This is all so inconvenient. Behavior like this does not become you, Gilda. I do hope this is not the consequence of some Wiccan spell."

Gilda and I looked at each other. When it became clear that she wasn't going to leap in, I said, "We were worried about Malthea, and now we know she's going to be all right. Our problem is what Gilda's going to do in the immediate future. I strongly suggest that she contact Sergeant Jorgeson."

She glanced at Fern, then whispered to me, "Does he know?"

"Know what?" said Fern.

"Not yet," I answered, "but it's a matter of time before his computer boys determine Nicholas's passwords and gain access to the files. It'll be better for you if you've already admitted all this."

"Admitted what?" Fern squawked, beginning to sound like a high-strung parrot with exceptionally acute hearing.

Gilda tried unsuccessfully to push her bangs out of her eyes. "There's more, Mrs. Malloy. I went back out there to talk to Nicholas."

"You people should have carpooled," I said irritably. "So were you there before Fern's purported arrival, after Malthea's purported departure, or sometime in between while Roy purportedly was shooting Nicholas?"

She ignored Fern's gasp and said, "The only person I saw was Sullivan walking across the pasture toward the house. He must have seen me, because he dropped to the ground like a sniper had nailed him."

"Sullivan Sawyer?" I said. "Are you sure?"

"He must have been going there for the same reason I was. When I knocked on the door of the study on the eve of the solstice, Nicholas was on the telephone. As I went inside, he said, 'As you wish, Sullivan,' and then hung up. He looked so angry that I pretended I hadn't heard anything."

"Eavesdropping is vulgar," inserted Fern. "I know you live in a trailer park these days. Did you grow up in one as well?"

"What if I did?" countered Gilda.

I clamped my hand on Gilda's shoulder to keep her on the couch. "Not everyone spends her childhood making daisy chains in the meadow, Fern. Are you ready to leave?"

"Poison ivy garlands seem more likely," Fern said as she buttoned her coat. "Yes, I am more than ready to leave."

"Then please wait by the elevator. I'll be there in a minute."

She opened her mouth to protest, then thought better of it and stalked out of the room. I listened as her footsteps diminished, then tightened my grip on Gilda's shoulder and said, "Did you speak to Nicholas?"

"I lost my nerve when I saw Sullivan. I pedaled home and stayed up half the night trying to find a spell that would prevent him from mentioning it at the celebration the next morning. It would have made Nicholas all the more determined to destroy me."

"What time did you arrive at his house?"

"I don't know," she said. "I headed out there at eleven, but whenever I saw a car coming, I dragged my bicycle into the ditch and squatted next to it."

"Did you recognize any of the cars?" I asked.

"I thought I saw hers," she said, pointing her thumb in the direction of the elevators. "There wasn't much moonlight, though, and I told myself I was mistaken. Was it really Fern? Had Nicholas threatened her, too?"

I briefly thought of Fern's deceased husband, then shook my head and picked up my purse. "You'll have to get a Ouija board and ask him yourself. Do you know where Roy is hiding?"

"Get your own Ouija board," she said, clearly offended by my remark. "Better yet, call a psychic at one of those one-nine-hundred numbers. You might get a real surprise."

"Roy needs to be in the psychiatric ward, Gilda. You said you talked to him earlier today. Aren't you worried that he might harm himself?"

She stood up and collected her green cap. "Group therapy three times a week isn't going to exorcise his demon."

I considering blocking the doorway, but to be honest, it was late and I was sick of them. "Will you go back to the sixth floor?"

"Like a good little girl?" Smirking, she pulled on the cap and tucked her hair under it. The result was lumpy but seemed to satisfy her. "No, I think I'll go out to the grounds, peel off these clothes, and recite the words of the Goddess. 'I who am the beauty of the green Earth, and the white Moon amongst the stars—'" She broke off as the doors of the ICU opened and a cart squeaked down the hall. "See you around, Mrs. Malloy," she said as she whipped past me.

"Not if I can help it," I retorted to an empty room. After a small debate whether I should straighten magazines and switch off the light, I went to the elevator and stood mutely next to Fern. We rode to the ground floor. The Hispanic family was no longer in the emergency room, but the woman with the baby was in the same place, partially covered with a blanket and snoring loudly.

I stopped at the reception desk and told a nurse about my encounter with Gilda D'Orcher in the ICU wing, then asked her to call security and the Farberville Police Department.

"I'd heard she was a patient on the sixth floor," the woman said with a malicious smile. "I'm not the only one who thought she should have been sent there a long time ago. The stories about her are enough to chill your blood. One of the orderlies swore he caught a glimpse of her in the basement with a black cat. Once she and her supervisor had an argument, and the very next day the supervisor slipped on a wet spot on the floor and broke her ankle."

I was hoping she would elaborate, but she picked up the telephone and punched a button. I pushed open the door for Fern and glowered at her back as she scurried toward the VW. Once we were buckled in and driving toward her neighborhood, I said, "Why did you go back to Nicholas's that night?"

Her nose rose imperiously. "I believe I've already explained it."

"No, you haven't," I said as I braked in anticipation of a red light. "The brandy decanter wasn't touched. The story you told me was at Malthea's behest, wasn't it? You and she were trying to help Roy. Why does she care so much about him?"

"I refuse to discuss it," she said with a sniff. "I have my reasons—and they are none of your business. I am very sorry you intruded on our winter solstice celebration, Claire. This is the first year we've had problems like this."

"Like murder?" I said bluntly.

"All this unpleasantness. Nicholas should have known better than to think he could . . ."

"Could what? Blackmail everybody? Could that be what put the damper on the festivities?"

"He was a gentleman. He would never stoop to that sort of thing."

"Then what?" I demanded, huffing and puffing and close to blowing her out of the car. "You did go there, although not to have a glass of brandy and a civilized conversation. Had Nicholas threatened to expose you, too?"

"Don't be absurd. I've done nothing wrong. You, on the other hand, are driving erratically. It's making me nervous. I can see I shall need a cup of valeriana tea before I can possibly fall asleep."

I gave up and drove her home without further attempts to elicit information from her. She might not have actually spent any time as a teacher, but she'd studied the techniques of classroom intimidation and paid careful attention.

"Good night," I said as I pulled up to the curb. "Can you drive yourself to the hospital tomorrow?"

"One would think." She climbed out of the car, gave me an enigmatic look, and went up the sidewalk to her porch. I waited until she was inside, then drove to the corner and obediently stopped in front of an octagonal sign requesting as much from me.

At this point, I'll admit, I craned my neck and made sure Roy was not hiding in the backseat. Rather than continue home, however, I pulled to the curb, cut off the engine, and sat back to think about what I'd heard—and what it might have meant.

If (with a capital *I*) Gilda had been telling the truth, Fern had been at the house and Sullivan had been going in that direction. What a busy night Nicholas might have had if he'd entertained each and every would-be caller. He must have begun to regret his announcement as cars, cyclists, and pedestrians crunched across the gravel forecourt in an endless parade. Which of them had been admitted? And what had he or she found? A blustery, self-righteous Druid or a corpse on the kitchen floor?

Roy should have been the central figure, but Malthea seemed to be popping up in the center of the vortex with every revelation. Thanks to Fern's uncharacteristic cooperation, I had a scanty notion of Malthea's history: college, a broken engagement, a career in teaching, retirement, volunteer work. Jorgeson might have a few more tidbits, but he wouldn't have ordered a full-blown background check on any of them unless fingerprints had matched a set in the FBI file.

At least I wasn't brooding about Peter, I told myself as I wondered if there was any way to get a set of Leslie's fingerprints. It seemed obvious that she was employed by the KGB, and used the trite St. Petersburg opera ploy to pass along state secrets to unshaven men named Vladimir and Uri. Myron was likely to be in on it. The wolfhounds undoubtedly had cyanide capsules embedded in their rhinestone-studded collars.

Clearly, I needed to go home and find something to read, if only the back of a cereal box or an insert in the newspaper announcing a Christmas Eve sale at a local discount store. I needed a cold drink and a hot meal. I needed to be sitting on the sofa when Caron came home.

Or maybe I needed a lobotomy, I concluded as I got out of the car, made sure the doors were locked, and walked back toward the duplex, careful to stay in the shadows.

Lights were on inside Fern's apartment; Malthea's, as expected, was dark. I asked myself where an Arch Druid might hide a front door key. Despite an escalation in the crime rate and admonishments from the chief of police, residents of Farberville continue to cloak themselves in a small-town mentality of trusting thy neighbor as thyself. However, there was no key under the mat or on the sill above the door.

I was groping the soil in a clay flowerpot when the porch light came on and Fern opened her door.

"Have you lost something?" she said.

I straightened up and brushed grit off my fingers. "My mind, for instance? I think that's obvious by now. No, Fern, I simply decided that I have to know more about Malthea in order to help her avoid spending the rest of her life in prison. She's maddening, but I like her."

"The rest of her life in prison?" Pulling a shawl more tightly around her shoulders, Fern came out onto the porch. "All she did was tell the police a little white lie about the brandy decanter. Surely that's not a crime that merits prison. A fine, perhaps, and certainly a scolding from a judge—but prison?"

"You haven't spoken to her today, have you?"

"No, I told you that when we first arrived at the hospital. Has she been accused of something?"

I gave her a short, sanitized version of Roy's latest confession. "And she wasn't in seclusion in her apartment, either," I added. "She followed me all over town this afternoon, then confronted me in the grove and demanded to hear exactly what Roy'd said. She refused to confirm or deny it. Sergeant Jorgeson had his doubts, but if the media get wind of this, the county prosecutor, who's never averse to publicity, may demand that she be charged. You'll have more tabloid reporters in your yard than you have dandelions in the spring. Your photograph—and Malthea's mug shots— will be on covers in every supermarket in the country."

Fern turned around and put her hand on the doorknob. After a long moment, she cleared her throat and said, "I was planning to pack a bag to take to the hospital tomorrow. Just a few things to make Malthea more comfortable, like her robe and slippers, toiletries, a crossword puzzle book. I'll get her key and do it now. If you'd like, you can come along."

Once we were inside Malthea's apartment, Fern murmured something and went into another room. I sat down at a small desk and began opening drawers. The first contained utility receipts, an expired library card, pencils with worn erasers, and a small box filled with discolored keys.

I moved along, discovering such keepsakes as matchbooks, calendars from the previous decade, postcards with illegible scrawls, packets of salt and pepper from fast-food restaurants, and leaky pens.

In the bottom drawer on the right, covered by notebooks and much-used folders, was a leather box. Feeling oddly guilty, I took it out and set it on the surface in front of me.

The top item was a neatly clipped newspaper article with a photograph of a smiling couple and a header that announced that Dr. Randall H. Tate and his wife, Dr. Brenda Cockburn-Tate, anthropologists at Farber College, had been awarded a grant from the National Geographic Foundation to study the Dayak of Borneo, an aboriginal people who lived in the tropical rain forests of the highlands. Dr. Tate was particularly interested in their centuries-old tradition of headhunting.

I put the article aside and took out a much smaller clipping concerning Dr. Tate's appointment as head of the department of cultural anthropology. Beneath it was a blurry snapshot of a man in his yard who appeared to be Dr. Tate at an age when he possessed a great deal more hair and at least one pair of bell-bottom jeans.

There were more snapshots of unknown people,

some grim and some smiling. The backgrounds were uniformly indistinct. I hurried through them, then froze as I came upon one of Roy. He was walking along a sidewalk, oblivious of the camera. After a bit of scrutiny, I decided that he was outside the used-book store on Thurber Street where he'd claimed Malthea had approached him.

Had she been stalking him?

I replaced everything in the box and returned it to the bottom drawer. I'd been through all the desk drawers, but Fern was packing at a charmingly slow pace. I went into the kitchen and eased open drawers until I found one filled with the sort of junk I keep in such a kitchen drawer. There were manuals from extinct appliances, virginal warranty cards, rubber bands, string, an empty roll of masking tape . . . and a brochure from an outfit called Psychic Confidantes. For a mere pittance of $3.99 per minute, any caller could, from the privacy of his or her own home, have a totally confidential session with a certified psychic. Answers to questions concerning romance, careers, and money were guaranteed one hundred percent.

Malthea must have believed this twaddle, I thought as I took out a deck of tarot cards and stared at the depictions of characters dressed in colorful costumes. Even "Death" was gaudy. Although I doubted conversations with a "Psychic Confidante" were covered by the rules of client confidentiality, it might prove difficult to subpoena a voice at the other end of the line with the name Divinia.

There was a 1-900 number written in ink at the bottom of the brochure. I copied it down on an old grocery-store tape, then put everything back and looked around for another place in which Malthea might have stashed something of note.

I was heading for the refrigerator (don't ask) when I saw Fern in the doorway.

"Did you find anything?" she asked.

"Photographs of Roy and a couple of clippings concerning his father. Why was Malthea so interested in them?"

"She was very disturbed when she first caught a glimpse of Roy in some shop, and asked the clerk about him. She did not lead him into satanism; she was trying to save him."

"Has she ever mentioned the Sisters of Illumination?"

"No, and she's never staggered in at dawn drenched in blood. That's all balderdash, and I'm disappointed that you would even ask such a question. She and I have a tacit agreement not to impose on each other, so I can't give you a detailed account of her daily activities. But I've never been given any reason to believe that she has an evil bone in her body. Roy has been experiencing nightmares, very likely drug-induced. He needs to be under the care of professionals."

I leaned against the counter and tried not to sound too frustrated. "Then why didn't she just say so?"

Fern looked away. "She is fond of Roy. I suppose she thinks her silence will in some way help him out of this dreadful mess. Is there any doubt that he shot Nicholas?"

"The evidence is there. What needs to be determined is if he's competent to stand trial. Once he's back in custody, there'll be a brief hearing at which his lawyer and the prosecutor will agree to a thirty-day period of observation at the state hospital. What happens after that is up to the psychiatrists."

"If he sticks to his story?"

"It's anybody's guess," I said honestly. "If a jury believes that Malthea took advantage of his vulnerability, she may receive a harsh sentence. He was very convincing when he told me. I almost felt as though I could smell a trace of sulfur in the air."

Fern picked up a small suitcase. "Then you are in need of a strong tonic to purge your system. I'd like to go to bed now. I doubt I'll get much sleep; I have many things to think about."

I trailed her out to the porch and watched as she locked Malthea's door, pocketed the key, and went into her apartment. The porch light flickered off. Being a perspicacious person, I realized that it was a not-so-subtle suggestion that I do the same.

As I drove home, I mulled over the significance, if any, of the two clippings and the photographs of Randall and Roy (*père et fils*, as it were). There was no way to question either of them and almost no point in questioning Malthea. Was it conceivable that she'd seen him drifting along Thurber Street and pegged him as a potential victim? Had the article about the Borneo sabbatical been in the newspaper before or after she approached him? Could Sullivan Sawyer have said something about his professor's son that led her to lurk near the bookstore and surreptitiously take the photograph?

I must have relied on automatic pilot because I was startled when I realized I'd parked in the garage. My car was not there, but Caron had more than two hours before she was due. I stopped by the retiree's apartment, handed him the keys and assured him that "my friend" was in good shape, then trudged upstairs.

Not more than two minutes after I'd turned on the lights and decided which frozen entrée might appeal, the doorbell rang. I stuck a chicken à la Popsicle in the microwave and went to the front door.

The man on the landing was a stranger, and decidedly strange. He wore a shabby overcoat bereft of most of its buttons, a beret that covered his forehead like a moldy blue pancake, and heavy, mud-caked boots. A backpack hung on one shoulder, a rolled-up sleeping bag on the other. His grayish yellow hair hung below his ears, and his white beard was scraggly and dotted with flecks of tobacco. Eyes that might once have been blue were faded into a dull, translucent gray. His nose, in contrast, was markedly red. There was a redolence about him— not of body odor or soured sweat, but of earthiness. I suspected bathing was not on his daily agenda.

"Ms. Malloy?" he said hesitantly.

"I'm Claire Malloy. Can I help you?"

He began to back away. "I knew it was a long shot, and I'm sorry to disturb you. The note was from someone named Caron Malloy. I looked her name up in the directory and found a listing for 'C. Malloy.' I've been sitting on the wall across the street for most of an hour waiting for someone to come home. I was kinda hoping that . . . well, never mind. I could have used the dough, but that's how it goes. Have a nice evening, ma'am. I'll be on my way now."

"Wait a minute," I said hastily. "You had a note from Caron Malloy? Who are you?"

"I guess you could say I'm Santa Claus."

# CHAPTER 14

"Won't you come in?" I said weakly.
"I don't want to disturb you. Do you know this Caron Malloy?"

"Rather well, I'm afraid. She's not here right now, but I'd appreciate it if you would explain why she sent you a note and promised you money. Would you like some coffee? It won't take a minute."

"That'd be nice." He dropped the backpack and sleeping bag on the landing and shuffled by me. "Nice place you got here, Ms. Malloy. Real comfortable and casual. I guess you decorated it yourself, huh?"

I gestured at the sofa. "Please sit down and I'll start the coffee. Shall I call you Mr. Claus, or may I be more informal and call you Santa?"

"I answer to Ed," he said as he sat down and pulled off his boots. Most of his blackened toenails were visible through holes, and one heel was covered by only a few crisscrossed threads. "Don't want to track up your floor any more than necessary. It's been a while since I was invited into a home like this. Most of the time I'm asked to wait on the back porch. Not that I mind, of course. I'll stand on my head and crow like a rooster if that's what it takes to get something to eat."

I caught the hint, and after I'd started the coffee,

made him several thick cheese sandwiches. When I returned to the living room with a mug and a plate, I found him reading the complaint. It clicked rather neatly. "You're the Santa who got sacked, aren't you?" I said. "How did Caron track you down?"

"When I filled out some fool form, I put the Salvation Army shelter down as my address. That's where I found a note late this afternoon." He chomped vigorously, and after several moments of masticating, said, "Thanks, Ms. Malloy. I know I'm making you uncomfortable, so just tell me to leave when it gets to be too much. I don't smell so good. I slurp when I drink coffee because of some dental problems. I can understand why you don't want me to hang around and embarrass you in front of your neighbors."

"No," I protested, uneasily wondering how hypocritical I, an avowed liberal, was at heart. He'd been a perfect gentleman thus far. He was down on his luck, but amenable, polite, and a great deal more sensitive than a lieutenant I knew on the Farberville detective squad. "Caron was a reindeer for a few days. I suppose she wanted to ask you about your stint in Santa's Workshop before she and Inez were hired. Did you have a problem with Ms. Portmeyer?"

Ed wiped his mouth with a napkin. "Not like those first girls had with her. They'd show up on time, put on those idiotic costumes, and smile like gargoyles. They weren't Fulbright scholarship material, but they tried as hard as they could. It didn't matter. Ms. Portmeyer gave 'em hell all day every day."

"What about you?" I asked.

"You heard how I got fired, right?" He waited until I'd nodded, then continued. "I have a problem with drinking, but I really needed this job and I was being careful. There may have been a day or two when I took a couple of swallows of whiskey, but facing a stream of greedy little kids and tight-assed mothers isn't all that easy. One kid gave me a notarized list, if you can believe it. Another wanted a week at a health spa. 'Ho, ho, ho,' I'd say, wishing I could turn my head and puke. But then along would come some kid who wanted a doll for his sister and a daddy who wouldn't hit them."

"The day you were fired, Caron said that she noticed you were unsteady."

"That I was, Ms. Malloy, and then some. I was cold sober when I got to the employee lounge that morning, mostly because I was broke. Portmeyer was in a real foul mood and started making nasty remarks about how sorry she was that she'd hired me in the first place. I was pretty sure I wouldn't last the rest of the week, much less until Christmas Eve, but I kept my mouth shut. Finally she left and I opened my locker to get out the Santa suit. Right there in front was a pint of whiskey. It wasn't my preferred brand, but I'm not as picky as I used to be."

"So you drank it," I said.

Ed took another bite of sandwich and washed it down with coffee. "Not right then, I didn't. I didn't dare go out to the Workshop with whiskey on my breath, not with Portmeyer waiting for one little mistake so she could fire me. I did okay most of the day, even with her watching me like a buzzard on a low branch. Every time I took a break, she'd follow me into the lounge and tell me how pathetic I was."

"What a dreadful woman," I said.

"It's amazing what you can put up with when you're desperate. Finally, late in the afternoon, she told me I could take a break and then added in a real sugary voice that I'd better make the most of it because it might be my last one. I figured I'd be fired at the end of the shift. Since I had nothing to lose, I opened the whiskey bottle. My nerves were so shot that I guzzled it. You know the rest."

"Where do you think the bottle came from?"

"I wasn't in the mood to worry about it," he said, sounding vaguely ashamed. "I didn't bother to use the padlock on my locker. Anyone who would steal my clothes needs them a lot worse than I do." He held up his foot and wiggled his toes. "It might be time to go by the thrift shop and treat myself to a Christmas present. Maybe I can find argyles this time."

"I wish I had some of my late husband's clothes," I said, "but I gave everything away a long time ago. How much did Caron promise to pay you?"

He tugged on his beard, surreptitiously watching me as he pretended to think. Then he sighed and said, "She didn't say, and I'd have settled for a couple of dollars. However, you've been so kind and generous that I won't accept anything. Like I said, most people won't even let me inside. I guess they're afraid I have fleas or lice. I do the best I can, but sometimes the shelter has to turn people away. Lots of women and children on the streets this time of year."

"Hey, Ed," I said, "would you like to take a bath here?"

"I don't want to impose, Ms. Malloy. You tell Caron that she can get in touch with me through the shelter if she has any questions. You two have a real good Christmas." He picked up the boots and started toward the door. "I'll put these on when I get outside. Thanks for the sandwiches and coffee. It's comforting to know there are still some decent people on the planet."

"Wait," I said as I scrambled to my feet. "It's not an imposition. There's a perfectly adequate bathtub begging to be used. Please let me do this small favor."

"You sure?"

I caught his arm and gently tugged him back inside. "I'm sure, Ed. You'll find clean towels in the closet and six or seven different types of shampoo. Caron never knows from day to day if she'll wake up with dry hair, oily hair, dandruff, or split ends. Help yourself and take your time."

He smiled. "Yeah, I worry about split ends, too."

Once he was in the bathroom and the water was gushing into the bathtub, I made sandwiches out of the remaining bread and cheese and left them in a sack next to his backpack. I crept back to the bathroom door and listened to contented splashing, then went downstairs and knocked yet again on the retired professor's door.

"You're still early," he said, waggling his finger at me. "Tomorrow at seven."

"Do you have any argyle socks?"

He looked blankly at me. "Argyle socks?"

"Yes. I'll replace them as soon as I have a chance, but I need a pair right now and it's too late to go to the store."

"Argyle socks?" he repeated.

"Santa Claus needs them."

"He does?"

"His are so full of holes that nine of his toes poke through. Please hurry; he'll be finished with his bath before long."

He licked his lips. "Santa, who is in need of argyle

socks, is taking a bath in your apartment. Is that an accurate assessment of the situation?"

I suppose he thought I'd been into a pitcher of my own creation, but I was reluctant to explain. "That, sir, is an accurate assessment of the situation. Do you have argyle socks or not?"

"Shall I wrap them?"

"No, that's pushing it. Just get the socks."

"Anything else?"

I thought it over for a moment. "A sweater would be nice."

"Argyle socks and a sweater," he murmured. "Does Santa need underwear and pajamas as well?"

The retiree looked like the sort to wear pajamas decorated with snowmen. "No pajamas," I said, "but underwear would be greatly appreciated. And a pair of lined gloves, if you have a spare."

"Mrs. Malloy," he began portentously, as though preparing to scold me for a poor semester test result, then shrugged. "Argyle socks, underwear, a sweater, and gloves. Any preference for the color of the sweater?"

Caron had gone through a brief period as a color consultant, but I hadn't paid much attention. "Just something heavy," I said meekly.

When I was back upstairs with the booty, I knocked on the bathroom door and told Ed the clothing would be on the floor outside the door. I then went into the kitchen, gazed longingly at the bottle of scotch I'd concealed behind the toaster, poured myself a cup of coffee, and called the police station. Jorgeson was not there, but the dispatcher promised to leave him a message that I'd called.

I was heating the entrée when Caron came in through the back door. "I'd like to speak to you," I said. "It seems you've been very busy for someone who was supposedly shopping at the mall."

"It was really crowded out there. Inez was so tired that I took her straight home. I'm famished. Will you stick something in the microwave for me?"

She made it out of the kitchen before I could reply. I was dutifully looking in the freezer when I heard her shriek; seconds later she skittered into the kitchen, and in a scandalized voice, whispered, "There's a man in the bathroom. He's taking a bath."

"It's the most logical room in which to engage in that particular activity," I said. "Do you want lasagna or beef tips with gravy."

"Mother, there's a man in the bathroom."

"You told me that, dear. Which will it be—lasagna or beef tips?"

"Why is he there?"

"Didn't you just say that he's taking a bath?" I said blandly. "If he were doing it in your bedroom, your alarm would be justified."

"Mother!"

I closed the freezer door. "You didn't recognize him?"

"No, I didn't recognize him—and I didn't stand in the doorway and introduce myself. Who is he?"

"Santa Claus."

"Why won't you answer my . . ." Her eyes widened. "Oh, that Santa Claus. How did he get this address? All I said in the note was that I'd go by the shelter in the morning."

"He found it in the telephone directory. How did you find *his* address, or those of the two girls who preceded you as reindeer at Santa's Workshop?"

"The shelter was a lucky guess," she mumbled, nervously watching the doorway that led to the hall. "I guess Ms. Portmeyer must have said something about the other girls, like where they lived and stuff."

"Did you have any trouble finding the little town?"

"Why do you think I went there?" she shot back, no doubt imagining herself tied to a stake as flames began to crackle around her feet. "I was trying to find a Christmas present for Peter. It was unbelievable at the mall. Inez said they took more than two hundred and fifty photographs today. It's no wonder she had a headache."

She'd managed to evade every one of my questions thus far. I took a deep breath and tried again. "What are you up to?"

"I can't tell you. Just trust me, okay?"

"I wish I could, but—" I broke off as the bathroom door opened and a disembodied hand scooped up the pile of clothing. I bit back a somewhat hysterical giggle and reopened the freezer door. "Do you still want something to eat?"

"Later," she said, glancing over her shoulder. "What did he tell you?"

I gave her a recap of Ed's story, and then threw in the anonymous ex-reindeer's for good measure. "Did Inez search Ms. Portmeyer's briefcase?" I asked. "Is that how you learned their names and addresses?"

"Not exactly. I didn't see a sleigh out in the yard when I got home, so maybe I should offer to drive Santa back to the shelter. Is that okay?"

"Whatever," I said, conceding defeat as graciously as I could. I retreated to the living room, and was gazing blindly at the Christmas tree when Ed, aka Santa Claus, came into the room. His hair was combed back, his beard trimmed and glistening. The sweater was tight but serviceable.

"Argyles," he said appreciatively. "Practically new, too."

"Caron's back, and will drive you to the shelter if that's where you're going."

He nodded. "It's too cold to sleep outside, so I guess I'd better see if they've found any spare cots." He gathered his things and went back through the apartment. I listened to a sibilant conversation in the kitchen, followed by the sound of the door closing. I bleakly wondered if I should have insisted that he sleep on the sofa. However, altruism has its limits—and allowing an unknown man to stay in the apartment overnight was beyond the pale.

I poured the drink to which I was entitled and settled down once again. Not a silent night, nor a holy one. Malthea was in the ICU unit, and Gilda and Roy were loosed on a populace unschooled in spells and demons. Caron would continue to be evasive until it suited her own purposes to be otherwise. Ed would end up under a bridge. My downstairs neighbor was apt to be on the telephone with the landlord, doing his best to terminate the lease so he could move out during the night. Furthermore, I began morosely, then caught myself and took a gulp of scotch.

No furthermores permitted.

I forced myself to think about what Gilda had said. Nicholas had called Sullivan and had a conversation that left at least one of them angry. Later Sullivan had gone to the house. As had Fern. As had Gilda. As had Roy. As had Malthea, or so she'd said. Only one participant thus far had not yet admitted to a late-night visit.

I looked up the Sawyers' telephone number and dialed it. When a child answered, I asked to speak to its mother.

"Who's this?"

"Someone who will sneak into your bedroom and shave your head if you don't put your mother on the line," I said matter-of-factly. I don't think I meant it.

The receiver clattered as it hit the floor. Moments later Morning Rose said, "Hello?"

I identified myself, then said, "I was trying to get everything straight in my mind about the night Nicholas was killed. You went back there, didn't you?"

"Wait a moment," she said, then yelled at her children to go to their rooms or face the specter of no rice cakes with peanut butter. When she came back on, she sounded fatigued. "I was there, but not at Nicholas's house. I was worried about Roy. He was positively gray when the party broke up. I didn't want him to take off, or start in on drugs and do something he might regret. I knocked on his door, but he wouldn't let me in. I guess I should have beaten down the door and stayed with him until he came to his senses."

"This was when Sullivan thought you were in the backyard?"

"I guess so. He was in his office working on an article about contemporary paganism for some anthropology journal. Why are you asking me this?"

"Symmetry," I murmured.

"Are you okay, Mrs. Malloy?"

I could tell she wanted to ask me if I shared Roy's fondness for Herbal Ecstasy or more potent hallucinogens. "I'm dandy, Morning Rose. Is your husband available?"

"No, he left about an hour ago to get some research

material from his office. He's probably still there playing games on his computer. I've forbidden him to play
any kind of militaristic games in the house; it gives the
children the wrong ideas about global harmony and
universal cooperation. Are you familiar with the writings of Marx and Engels, Mrs. Malloy?"

"Long before you donned your first environmen-
tally correct diaper, Morning Rose." I hung up and sat
back, wondering if I should contact each and every
member of the Mormon Tabernacle Choir to find out
who else had returned to Primrose Hill on the night in
question. The crew of the SS Enterprise. The cast of
whatever constipated musical was currently reigning
on Broadway.

Caron seemed to be having problems finding the
Salvation Army shelter, or perhaps in disentangling
herself from Santa Claus. I wasn't especially worried
about her, except in a generic sense. No police officers
had loomed at the door thus far. No ambulances had
wailed in the distance. Ed may not have been a CEO
or a part-time brain surgeon, but I was confident that
he was basically benevolent. If I was wrong, he would
be sorry if he made an attempt to intimidate Caron
into forking over money. He'd have better luck trying
to wheedle her into promising him her firstborn child.

I listened to classical music drifting through the
vents along the floorboards as I wandered around the
room. It was not yet ten o'clock, and I knew no visions
of sugarplums would be dancing in my head anytime
soon. The telephone sat in splendid silence, but I kept
glancing at it as if it might leap across the carpet and
attach itself to my neck like a vampire bat.

I finally decided to walk off my tension. I wrote a
note for Caron, then put on my coat and headed across

the campus lawn. For the record, I was not worried
that any of the Druids would spring out of the shadows and wrestle me to the ground, salivating wildly
and wielding a butcher knife. That only happens in
fiction.

I walked along the sidewalk, my hands in my pockets and my face furrowed unattractively as I tried to
make some sense of the muddle. The most obvious—
and simplistic—solution was to accept Roy's confession and write him off as a deeply disturbed kid. But
why hadn't Malthea protested? Why hadn't she re-
sponded with indignation instead of doing everything
she could to bolster Roy's various stories?

Moving briskly, I veered around the dark student
union and headed in the general direction of the law
school. The cold wind stung my ears and chapped my
cheeks, but the sheer sense of motion felt good, as if I
were accomplishing some minor Herculean task. And,
yes, I seemed to be closing in on the social sciences
building, where I might find a certain person blipping
evil invaders on his computer.

There were several lights on inside the building. I
went inside, paused to rub my hands together until
they tingled, and then found a placard listing office
numbers. Sullivan had not warranted an office of his
own, but I was familiar enough with the ways of aca-
demia to suspect he would have a cubicle in the vicinity
of the department. I took the elevator to the third floor.

The floor was adequately lit but very quiet. After
several moments of questioning my wisdom—and de-
termining that it was, as always, impeccably correct—I
tried a couple of corridors and finally found one emblazoned with multicolored flyers announcing glorious opportunities to sift sand in Turkey or study the

richly diverse subcultures of Paris and Rome. Airfare not included.

The sound of clicking keys indicated that at least one creature was stirring. I went through the main office and into a large room with tables lining the walls, a hodgepodge of chairs, stacks of papers and folders, a grid of overflowing mailboxes, and a graduate student hunched in front of a computer. On the screen entities resembling Ping-Pong balls drifted downward. One exploded.

Sullivan chortled. "Gotcha, you bastard."

"I hope I'm not interrupting," I said.

He spun around and gaped at me. "I—I didn't hear you come in. What are you doing here?"

"Morning Rose thought you might be here. Do you mind if we talk?"

"I've already told you that I don't care what happens to Roy. He confessed, didn't he? Why isn't that enough? Are the authorities waiting until he kills someone else before they arrest him?"

"They'd very much like to arrest him at this point," I said, "but he's unavailable. Why did you go to Nicholas's house after the disastrous party?"

My abrupt change of topic proved effective; he stared at me for a long moment, seemingly doing his best to ascertain what I knew—and what I didn't. I waited with the appraising stare of a distaff Perry Mason.

"Who says I did?" he said carefully.

"That doesn't matter, does it? Nicholas called you around seven o'clock. The conversation ended abruptly. You went there later to confront him."

"No, I didn't."

Perry Mason's witnesses always broke down on the stand and confessed seconds before the commercial.

Sullivan must not have been a fan of the show. "Yes, you did," I said chidingly. "A little after eleven o'clock, wouldn't you say? You came across the pasture on foot."

"So that was Gilda," he said, putting his elbow on the table and massaging his forehead with his fingertips. "I didn't think she saw me."

"Well, she did. What happened after that?"

"I don't have to answer your questions, Mrs. Malloy, but I will say that I did not set foot in Nicholas's house." He leaned forward and punched a button to shut down the computer, then stood up. "I'm going home. If the police want to talk to me, that's where I'll be. If you want to talk to me, too damn bad."

"Did Nicholas find out some dirty little secret about you?" I persevered as I followed him back into the corridor. "Did you falsify your résumé or forget to mention a felony conviction?"

"You are more than welcome to verify every name, date, and letter of recommendation included in my résumé. In the meantime, will you please just leave us alone? The children are already upset as it is. Nicholas allowed Cosmos to play on his computer. He gave Rainbow a robe that was supposedly an exact replica of those worn by Druid priestesses two thousand years ago. Morning Rose is worried sick about Roy. I'm more worried about what Dr. Tate will say when he gets back from Borneo and hears that I threw his son out of my house." He locked the office door, put the key in his pocket, and walked rapidly toward the elevator. "I have nothing else to say."

Amateur sleuths cannot be bashful. "If you didn't go there to speak to Nicholas, why did you? Certainly not to make sure Roy was not unduly disturbed, since you've made it clear you're not concerned about him. Morning Rose was, though. Were you following her?"

"*Nothing else*, Mrs. Malloy. Which word is causing you problems?"

I glanced at the lighted numeral above the elevator doors, trying to assess how much time I had. There were other people on the move in the building, but with only five floors, time was of the essence. "Morning Rose said she went to Roy's apartment but he wouldn't let her in."

"My wife was in the backyard, capering around stark naked and chanting. I was in my office at home."

"You just admitted Gilda saw you."

"Isn't she currently confined in the psychiatric ward? Not much of a witness, is she? Your only other witness claims to have been ripped apart by an Egyptian demon and admitted that he killed a man in cold blood."

I was casting about for an adequately scathing response when the elevator doors opened. Sullivan stepped just inside, blocking my entrance, and stood there glaring at me until the doors closed.

The elevator descended to the first floor, then came back up to fetch me. By the time I arrived outside, Sullivan had disappeared either down one of numerous dark sidewalks or around the building to the parking lot. The sound of a car starting suggested the latter.

"Jorgeson has the weapon," I said out loud as I headed home. "It belongs to Roy's father and has Roy's fingerprints on it. Roy confessed. Just because there was need of a pagan traffic controller before the murder doesn't mean that Roy didn't do it. A shoplifter in a grocery store doesn't negate an armed robbery an hour later."

A flutter of motion in my peripheral vision indicated my grousing had roused a couple who thought the lonely campus provided a safe place to advance their relationship. I did not apologize or make sure they planned to engage in safe sex, but instead continued along the sidewalk.

I stopped on the porch to collect my mail, the usual collection of bills and flyers, and opened the door.

A hand caught the door before I could close it.

# CHAPTER 15

"Mrs. Malloy," Morning Rose said with enough ill-contained urgency to awaken drunks dozing on barstools across the street from the Book Depot. "Thank God you're here! I didn't know what else to do. I'm so frightened."

I'd put the poor retired professor through quite a bit already, so I motioned her inside. "Let's go upstairs," I said in a low voice. "Then we'll talk."

"There's no time for that," she said.

"Ah, but there is. I have no desire to go dashing into the night on some foolish mission, so I have all the time in the world."

"It's Roy. He's going to kill himself if we don't find him." She pulled a folded paper out of her pocket and offered it to me. When I didn't accept it, she said, "I found this under our front door. The minute that Sullivan got home, I hurried here. You have to read it. He's serious—"

"Call the police."

"I don't dare," she said as she sank to her knees and covered her face with her hands like a seduced maiden in a Greek tragedy who'd just realized the baby might be born with feathers. "The minute he sees them, he'll put the gun to his head and pull the trigger. He's sick,

Mrs. Malloy. We have to find him and get him back
to the psychiatric ward where he can be restrained.
How did he get out of there? Don't they realize he's
suicidal?"

I plucked the letter out of her hand and read it under the glow of the forty-watt bulb the miserly landlord favored. Most of it was written in an illegible
scrawl that would have exasperated Fern, but I could
decipher the phrases "can't face the torment" and
"better off dead."

"Just what are you planning to do?" I asked Morning Rose. "Roy left the hospital hours ago. He could be
anywhere."

She looked up at me. "I think I know where he
stayed after he left the carriage house."

"So alert the police. They're trained to deal with
emotionally disturbed people. They'll walk softly and
carry big butterfly nets."

"I'm the only person who can talk him into going
back to the hospital. If anyone else approaches him,
he'll snap like a twig. You have to help me save his
life!"

"No, I don't," I said, shaking my head. "He's a confessed murderer and quite possibly a dangerous
schizophrenic. I'm not about to go track him down in
a dark alley and suggest he turn himself in. I've done
that several times, and I'm tired of it."

"He's not in an alley," she said as she stood up and
caught my hands. "I think Roy broke into one of
Nicholas's rental properties. He's done repair work in
many of them, and he knows which are likely to be
empty over the Christmas break. You can stay in the
van, Mrs. Malloy. If there's a light, I'll get out and ring
the doorbell. As soon as you see Roy at the door, you

can drive to a telephone and call the police. That'll give me time to convince him to come quietly." She squeezed my hands so tightly that I winced. "He won't hurt me. I can get the gun away from him and calm him down so that he won't—do something foolish."

"Jorgeson can arrange for an unmarked police car to take you around the properties."

"No," she said with a frustrated groan. "What if Roy looks at the car and sees an unfamiliar driver? He'll panic and blow out his brains. If he sees you, he might not be so impulsive. He's trusted you in the past. You don't have to set one foot outside the van. You'll be at least twenty feet away with the engine running. I wouldn't ask you to do this if I thought you'd be in any danger. What's more, the odds that we'll find him are infinitesimal. Nicholas owned houses and apartment buildings all over Farberville. I only know the few that Roy mentioned."

"Have Sullivan go with you."

"Roy knows how much Sullivan despises him," she said, lapsing back into urgency and doing so much damage to my hands that I could never become a renowned concert pianist (it was on my midlife-crisis list). "An hour is all I ask. If I haven't found Roy by then, I'll go home and light candles for him. He'll need all the help he can get."

"Let's not get overly dramatic," I said as I jerked my hands free before she completely mangled them.

"He's the same age as your daughter, isn't he? You wouldn't hesitate to save her, but Roy's mother isn't as compassionate. She got drunk every day and slept with anyone who'd have her. Roy came home from school one afternoon and found her in bed with the preacher from—"

"You've made your point. All right, Morning Rose, we'll drive by the rental properties and look for lights. Not all the tenants are students, however, and not all the students leave town for the holidays, so you're likely to find yourself apologizing to people for disturbing them at this hour. I will remain in the driver's seat. We will do this for no more than an hour."

"Oh, thank you," she gushed, looking as if she might give me a warm Wiccan hug.

I stepped back so abruptly I almost fell off the edge of the porch. "Where's the van?"

"Just around the corner. Please, let's hurry."

I followed her through the yard, debating if I should congratulate myself on this spontaneous enterprise or drive to the hospital and inquire into vacancies on the sixth floor. The van reeked of patchouli oil and dried peanut butter. It had a stick shift, but I'd mastered that earlier. "Where do we start?"

"Nicholas owned all the houses in our development," Morning Rose said.

"And the duplexes and houses on Malthea's street," I countered. "Let's go there, and work our way toward your end of town."

"Okay," she muttered, apparently having lost her missionary zeal between the porch and the passenger's seat.

I drove slowly down the pertinent street, noting that Fern's lights were on and Malthea's off. Almost all the other houses were dark, and there were only two cars parked along the curb in the four-block stretch.

"Roy could be inside any of these houses," I said. "What he's really interested in is somewhere warm to sleep. Maybe he realized that it wouldn't be wise to turn on the lights and advertise his presence."

"He's not thinking clearly."

"I agree with that," I said as I turned toward the south part of town. "Any other properties between here and your area?"

"Nicholas bought Malthea's house next to the cemetery. Roy mentioned that when he went there to rake leaves, the two girls renting it tried to get him to drink wine with them. Undergraduates, likely to go home for Christmas."

"Where's the house?"

She directed me to a narrow street that ran along the back side of the cemetery. "That's it, I think," she said, pointing at a shabby little house set well away from the streetlights. "Stop here and I'll check it out. Keep your door locked, Mrs. Malloy, and if anything strange happens, don't come after me. Get away and call the police."

I watched her creep across the yard, peer into a darkened window, and then vanish behind an unruly barrier of bushes. Five minutes later she had not reappeared. Nothing whatsoever, strange or mundane, had happened.

I turned off the car's engine and rolled down the window. In a more congenial season I would have heard crickets, birds, tree frogs, raucous music from the beer garden, and the mating calls of students in the apartment complexes on the next block. The only thing I could hear now was the rumble of traffic several blocks away.

I rolled up the window and looked at the cemetery beyond a crumbling rock wall. Moonlight glinted off

marble and granite monuments as if they were chis-
eled blocks of ice. Wind riffled branches of trees that
had been there longer than the current tenants.

Morning Rose did not return.

I hummed my way through the theme songs of
*Gilligan's Island* and *The Brady Bunch*. I attempted the
graduation processional but gave up after a few bars. I
had a paperback in my purse (dedicated mystery fans
always do), but I didn't have a flashlight and it was
too dark to see the print, much less read it.

She did not return.

I contemplated how I'd explain her absence to her
children on Christmas Eve. "Your mommy," I'd say,
blinking back tears, "was a compassionate woman
who sacrificed herself to save a young boy. She was an
angel of mercy."

Still no Morning Rose.

Something was wrong, but I wasn't willing to leave
the van to investigate. I finally decided to wait five
more minutes, then go to the bookstore and call the
police. They'd most likely find Morning Rose on the
ground with a sprained ankle or wandering like a
wraith through backyards at the end of the block,
plaintively bleating Roy's name. I'd feel silly, but not
stupid.

I was rehearsing my remarks to the 911 dispatcher
when two clinging figures came slowly across the yard.
As they reached the street, I could see that Morning
Rose had her arms around Roy and appeared to be
supporting him. He was hunched over as though he
were in the throes of a violent gastric attack, his face
masked by his hair, his arms limp at his sides.

"I found him," she called, "and he's agreed to be
taken to the hospital."

The back door of the van slid open. She helped Roy inside, closed the door, and climbed into the seat next to me. "Everything will be fine," she said, twisting around to look at him. "You'll be safe. If they let me, I'll sit in your room the rest of the night, just in case you have . . . a nightmare."

The wisest thing to do was to get him to the hospital as quickly as possible. Rather than questioning Morning Rose about such minor issues as the whereabouts of his purported gun, I started the engine. "We should be there in fifteen minutes."

"I won't be safe at the hospital," Roy said dully. "Malthea's there, so she can tell Ambesek where to find me. I'm going to die. Why didn't you let me go without the agony?"

I pushed down on the accelerator. "Ten minutes, maybe less if we don't hit any red lights."

Morning Rose tried to smile. "You'll be fine, Roy."

I was about to reiterate the sentiment when I felt the barrel of a gun pressed against my neck. My foot slipped off the pedal, inadvertently hit the brakes, and brought the van to a shuddery stop in the middle of Thurber Street.

"Start the car," Roy said in a crisp, cold voice. "If that happens again, you can stand under the mistletoe and kiss your ass good-bye."

"Roy!" yelped Morning Rose. "You said you were unarmed."

"Yeah, but everybody knows I'm crazy." He increased the pressure on my neck. "Drive to the grove. I've got things to do that aren't permitted in the psych ward."

I did as ordered. Morning Rose sat silently, her hands writhing in her lap and her eyes lowered. I was as angry at her as I was at Roy, but there was no point in scolding her for falling for his ploy. Wiccans could be as obtuse as the rest of us.

"What things?" I asked Roy as I drove through town.

"I'll tell you when we get there. Now shut up and don't do anything impulsive, like run into a parked car. I don't want to hurt you, Mrs. Malloy, but I will."

"Haven't we been through this before?"

"Someone must have rewound the tape," he said. "Just drive—okay?"

We arrived without further conversation. I couldn't tell what was going through Morning Rose's mind, but I doubted she would be useful in a confrontation. Spells weren't likely to deflect bullets.

"Here we are," I said brightly as I pulled over to the fence. "Shall I pick you up later?"

"Get out of the car," Roy said, unamused. "Morning Rose, take the key. We're all going for a stroll."

It was not an appealing idea. I climbed down from the seat, went around the front of the van, and waited as Morning Rose pretty much slithered out of her seat. Roy caught her before she fell to the ground.

"Get a grip," he snarled. "I'm not going to sling you over my shoulder and carry you."

She touched his face. "You swore you'd go to the hospital, Roy. It's not too late. Why don't we all get back in the van and—"

She gasped as he lightly slapped her.

He waved the gun at the trees in the distance. "Let's go."

We stumbled across the pasture and into the woods. Roy prodded me with the gun whenever I faltered, and we eventually found the clearing. The altar reminded me of the gravestones in the cemetery, white and cold, eternally lifeless.

"What are you going to do?" Morning Rose asked Roy in a timid squeak.

"I hate to put it this bluntly, but I'm going to shoot Mrs. Malloy."

"What?" I said, staring at him. "What's your beef with me? I've been trying to help you ever since all this started, for pity's sake. I've listened to your confessions, held your hand while you were interrogated, and pleaded your cause with Sergeant Jorgeson. This is not the best way to express your gratitude, Roy. I don't expect flowers and candy, but a card might be in order."

"You know too much."

"All I know is what people have told me, and most of that has been untrue. I may not believe in demons, and I may have my doubts that Malthea's a priestess in some screwy cult, but . . ." I broke off and sat down on the stump, which was getting as familiar as my living-room sofa (although not as comfortable). "How do you know Malthea's in the hospital?"

For the first time since I'd met him, he smiled. "Maybe a little messenger from hell told me. Now move over there next to the altar. It's time someone put it to good use."

"I can think of no reason why I should cooperate," I said, staying where I was and crossing my arms. "You can kill Morning Rose and me, but you know perfectly well that you won't get away with it. If you're found guilty by reason of insanity, they'll lock you up in a hospital until you've quit foaming—then lock you up in a prison for the rest of your life. There won't be any 'sick little boy' defense."

Morning Rose moved toward my side, her eyes enormous in the shadowy light. "But that's what he is, Mrs. Malloy. Once he's had proper treatment, he'll be able to make a plea for leniency and serve only a small sentence. He's not a hardened criminal."

"Is that what you want as an epitaph on your headstone?" I asked her. I grabbed her shoulders and spun her around so that she was facing Roy. Without releasing her, I added, "See that gun in his hand? He's going to shoot you."

"Let her go," Roy said.

She began to squirm, but I dug my fingernails into her flesh. "Or maybe he won't shoot you," I said slowly. "The only members of your group who know that Malthea's in the hospital are Fern and Gilda. I'm going to assume Roy has not been in communication with either of them this evening. He must have learned this from you, Morning Rose. How did you find out? Did you see the ambulance go up the driveway at Primrose Hill?" She nodded. "But that wouldn't explain why you knew it was there for Malthea. Was it because you were responsible for the assault in the study?"

Roy leaned against the altar, rather casually, in my opinion, for someone who intended to cover it with bloodstains. Without letting the gun bobble even for an instant, he pulled a cigarette pack and a lighter out of his pocket. "Very good, Mrs. Malloy. Now let her go."

"Not just yet," I said as my fingers began to protest. "Gilda told me that Nicholas had evidence that would cause her to lose her job and possibly face criminal charges. That's why she tried to break into the house earlier—to find the evidence. It's also why Malthea did the same thing a few hours ago, and, apparently, did Morning Rose. What is it?"

"You haven't proved I was there," said Morning Rose sulkily.

I shook her as I would a mysterious package beneath a Christmas tree. "Malthea seems determined to protect Roy, and not in order to hide any association with a satanic cult."

"Don't be so sure," he said as he lit the cigarette.

"But you did kill Nicholas," I continued. "Why?"

"Because," he said in a whiny falsetto, "I'm a victim, too. My father rejected me and my mother neglected me. The preacher used to beat me with a strap. I know I shouldn't have taken drugs, ma'am, but I was all alone and so confused. I guess I was beggin' for help."

"Roy," Morning Rose said, "this has gone on long enough. You've got a gun, and you should be able to find a way to use it."

I abruptly shifted my arms to her waist and grasped my wrists, pulling her against me. "The bullet will penetrate both of us. Waste not, want not."

"Don't make this any harder than necessary," he said as he approached.

"I'm not going to make it any easier than necessary," I said, calculating the distance. "I shouldn't do that, should I, Morning Rose?"

"No," she said in a thin voice.

"I didn't hear you," I said, vigorously administering the Heimlich maneuver to help her cough up a lie.

"No!" she wailed.

Roy was no more than a yard away, the gun a shade closer. I took a breath, shoved Morning Rose into him, watched both of them flounder backward against the altar, then darted into the woods. A shot ricocheted off a branch above my head, but I kept stumbling through trees and bushes. The sounds of thrashing and cursing made it clear that Roy was on his feet and coming after me.

It occurred to me that he was tracking me by the same noises. I crawled under a low fir, pulled my legs against my chest, and buried my face in decayed leaves and what smelled like the remains of a dead animal. The most minimal movement had exposed the amorous couple on the campus; I did not so much as blink. Footsteps crunched nearby, then moved away.

One of the egregious errors common to movies is for the fugitive to hear noises diminish, scramble to his or her feet, and go thundering onward, alerting the hunter to redirect the search. I stayed put, making no effort to do anything but listen for the most minute sound. When I felt the tingling onset of a sneeze, I clamped my nose between my thumb and forefinger and breathed carefully through my mouth. Something tickled my ankle. I told myself it was a leaf.

After ten minutes or so, a muscle in my calf began to quiver, warning me that a cramp was imminent if I didn't move. I stood up and wiped primordial ooze off my eyelashes and forehead. The road was to my right. Roy could be anywhere, but there was no future in freezing under a thicket. I kept a goodly distance between myself and the grove as I skulked from tree to tree like a spy in a cartoon.

When I arrived at the edge of the pasture, I could see the van where I'd parked it. Regrettably, this implied they were still in the vicinity. Loping like a hound, I made it to the road and squatted behind the scanty cover of a fence post. The van appeared to be empty. No one emerged from the woods behind me. I caught my breath, counted to ten, and then ran across the expanse of muddy ruts and flung myself into the stubble. I raised my head and peered over my shoulder, but the pasture remained a placid sea of weeds.

The stubble, on the other hand, was jabbing me most rudely in places never intended to be jabbed. Rather than make my way down the road, I decided to head for Nicholas's house. I could break another window if necessary, make a terse telephone call, and then hide in the garden until a patrol car came racing up the driveway. This would be one 911 call that required no rehearsal.

I took one final look at the woods, then ran toward the house, staying as low as I could and taking an impressive number of belly dives as I stepped in holes and caught my foot on obdurate vines. I was beginning to feel a bit optimistic when the headlights of the van came on and illuminated the pasture. I flattened myself and uttered a choice word.

After a moment, I looked back and saw a figure silhouetted against the headlights. Roy was halfway across the pasture and coming toward me. I couldn't see the gun, but it did not seem prudent to linger. I scrambled to my feet and ran toward the poplars delineating the driveway, fully expecting to feel an explosive pain in the middle of my back.

I arrived in the forecourt and paused. Roy would hear the breaking of glass and be inside the house before I could find the telephone in the dark. He would be less than empathetic. A bullet hit the front of the house, reminding me that I was unnecessarily exposed. The doors of the carriage house were ajar. I slipped inside and peered through the crack.

This time I could see the gun in his right hand as he came into the middle of the forecourt. He peered at the house, his head tilted as he listened for the sound of my footsteps. I edged backward and promptly bumped into the hearse. I remembered the storage room on one side, but it was very much a cobweb-festooned dead end.

The windows of the hearse had been down when I'd last looked inside it for Roy, and they still were. I slithered into it and crouched on the seat, praying the police had not removed the key from the ignition switch. My heart quickened as I felt it.

I eased into position in front of the steering wheel and located the pedals on the floorboard. Hoping Roy was the sort to keep his vehicle tuned and with adequate fuel, I switched on the engine. It began to purr most endearingly. My only chance to get it into reverse was to turn on the lights, and after a moment of fumbling, I yanked the right knob. The door behind me squealed as it was dragged open. I could see Roy's face in the red glare of the taillights.

I shifted it into reverse and jammed down the accelerator. Roy tried to leap out of the way, but he was only partially successful and went flying into the air, his arms flailing and the gun sailing into the darkness. I leapt out of the hearse. Roy lay a good ten feet away from the point of impact. Blood dribbled out of the corners of his mouth, indicative of internal injuries. I knelt and listened to his laborious breathing.

"Sorry about that," I murmured, then opened the back doors of the hearse. "Let me give you a lift back to town, Roy. It's the least I can do."

# CHAPTER 16

"Would you rather have coffee?" Jorgeson asked as he handed me a can of soda from the machine in the emergency room. "The cafeteria's closed, but we can find a pot somewhere."

"I don't want anything," I said, exploring scratches and abrasions on my heretofore flawless face. It was well past midnight, and Jorgeson and I were the only people in the room. He was in need of a shave; I suspected I looked as though I was the loser in a mud-wrestling competition. I'd called Caron and made sure she was home; she'd been grudgingly pleased to hear from me. "What about Morning Rose? Have you found her?"

"Let me check." He went to the pay phone and had a muted conversation. When he returned, he said, "She called in a few minutes ago and demanded that we send dogs and a helicopter with searchlights to the woods to rescue you. The dispatcher assured her that everything was under control."

"I wish it were," I muttered.

Jorgeson overlooked my petulance. "What exactly did the staff say when you pulled up at the entrance in a hearse?"

"I told them the body was in the back. They were

hesitant to open the doors until I'd explained that I wasn't looking for the morgue. A sense of humor does not appear to be a prerequisite for employment."

His lips twitched momentarily, but he was too tired to produce a smile. "Okay, Mrs. Malloy, I have a reasonably clear idea of what happened. An officer will stay with Roy until we figure out what to do with him."

"Both of them may need demonproof vests. Can you assign an officer to Malthea's room, just to be on the safe side?"

"I've already done it. There's no reason for you to stay here any longer. I'll have someone drive you home. You'd better see if Caron can handle the bookstore tomorrow, because it's going to take a long time to get your statement. The prosecutor may decide to sit in on it. That means the media won't be far behind."

"They might have a better story if Roy truly were certifiable, but he's not. It's an act, Jorgeson. He's convinced that he'll be tried as a juvenile, incarcerated until he's eighteen or, at worst, twenty-one, and then be released. Presuming his father can afford it, an expert will testify about diminished responsibility and the effects of long-term abuse. Roy'll get a slap on the wrist. What he deserves is an Oscar."

"Best actor in a bad movie?"

"And the Oscar for best director should go to Morning Rose Sawyer. She was using him to reenact some Wiccan mythology involving the sacred marriage between the Mother Goddess and the Horned God, whatever that is. The sexual undertones have been obvious all along. Considering her track record, one shudders to think what might have resulted from this union." I disengaged a leaf from my hair and dropped it in a trash receptacle. "Sullivan suspected something, which is why he followed her. Nicholas must have seen her entering and leaving the carriage house late at night and realized what was happening. He was going to expose them before he went to Wales."

"Roy's only sixteen," Jorgeson said, grimacing. "She's thirty-four. That's sexual misconduct, or maybe even violation of a minor, a felony, if the prosecutor can show she was acting as a temporary guardian when the affair started. I can't see her going to prison because of it, though. He's twice her size and could buy liquor without being carded. A fragile boy he's not."

"She could hardly have consulted a lawyer, and she must have read about some recent cases in which the older woman received a substantial prison term. She had to worry about her husband, too. If he believed whatever evidence Nicholas had, he'd divorce her and get custody of the children. If you were a judge confronted with a diligent graduate student and a self-admitted witch who frolics naked in the backyard and seduced a teenage boy, what would you do?"

"So she encouraged Roy to kill Nicholas Chunder?"

I put down the can of soda. "Nicholas said something to them before the party, then went so far as to call Sullivan and repeat it. Morning Rose must have thought her only way to avoid prosecution and divorce would be if Roy killed Nicholas and, if necessary, confessed. When the burglary theory didn't hold up, and then the homosexual advances theory fell apart, they moved right along to the next one. You have to give them credit for flexibility."

Jorgeson picked up the soda I'd rejected and took a swallow. "But it required Malthea's cooperation. How could they know she wouldn't deny it? There was no way they could prove these ludicrous accusations."

"You'll have to ask them," I said with a yawn. "I'm not accustomed to being chased by a demon, Jorgeson. I need to bathe, dab cream on my cuts, take two aspirin, and go to bed. I'll call you in the morning."

"What were you babbling about last night?" demanded Caron as I hobbled into the kitchen the next morning. "Considering how awful you look, it's no surprise you were at the hospital. Shouldn't they have kept you for observation pending cosmetic surgery?"

I gave her a hooded look and poured a glass of orange juice. "Mr. Mortician decided to live up to his nickname, and did his best to let me be his first customer."

"Roy Tate? What were you doing with him?"

I told her what had happened. When she stopped sputtering indignantly (and swiping at a tear or two, although she will never admit it), I added, "It's over now. They got swept up into something that made them feel omnipotent and exotic—or maybe they were looking for an excuse to behave badly. If you must join a cult, dear, please let it be nothing more nefarious than a sorority. I'll have you kidnapped and deprogrammed in no time."

"Very funny," she said. "Are you sure you're okay?"

"I did damage to some muscles I didn't know I had, but I'll be fine in a day or two. Tonight's Christmas Eve. I absolutely have to stop downstairs and have a cup of cheer, and then I suppose I'll go to Luanne's party. You don't have to come along, but we will be having dinner there tomorrow afternoon."

"What time are you going downstairs?"

"Seven," I said, eyeing her suspiciously. My social

agenda is rarely of any importance in her overall scheme of the universe; the only time she inquires is when she's scheming to get the car. "Why?"

"No reason."

Although I knew it was futile, I waited for a moment in case she chose to be more forthcoming. She did not. I told her she'd have to open the Book Depot and stay there until I'd finished at the police department, and then compounded the crime by telling her she might be stuck most of the day.

Caron goggled at me as if I'd revealed a secret hankering to take up skydiving. "But I have important things to do. I haven't finished shopping. I just know Inez is going to get me this pair of earrings I found out at the mall, and that means I have to give her this dorky scarf that makes her look like she's being throttled by a paisley boa constrictor. And I haven't found anything decent for Luanne. I think she may give me this nifty beaded purse. I can't just give her a coupon to rent a video."

"I'm charmed by this display of selfless generosity," I said as I put on my coat. "Shall we go? I'd like to get this over with."

"I suppose."

She rolled her eyes and sighed all the way to the car, but restrained herself from attempting to convince me that shopping had priority over making a statement at the police department. An atypical display of maturity on her part.

"So," I said, frowning as I noticed how little gas was in the tank, "what did you and Ed find to talk about last night?"

"Nothing. I took him to the shelter and dropped

him off, then went to Carrie's for a few minutes. She
has this really cool computer."

And I could hire eight tiny reindeer to pull the car to
the gas station when I ran out of gas. "You must have
had a reason for wanting to talk to him. You left him a
note, after all." I paused to consider an earlier remark.
"How could you have done that without knowing his
name?"

Caron turned her head to look out the window. "He
must have mentioned it. I just wanted to ask him a
couple of questions—okay? We did not bond. The
only thing we have in common is that we were both
fired by a woman with plutonium implants. How long
is this statement going to take?"

I dropped her off and continued to the police station. Jorgeson managed a wan smile as I came into his
office. "We've got to start keeping regular office hours,
Mrs. Malloy. My wife is so mad that she's threatening
to book a Caribbean cruise. What am I supposed to do
for three days while she throws up in the sink? Play
shuffleboard with pink-haired ladies from Miami?"

"Is Morning Rose in custody?" I asked.

"Yes, and we're making some headway with the
computer files. Chunder recorded every last detail,
from what he spent on postage stamps to when he last
spoke to his accountant. I won't be surprised if he kept
notes about when he saw Morning Rose sneaking into
the carriage house for late-night sessions. Last month
he made a long-distance call to a seedy motel in Mis-
souri, and not because he wanted a reservation. Someone there should remember them. It'll take a few days
to reconstruct the evidence, but we will."

"How's Sullivan taking it?"

"He is not a happy man. He's admitted he thought

there might be something going on between the two of them, and that's the real reason he made Roy move out of the house. He told Chunder that his wife was just being supportive, but he knew she wasn't always in the backyard like she said she was. Corporal Billsby is not a happy man, either. We left him at the house with the two children. He's already called twice to beg for relief, but I think it'll be good for him. A young man like that can stand to build some character."

"And Roy?" I said, waving off a uniformed officer who was headed toward me with a cup of coffee.

Jorgeson rocked back in his chair. "He has a couple of broken ribs, a ruptured spleen, and a lot of bruises. When he's ready to be transferred back up to the psych ward, he'll remain under full security. The shrinks will wear him down eventually, and he and Morning Rose will be slathering the blame on each other like whipped cream on pumpkin pie." He took a couple of antacid tablets from a roll and offered it to me, but I shook my head. "Gilda seems to have packed up and left town. The manager at the trailer park thought he saw candlelight in her trailer late last night, but he was entertaining a widow. They were doing the lambada and he didn't want to lose the beat."

I imagined Gilda on her bicycle, a suitcase strapped on the back, her coattails flapping in the wind as she pedaled down the road in search of yet another hospital in need of her services. "What will you do about her?"

"We'll find her," he said flatly. "Now, Mrs. Malloy, we need your statement so you can get out of here. I hope the lieutenant doesn't blame this whole thing on me. That first morning I should have sent you home instead of asking for your help. You came damn close to getting yourself killed."

"I did no such thing," I replied tartly.

"Whatever you say."

"And the lieutenant has no one else but himself to blame for this. If he hadn't goaded me into doing something uncharacteristic, none of this would have happened. I hope you will make that clear when you speak to him."

He gave me the same sad look he'd given me when I'd blurted out my woes. "If he calls, I'll do my best."

I spent the next three hours relating the events of the previous evening, struggling to repeat verbatim conversations with Fern, Gilda, Sullivan, Morning Rose, and most painfully, Roy. Yes, he'd said he was going to shoot me. No, he hadn't said he was going to kill me, but his intent was hard to miss. No, Morning Rose hadn't admitted any collusion, but the headlights on the van had come on when Roy was already in the pasture. She'd driven away while I was loading Roy into the hearse.

By the time I was finished, my face felt as if it were caked with clay. My eyes were gritty, my tongue fuzzy with exhaustion. I declined Jorgeson's final offer of coffee and put on my coat.

He walked me to the front door, raised his hand as if to pat my shoulder, then thought better of it. "Merry Christmas, Mrs. Malloy," he murmured.

"You, too." I went to my car and sat for a long while, overwhelmed by the sheer nastiness of the crime. The only one of the Druids who'd behaved honorably was Nicholas Chunder, and he was dead. He'd been partially responsible, of course; he'd hoarded his information instead of simply informing the appropriate authorities. I hoped he'd enjoyed his final opportunity to flaunt his power over the members of the Sacred Grove of Keltria. It certainly hadn't ended well for him.

Caron would be chewing her fingernails by now, but I wasn't ready to spend the rest of the afternoon brooding over unanswered questions. I drove to the hospital, went through the conventional entrance, and asked a volunteer behind a computer for the number of Malthea's room.

The woman, seventyish and as petite and perky as any of Santa's elves, punched buttons, then beamed at me. "She went home this morning. I hate the idea of anyone spending Christmas in a hospital, don't you? Carolers come by, and the auxiliary decorates the nursing stations and puts candy-cane reindeers on the meal trays, but it's just not the same as being surrounded with family members and close friends."

I read her name tag and reciprocated with a warm smile. "May I use your telephone, Bea?"

"Normally, it's not allowed, but since it's so close to Christmas . . ." She looked as though she sincerely believed there was a manger in the nursery and shepherds keeping watch over their flocks in the parking lot. "Go ahead."

I called Jorgeson. "Do you know that Malthea left the hospital?"

"The officer assigned to her door called in a few minutes ago. She persuaded him to go down to the cafeteria to get her a cup of hot chocolate. Someone from housekeeping had just shown up to clean her room, so he figured she'd be okay for ten minutes or so. When he returned, her clothes were still there. He alerted hospital security, and they wasted an hour doing a floor-by-floor search for an elderly woman in a

robe and slippers. I've sent a patrol car to her apartment to pick her up."

"Ask the officers to wait at the corner," I said.
"Leaving the hospital without authorization is not a
crime. I'd like to talk to her."

Jorgeson agreed. I hung up, thanked Bea, and drove
to the duplex. I knocked on Malthea's door, and when
no one answered, pounded on it with my fist until my
hand throbbed.

Fern opened her door. "She's gone, Claire."

"Gone where?"

"I couldn't say."

I hit the door one last time, then let my hand fall.
"Did you pick her up at the hospital?"

"Is that against the law?"

"No," I said. "May I have a cup of tea?"

"Yes, of course," she said, gesturing for me to come
inside. "Malthea did indeed ask me to fetch her from
the hospital. It was rather exciting to wait by the door,
the engine racing, my palms perspiring; I felt like I
was at the wheel of the getaway car during a bank robbery. I expected her to come running out the door with
security officers hot on her heels, but she strolled out
to the car and suggested we go home."

"In street clothes?"

Fern busied herself with the teapot. "Yes, I suppose
so. She wasn't wearing one of those gowns that ex-
poses one's privates to all and sundry."

"Gilda's doing?" I persevered.

"Gilda may be a Wiccan—and what an unreliable
lot they seem to be—but she has deep loyalties to the
grove. I'm not saying that she provided Malthea with
clothes, but it might have happened that way. In any

case, I brought Malthea home. Twenty minutes later she loaded several suitcases and boxes into her car, came to the door and hugged me, and promised to keep in touch. She made me swear to see to Merlinda. Before I could question her as to her plans, she left. Just like that."

A teacup slipped out of Fern's hand and shattered to the floor. She mumbled an apology and went into the living room. I picked up the sizable pieces, then found a broom and a dustpan and swept up the slivers. I found another teacup, fixed a tray, and took it into the living room, where I found her huddled on the sofa, a shawl around her shoulders.

"Here," I said as I gave her a steaming cup. "Malthea's not in any trouble, and neither are you. Morning Rose and Roy are in custody. It's over."

"What about Cosmos and Rainbow?" she asked.

"Sullivan may have suspected what was going on, but he won't be charged. You and Malthea knew, didn't you?"

"We weren't sure. We were worried that . . . Roy might be engaged in something beyond his years, but we couldn't ask him. It would not have been seemly for two old ladies to broach the subject. A boy his age can't believe that our generation ever experienced sexual intimacy. It makes one wonder where they think they came from, doesn't it? All this modern openness about sex, and they're clinging to storks and cabbage patches. Have they no idea what Adam and Eve did after they ate the apple?"

I paused, wondering if Caron had ever envisioned me in bed with her father. She most likely preferred to see herself as the consequence of immaculate conception.

"Why," I asked, "were you and Malthea so worried about Roy?"

"There was no one else to worry about him except the two of us. His parents had abandoned him, and he had no one else to fall back on for support and guidance. It would have been so much better if he'd gone to Borneo. He would have been much safer among headhunters than . . ."

"Why did Malthea leave?" I asked bluntly.

Fern pulled the shawl more tightly around her and took a sip of tea. "I don't know."

"Did she do it so she won't have to testify against him?"

"Testify about what?"

"Testify that she had nothing to do with Nicholas Chunder's murder," I said. "I know she didn't, and so do you. Why did you and she lie about it, Fern? He's a punk. He may have had a tough life, but so have a lot of other kids. My daughter's made it thus far with only a scrape or two. Families aren't perfect these days; we adapt to reality and do what's necessary to get by. I could understand if Malthea was concerned about Roy, but . . ."

"Of course she was," Fern said. "We both were."

"She's his grandmother," I said, wondering why it had taken me so long to arrive at the realization.

Fern snatched the teacup from my hand and banged it down on the tray. "That's absurd. Malthea never married, so how could she have had a child? Even if she had, the child would have been put up for adoption and that would have been the end of it. There could have been no reconciliation. If you don't mind, I'd like to go out to my greenhouse and mist the asparagus ferns. They require daily attention to maintain their vitality." She threw aside the shawl and stood up. "I will not be able to continue to live here in the future, Claire, so this had best be good-bye."

"Where will you go?" I asked as she literally propelled me to the front door.

"It's under control. Malthea left this for you." She pushed a folded piece of paper into my hand. "Good night, Claire."

The door closed in my face, and seconds later, the porch light went out. I stood there for a moment, trying to determine if I'd actually learned anything I hadn't already subconsciously suspected. Adoption papers were sealed; not even Jorgeson could ever prove that Malthea was the mother of one of Roy's parents, most likely Randall. Scrutinizing the photographs in the leather box would serve no purpose, even if it was still in the desk drawer. I knew it wasn't.

I wished Malthea had stayed around long enough to say good-bye, but I could understand her reasons for leaving. At some point, she would see an article in a newspaper that revealed the ugly plot and realize that she was no longer implicated. But perhaps by then she would have found a happier grove, where mistletoe and mead were abundant.

Something furry curled around my ankle, and I'm sorry to admit that I let out an unnecessarily loud shriek. Fern's door flew open and she came onto the porch.

"Merlinda?" she said, scooping up a bundle of black fur that resembled a cat. "Did she hurt you? Well, let's just have a nice saucer of milk."

This time the door slammed closed.

I walked slowly to the car, then paused under the streetlight to unfold the slip of paper. The writing was unsteady but legible: "As Mumsy always said, generalizations aren't worth a damn." Grinning despite myself, I glanced up at the moon and wished her well.

I went to the Book Depot and relieved Caron. She claimed some life-threatening need for the car. Rather than argue, I gave her the keys and went into the office, sat down, and tried to find a reason to call Jorgeson and tell him that Malthea had left town. She wasn't really a witness, I told myself—or at least not a vital one. The charges would not culminate in a trial. Plea bargains, minimal sentences, community service— and Morning Rose and Roy would be freed to resume their unhealthy alliance until she found another candidate for Horned God. Sullivan and the children would survive. I hoped Nicholas Chunder had left arrangements to have his ashes sprinkled in Wales.

"What's wrong with you?" asked my science-fiction hippie as he came into the store.

"Holiday blues," I said. "Need another book for your new friend?"

"No," he said, turning red in those patches of skin that were visible above his beard and below his beetlish brow. "I have something for you. I know that you think I steal books, and maybe I do, but not very often. Anyway, you don't ever embarrass me like some of the shopkeepers do. You don't snicker when I come in or trail me around like I was some sort of thief."

"Should I?"

"Yeah, maybe. Anyway, I wanted to give this to you." He dropped a tissue-wrapped package on the counter, then winked and went out the door.

I unwrapped the paper and found a crystal figurine of a magician, no more than an inch high (and therefore easy to slip into a pocket). I'd seen similar figurines at the gallery just across the tracks, and made a note to return it after Christmas. I would not explain.

Jorgeson came into the store late in the afternoon, the tinkle of the bell above the door a good deal livelier than his expression. "Here," he said, handing me a package wrapped in foil. "I want you to know how much I appreciate what you went through. I was out of my league, and you saved me from making a fool of myself. We didn't always see things the same way, Mrs. Malloy. You could have told me to take a flying leap, but you didn't."

"Jorgeson," I said, "you didn't have to . . ."

"It's just a fruitcake. My wife said I should get you perfume or something, but everybody likes fruitcake. Right?"

"Absolutely," I said, nodding forcefully. "I love fruitcake, and so does Caron."

He turned his back and picked up a paperback from the rack. "The lieutenant called this afternoon. He's going to take a three-month leave of absence. He said he'd been under a lot of pressure and needed a break."

"Oh, really?" I said evenly.

"I don't think it means anything," Jorgeson said as he turned around and looked at me. "Things have been pretty hectic for the last couple of months. All of us need a break, but we need our salaries, too. The lieutenant's in a different situation."

"Independently wealthy, for instance?"

"I suppose he is. He said he's going to call you this evening and explain things. I just thought I might warn you so you won't . . ."

I realized he wanted me to say something, but I

picked up the package and looked at my distorted reflection. After he'd left, I took the package into my office, set it on the desk, making sure it was in the exact middle of the blotter, and went back out in hopes of selling one last book. I can offer no excuse for what I decided to do at that moment, except to say that I was somewhat lower than a pregnant sow's belly. I took out the scrap of paper on which I'd written the number of the Psychic Confidantes number and dialed it.

"Hullo?" said a squeaky voice.

"I'd like to speak to Divinia," I said.

"As soon as I heard the phone ring, I knew that," she said. "Can you hold on for a second?" She put her hand over the receiver and yelled, "Go vacuum in the bedroom, honey, on account of I got a call."

"Is this Divinia?" I asked.

"No, she ain't available. We've got this deal where all her calls are transferred to me when she can't answer. Are you one of her regulars?"

"Shouldn't you know that?" I asked.

"Oh, I do. Divinia's not doing so well at the present time, but she'll be on in a few days. What can I do for you? Got problems with your boyfriend? That's my specialty."

"What makes you think I have a boyfriend?"

"Everybody who calls Psychic Confidantes has a boyfriend. Tell me his name and I'll do a reading."

Although I knew the meter was ticking at approximately four dollars a minute, it was beginning to amuse me. "You're a psychic. You tell *me* his name."

"I don't got time to play games. Call Divinia when she gets back. In the meantime, don't trust what he says about other women, but don't be surprised if he shows up with a real nice Christmas present. He's real sorry about what he did."

"What did he do?"

"You don't want to know."

She hung up, leaving me holding the receiver against my ear and feeling foolish. I locked up and walked back to the apartment.

I had an hour before heading downstairs for a cocktail and mindless chatter, to be followed by white wine and more mindless chatter. I made a drink and took it into the bathroom, where I could find some solace in a bath and a book.

I was somewhat submerged in both when I heard the back door open and more than one pair of feet tromp into the kitchen.

"Mother?" called Caron.

"Yes, dear?" I replied without enthusiasm.

"We've got company. You'd better get dressed."

As much as I wanted to sink beneath the water and find out how long I could hold my breath, I climbed out of the bathtub and put on my clothes. They were not what I had intended to wear to the retiree's party, but I had no desire to be spotted sprinting down the hall to my room in the wherewithal. Skyclad, so to speak.

I was not prepared for the crowd in the living room. Caron and Inez were whispering by the door. Luanne was seated on the sofa as though it were a throne and she were awaiting an audience with an endless line of courtiers. One of them might have been Ed, who was hovering near the doorway to the kitchen.

"Hey," he said lamely.

Caron came over to my side. "Don't be mad at me, okay?"

"If I'd known we were having a party, I would have bought some eggnog."

"It's not a party."

Luanne looked back at me. "But it will be shortly, Claire. Come sit down next to me. Caron has something she wants to show you."

I glanced at Ed. "Shouldn't I make coffee or something?"

"Sit," Luanne said, slapping the cushion. "Caron has a Christmas present for you. You may be of the traditional school that believes presents can only be opened on Christmas morning, but we took it to a vote and decided that you deserve to receive it tonight."

"We?" I said as I sat down.

Ed cleared his throat; if he'd had a forelock, he would have tugged it. "I shouldn't be here, Ms. Malloy. I'll just be on my way."

Caron hurried across the room and poked him in the chest. "You'll do no such thing. I told you that I need a Santa Claus when I give this present to my mother. Is it asking too much for you to stay for ten or fifteen more minutes? I'll pay you for your time if that's what you want."

"You know that's not why I said that."

"Then let's not play Mr. Sensitive," she said acerbically. "Would it be too much trouble for you to sit down on the sofa?"

"Maybe I should stay over here," he said.

"Whatever." Caron turned around and looked at me. "I borrowed a video camera from Rhonda and made a tape. I think you'll enjoy it."

Inez slipped a cassette into the VCR, pushed buttons, and then stepped back. We all seemed to be holding our collective breath as static flickered and then materialized into a jerky scene of a child on a swing set.

"This," Caron said, "is Morgan Connolly, less than twenty-four hours after her supposed traumatic experience at the mall. Note, if you will, her smarmy smile and lack of reluctance to engage in strenuous physical activity."

"Caron," I began, "our lawyer said not to—"

"And here is Morgan, doing cartwheels. My goodness, was that a somersault? How could a child with these injuries perform so vigorously? Is it possible that she wasn't quite so injured as they claim?"

"One wonders," Luanne drawled. "She does appear remarkably fit, doesn't she?"

I knew something was expected of me, but I couldn't buy into their rosy glow. "This doesn't prove she didn't experience mental anguish. All it takes is one psychologist and—"

"And now what do we see?" Caron said as the flickering screen once again came into focus. "Why, it's Mrs. Claus knocking on a front door. The door opens, and it's Morgan's father, Eric Connolly. He's hugging her, and she's kissing him on the cheek. Now we have Suzanne Connolly, mother of the victim. She's hugging Mrs. Claus, too. Is this a warm reunion or what? You'd almost think these were old friends, wouldn't you?"

The tape dissolved into static.

"What's more," Caron continued as she positioned herself in the middle of the room, "it occurred to me that Morgan's performance was a bit too slick, as if she'd done it more than once. It hadn't worked the first time, so Ms. Portmeyer had to invent reasons to fire Santa and the reindeer. I didn't get a chance to ask the two girls if they recognized Morgan, but Ed did."

"That's right," he said. "Two days before I found the whiskey bottle in my locker, the same little girl pushed her way to the head of the line and then scrambled past the two reindeer and ran toward me. They just stared at her. She knocked over a couple of elves, kicked me in the shins, and yanked my beard so she ended up with a fistful of hairs. Portmeyer finally intervened and led her back to the fence."

"And found a set of new employees so she could try again," I said. "Let's gift-wrap the cassette before we take it to Franklin."

Luanne slapped my leg. "Party time! Come on, Ed, you can help me cut up cheese and crank up the gramophone. Caron, are you and Inez going to come?"

"No, thank you. We're going to another party."

"Whose?" I asked.

"Rhonda's having a few people over to string popcorn and dumb stuff like that. Trust me when I say I'll be home early."

I waited until Luanne and Ed had clattered down the stairs. "Why are you invited?"

Caron's lip slid out. "Why shouldn't we be? I mean, we may not be going steady with football players, but we don't drool when we drink cranberry punch."

Inez sighed. "Louis Wilderberry's sister told Emily that he's giving Rhonda a gold bracelet for Christmas. She'll probably be wearing it tonight so we can all go blind admiring it."

"There's more than one plum in the pudding," Caron said archly. "Or I guess there is, anyway. I've never had plum pudding."

I did not allow myself to be diverted into a culinary conversation. "Why did she invite you?"

"I decided that since it's the Christmas season I'd forgive her for all her bitchy comments. I went over to her house, and as a gesture of goodwill, offered to write her term paper for history."

"If she loaned you the video camera," Inez contributed, then edged around the back of the sofa. "I'm sure she would have anyway."

"What's the topic of this paper?" I asked Caron.

"Something about the influence of sixteenth-century exploration on the cultures in Latin America."

"You don't know anything about that. Are you planning to do research as a further gesture of goodwill."

"Don't make me laugh," said Caron. "Rhonda knows less than I do. She thinks they used to speak Latin, if you can believe that. I'll make up a bunch of stuff. As long as I stick in a lot of dates and peculiar names, she'll never know the difference."

"Her teacher will," I pointed out dryly.

"School will be out before Rhonda gets her report card. I'm thinking about getting a summer job in Zion National Park. I don't know where it is, but it sounds like the sort of place nobody can find, even with a map."

I gestured for her to sit down beside me. "Thanks for the videotape. That was smart work on your part."

"I thought so. Actually, Luanne had a couple of suggestions, like staking out Morgan's yard with the video camera, and Inez helped, too."

"By searching Ms. Portmeyer's briefcase?"

"Oh, no," said Inez. "The mall let her use a little office off the lounge. All I did was look at some folders on her desk while I was supposed to be getting a package of film. Looking's not the same as searching, Mrs. Malloy."

"No, dear," I said, "it's certainly not."

After they'd gone, I changed into a red fleece jumpsuit in honor of the holiday, did what I could to cover the scratches on my face, and applied bright red lipstick in hopes that it would make me look merry and bright.

I was unplugging the lights on the Christmas tree when the telephone started to ring. I straightened the packages, tucked the foil-wrapped fruitcake under my arm to give to Ed when I got to Luanne's, and turned off the living-room light. The telephone was still ringing as I went down the steps for a Jingle Bell Bazooka.

**Keep reading** *for an excerpt from*
*Joan Hess's next Claire Malloy mystery...*

# DAMSELS IN DISTRESS

*Coming soon in hardcover from St. Martin's Minotaur*

"Good morrow, Kate, for that is your name, I hear."

I blinked at the young man in the doorway. "Well have you heard, but something hard of hearing. They call me Claire Malloy that do talk of me."

"You lie, in faith, for you are call'd plain Kate, and bonny Kate, and sometimes Kate the curst, but Kate, the prettiest Kate in Farberville. Kate of Kate Hall, my superdainty Kate, for dainties are all Kates, and therefore—"

"Mother," Caron said as she came out of my office, "who is This Person?"

"I have no idea," I admitted.

The peculiar man came into the bookstore and bowed, one arm across his waist and the other artfully posed above his head. He was dressed in a white shirt with billowy sleeves, a fringed leather tunic, purple tights, suede boots with curled toes, and a diamond-patterned conical cap topped with a tiny bell. His brown hair dangled to his shoulders, rare among the traditionally minded Farber College students. "Perchance miladies will allow me to maketh known myself?"

"This milady thinks you ought to maketh known thyself to the local police," Caron said, edging toward me. "Start with the Sheriff of Nottingham."

He stood up and swept off his cap. "Pester the Jester, or Edward Cobbinwood, if it pleaseth you all the more."

"Not especially," I said. "Would you care to explain further?"

"Okay, I'm a grad student at the college and a member of ARSE. I was assigned to talk to all the merchants at the mall and on Thurber Street about the Renaissance Fair in two weeks. We'd like to put up flyers in the store windows and maybe some banners. Fiona is hoping you'll let us use the portico in front of your bookstore for a stage to publicize the event."

"A Renaissance Fair? I haven't heard anything about this." I noticed Caron's sharp intake of breath and glanced at her. "Have you?"

She nodded. "I was going to tell you about it when you got home this evening. The AP history teacher sent a letter to everybody who's taking her course in the fall. We have to either participate in this fair thing or write a really ghastly midterm paper. I don't think she should be allowed to blackmail us like this. Inez and I are going to get up a petition and have everybody sign it, then take it to the school board. I mean, summer is supposed to be our vacation, not—"

"I get your point," I said.

"Look not so gloomy, my fair and freckled damsel," added Edward Cobbinwood. "It'll be fun. We put on a couple of Ren fairs when I was in undergraduate school. It's like a big costume party, with all kinds of entertainment and food. ARSE will stage battles, and perhaps a gallant knight in shining armor will fight for your honor."

Caron glared at him. "I am perfectly capable of defending my honor without the help of some guy dressed in rusty hubcaps."

"What's ARSE?" I asked.

"The Association for Renaissance Scholarship and Enlightenment. It's not a bunch of academics who meet once a year to read dry papers and argue about royal lineage or the positive side of the feudal system. Anybody can join. The country is divided into kingdoms, counties, and fiefdoms. The local group is Avalon. There are just a few members in town this summer, but when the semester starts in September, Fiona says—"

"Fiona Thackery," Caron said with a sigh, not yet willing

to allow me to dismiss her imminent martyrdom. "The AP history teacher. I'm thinking about taking shop instead. I've always wanted to get my hands on a nail gun. Or if I take auto mechanics, I'll learn to change tires and . . . tighten bolts and stuff like that. That way, when your car falls into a gazillion bits, I'll know how to put it back together. That's a lot more useful than memorizing the kings of England or the dates of the Napoleonic Wars."

"You're taking AP history," I said. "If you want to work at a garage on the weekends, that's fine with me."

She gave me a petulant look. "Then you can write the midterm paper. Compare and contrast the concepts of Hellenism and Hebraism in *The Divine Comedy* and *The Canterbury Tales*. Cite examples and footnote all source material. Five thousand word minimum. Any attempt at plagiarism from the Internet or elsewhere will result in a shaved head and six weeks in the stocks."

I cupped my hand to my ear. "Do I hear the lilting melody of 'Greensleeves' in the distance?"

"The only recorder I'm playing," Caron said sourly, "will have a tape in it."

Edward seemed to be enjoying the exchange, but fluttered his fingers and strolled out of the Book Depot to bewilder and beguile other merchants along the street. He must have had a recorder tucked in his pocket, because we could hear tootling as he headed up the hill. It may have been "Greensleeves," but it was hard to be sure. I hoped he wasn't a music major.

"Goodness gracious," said Inez Thornton as she came into the bookstore. Her eyes were round behind her thick lenses. "Did you see that weirdo in the purple tights?"

Inez has always been Caron's best friend through thick and thin (aka high crimes and misdemeanors). Caron, red-haired and obstinate, faster than a speeding bullet except when her alarm clock goes off in the morning, able to leap over logic in a single bound, is the dominant force. Meek, myopic Inez is but a pale understudy in Caron's pageant, but equally devious. Encroaching maturity tempers them at times. There are, of course, many other times.

"Tell me more about the letter from your history teacher," I said.

Caron grimaced. "This Renaissance Fair sounds so juvenile. Everybody has to dress up as something and go around pretending to be a minstrel or a damsel or a pirate or something silly like that. There's a meeting tomorrow afternoon at the high school so we can get our committee assignments. It's like Miss Thackery thinks we're already in her class. She shouldn't be allowed to get away with this. It's—it's unconstitutional!"

"That's right," said Inez, nodding emphatically. "Aren't we guaranteed life, liberty, and the pursuit of happiness?"

"I'm not sure reading Chaucer and Dante will make you all that happy, but you never know," I said. "You'll find copies on the back shelf. Help yourselves."

Rather than take me up on my generous offer, they left. I would have felt a twinge of maternal sympathy had they not been muttering for more than a month about how bored they were. I'd never been to a Renaissance Fair, but I supposed it was similar to a carnival show, with tents, booths, and entertainment—not to mention men clad in armor made of aluminum foil, bashing each other with padded sticks.

Pester the Jester did not reappear, to my relief. I've always been leery of men in tights, especially purple ones (tights, not men). The few customers who drifted in were dressed in standard summer wear and more interested in paperback thrillers and travel books than in Shakespeare. Business is sluggish in the summer, when most of the college students have gone home and their professors are either wandering through cavernous cathedrals in Europe or sifting sand at archeological digs. The academic community as a whole comprises nearly a quarter of Farberville's population of 25,000 semi-literate souls. Their civilian counterparts tend to do their shopping at the air-conditioned mall at the edge of town when the temperature begins to climb.

At 6:00 P.M. I locked the doors and went across the street

to the beer garden to meet Luanne Bradshaw, who owns a vintage clothing shop on Thurber Street. It could have been a hobby, not a livelihood, since she not only comes from a wealthy family on the East Coast but also divorced a successful doctor and left him barefoot in the park—or, at least, penniless in the penthouse. However, she chose to rid herself of most of her ill-gotten gains via trusts and foundations, dumped her offspring on the doorsteps of prestigious prep schools, and headed for the hinterlands. Farberville definitely falls into that category. Despite being in the throes of a midlife crisis that may well continue until she's ninety, she's disarmingly astute.

She was seated at a picnic table beneath a wisteria-entwined lattice that provided shade and a pleasant redolence. Her long, tanned legs were clearly visible in scandalously short shorts, and her black hair was tucked under a baseball cap. As I joined her, she filled a plastic cup with beer from a pitcher and set it down in front of me.

"You didn't mention Peter when you called earlier," she said by way of greeting. "Are you having prenuptial jitters? It's unbecoming in a woman of your age."

"My age is damn close to yours," I said, "and I'm not the one who scrambled all over the Andes with a bunch of virile young Australian men for six weeks."

"I kept claiming I needed to rest just so I could watch their darling butts wiggle as they hiked past me. So what's going on with Peter?"

"The captain sent him to FBI summer camp so he can learn how to protect our fair town if the terrorists attempt to create havoc by jamming the parking meters. It's a real threat, you know. The mayor will have to flee to his four-bedroom bunker out by the lake. The Kiwanis Club won't be able to have its weekly luncheon meetings at the diner behind the court house. The community theater won't be able to stage its endearingly inept production of 'Our Town' for the first time in nineteen years. All hell could break loose."

Luanne failed to look properly terrified. "How long will he be gone?"

"Three weeks at Quantico, and then a week at his mother's."

"Oh," she murmured.

I took a long swallow of beer. "It's not like that. She's resigned to the idea that Peter and I are getting married, or so he keeps telling me."

"But she's not coming to the wedding."

"No, she's not," I said. "She always goes to Aspen in September to avoid the hurricane season."

"Rhode Island is hardly a magnet for hurricanes, but neither is Farberville," Luanne said as she refilled her cup and mine.

"It's a tradition. She goes with a big group of her widowed friends. They take over a very posh condo complex and party all day and night. Besides, it's not as if this is Peter's first marriage—or mine. I'd look pretty silly in a flouncy white dress and veil, with my teenaged daughter as maid of honor. There's no reason why she should disrupt her long-standing plans for a simple little civil ceremony in a backyard."

"She's probably afraid she'll have to eat ribs," said Luanne, "and toast the happy couple with moonshine in a jelly jar. Have you spoken to her on the phone, or received a warm letter on her discreetly monogrammed stationery?"

The topic was not amusing me. "Not yet. Peter thinks we ought to give her some time to get used to the idea, and then go for a visit. Will you loan me a pair of jodpurs?"

"Yes, but they'll make your thighs look fat."

I brooded for a moment, then said, "Did you happen to encounter Pester the Jester this afternoon?"

"Oh my, yes. I couldn't take my eyes off his codpiece."

I told her about the letters Caron and Inez had received from the history teacher. "They're appalled, of course, and were rambling about their constitutional right to spend the summer sulking. I didn't have the heart to remind them that they'd already had their fifteen minutes of fame a month ago, when they were interviewed by the media after that unfortunate business with the disappearing corpse."

"Fame is fleeting," Luanne said.

We pondered this philosophical twaddle while we emptied our cups. The remaining beer in the pitcher was getting warm, and a group of noisy college kids arrived to take possession of a nearby picnic table. I told Luanne I'd call her later in the week, then walked the few blocks to my apartment on the second floor of a duplex across the street from the campus lawn. A note on the kitchen table informed me that Caron and Inez had gone out for pizza with friends. It was just as well, since my culinary interests were limited to boiling water for tea and nuking frozen entrées. In the mood for neither, I settled down on the sofa to read. I hoped Peter would call, but as it grew dark outside I gave up and consoled myself with images of him on the firing range, learning how to take down grannies with radioactive dentures and toddlers with teddy bears packed with explosives. Or librarians and booksellers who refused to turn in their patrons' reading preferences to cloak-and-dagger government agencies.

What I did not want to think about was the wedding, scheduled for early September. Not because I was having second thoughts, mind you. I was confident that I loved Peter and that we would do quite nicely when we rode off into the sunset of domestic bliss, which would include not only more opportunities for adult behavior of a most delectable sort, but also lazy Sunday mornings with coffee, muffins, and *The New York Times*, and occasional squabbles over the relative merits of endive versus romaine. He'd been suggesting matrimonial entanglement for several years, and I'd given it serious consideration. But after my first husband's untimely and very unseemly death, I'd struggled to regain my self-esteem and establish my independence. I hadn't done too well on the material aspects, as Caron pointed out on a regular basis. However, the Book Depot was still in business, and we lived on the agreeable side of genteel poverty.

A distressingly close call with mortality had led me to reassess my situation. The emotional barrier I'd constructed to protect myself collapsed during a convoluted moment when a hitman had impolitely threatened to blow my brains out (not in those exact words, but that was the gist of the message). If commitment meant sharing a closet, then so be it.

The problem lay in my inclinations to meddle in what Lieutenant Peter Rosen felt was official police business. It wasn't simply a compulsion to outsleuth Miss Marple. In all the situations I'd found myself questioning witnesses and snooping around crime scenes, I'd never once done so for my personal satisfaction—or to make fools of the local constabulary. It just happened. Peter, with his molasses brown eyes, curly hair, perfect teeth, and undeniable charm, never quite saw it that way. He'd lectured me, had my car impounded twice, threatened me with a jail cell, and attempted to keep me under house arrest. One had to admire his optimism.